SHANNON McKENNA

EDGE OF *Ruin*

Introduction

The D'Onofrio sisters—Nancy, Nell, and Vivi—have never been in trouble this deep.

Already, they're grieving the wrenching loss of their beloved adoptive mother Lucia, killed a few weeks ago in a home invasion. But it is quickly becoming clear that Lucia's murder was not random at all. It's connected to some terrifying secret—one that she took to her grave.

Whoever attacked Lucia now seems convinced that her bewildered adopted daughters can reveal this secret—which, of course, they can't. Already Nancy and Nell have beaten off several violent attacks, with the fortuitous help of their hyperprotective new lovers. Thank God for Liam and Duncan.

But Vivi is still out there on her own, trying to stay a step ahead of those murdering bastards. Because Lucia's killers are still on the prowl—and ruinous danger seems to follow Vivi wherever she goes ...

Chapter One

Vivi

I had to just grit my teeth and face it. The van was stuck.

I'd been spinning my tires in sloppy mud for over fifteen minutes now, and my poor old Volkswagen van was groaning and lurching with the strain. I had to suck it up, and devise an adult solution, probably one that required spending money I could ill afford. It also involved looking stupid and feckless in front of a bunch of people that I had never even met, which made me wince and cringe. Alas, poor me.

I killed the engine, shoved my tangled red hair back behind my ears, and pounded on the steering wheel with a grinding shriek of frustration. I was all alone, aside from my long-suffering dog, Edna, so I could throw a discreet little tantrum. Edna would never tell.

Didn't make me feel any better, though. The world outside the rain-sluiced windshield was a wavering blur of greens. Lightning flashed. I braced myself for the huge crash ... and

Edna yelped when it jolted us, scrambling frantically into my lap.

I petted the quivering dog. "Easy, honey girl," I crooned. "It'll be over soon. We'll get through it. We always do."

A hopeful thought, but I would still be in a very sticky jam when the storm was over. Perhaps an even stickier jam, depending on how much water was still in the sky, still getting ready to fall on top of me. This road could slide right off the mountain and bury us under tons of mud.

Which struck me as a train of thought to avoid right now.

It had seemed like a good idea last night to just push on, rain and all. Truth was, I'd been simply too scared to stop driving.

Too much tragic, horrible, terrifying shit had happened recently. The most horrific being that my adopted mother, Lucia D'Onofrio, had been murdered some weeks before.

That calamity had knocked me and my two sisters all onto our asses.

To make matters worse, my two sisters, Nancy and Nell, had both been attacked, multiple times. We had finally managed to conclude, mostly based on the meager crumbs of information the attackers had let drop when they kidnapped Nell, that our enemies were looking for some mysterious art object, something hidden decades ago in Italy, before the Second World War. As far as we could tell, everyone who knew where this thing was, or hell, even *what* it was, had long since died.

The killers had tried to get information from Lucia, but they had failed utterly. Lucia had died without giving it to them. Because Lucia was a boss. Fierce. Indomitable. My role model, my hero.

After that, infuriated by their failure, those murdering

assholes turned their sights on us. Lucia's clueless adopted daughters, who knew jack shit about Lucia's mysterious past.

It was hard to argue with stomach-churning fear when I was all alone, no one to act tough and fearless for. Only Edna knew the truth, and bless her sweet heart, she did not judge me. She just panted her hot, fishy breath heavily into my face and offered her solid, comforting presence like the very good girl that she was.

Edna's silken, chocolate brown fur had soaked up many tears I wouldn't show to anyone else. But even with my trusty dog at my side, I hadn't been able to face a roadside motel with a single door lock between me and the night, which was all I could afford. And I was the only D'Onofrio chick that didn't have a big, vigilant, protective guy giving the hairy eyeball to every stranger within shouting range of his new lady.

Which made me the obvious soft target. On my own, as always.

Not that I begrudged my sisters their good fortune. They both deserved to have a tough, devoted, foxy guy worshipping at their shrines. In fact, Liam and Duncan still didn't know how lucky they were in their fabulous new fiancées. They were going to be discovering it for the rest of their lives. Those men had been tongue-kissed by Fate.

I was intensely grateful for those guys, and what they had done for Nancy and Nell. Both men were tough, vigilant, and battle-tested. My sisters were as safe with Duncan and Liam as they could possibly be in these strange days. But as for me, well. I was feeling very solitary and unworshipped. I had been feeling that way even before Ulf Haupt and John the Fiend, a.k.a. Snake Eyes, started attacking the D'Onofrio women.

I was a generally cheerful person, and I made a real effort to keep it positive. But under these conditions, it was almost impossible to keep my chin up.

Both of my sisters had tried to persuade me to stay with them until we figured out what to do about our bloodthirsty enemies. But who knew how long that would take?

That solution struck me as nonproductive, unsustainable, and ultimately embarrassing. How long could a woman realistically sit around like a bump on a log in her sister's home, bored out of her mind, not working, not making art, being a financial drain and a big fat fifth wheel?

No way. I just couldn't. I would go mad. I would start to misbehave.

Besides, I really missed my dog. She'd been boarding with a friend of mine who lived out in the country since things got weird, but my sweet girl belonged with me. I'd never committed to anything in my life the way I'd committed to Edna. Every day I had forced her to wait for me had hurt me just a little bit more.

Nah, I just had to muddle on somehow. Even with all the grief and jealousy and confusion and stalking fiends. I was plenty stubborn. It was a D'Onofrio thing.

I stroked Edna's floppy, velvety soft ears, and buried my face against her silky fur. It calmed me down and let me breathe a little deeper as I peered out at the heavy, swollen gray sky. I supposed I could call my new mysterious landlord Jack Kendrick, Duncan's old friend from his stint as a field agent in the NSA. Kendrick was liable to know how to begin solving my complicated logistical problems.

But oh, God. How freaking embarrassing was that.

I checked my phone. Well, hell. There was no coverage out here anyway. That settled that. I was utterly lost in the ass end of nowhere.

Which was the whole idea, of course. To hide out somewhere remote, lost, trackless, where Ulf Haupt and Snake Eyes John would never think to look for me.

I'd made it to the town of Silverfish, Oregon at around two in the afternoon, if one could even call the place a town. It wasn't much more than a wide spot on the road. Through the torrents of rain, all I saw was a convenience store, a gas pump, a bait and tackle shop, and a boarded-up old Dairy Queen.

I had followed the directions, which I'd been advised to print out, since the place was out of the reach of GPS, and made my way onto progressively smaller roads, finally arriving at a dirt track with a hand-painted sign that read MOFFAT'S WAY. The directions offered nothing more. At that point, it was straight on til morning.

But Moffat's Way wasn't a driveway, it was an old logging road, deeply rutted and frighteningly steep. By the time I had realized how rough the road was, those ruts had become streams, with no place anywhere wide enough to turn around.

Then I made a sharp turn into a deep puddle, sank into the mud at a terrifying tilted angle, and that was that.

I leaned my hot cheek against the cool window, mind racing. Still procrastinating. Edna stuck her nose into my hand, gave it a sloppy, comforting lick, and then started enthusistically in on the side of my face.

Who knew how much farther this road went on before it came to Jack Kendrick's land? I hadn't bothered to inform myself about such nitpicky details. I just figured, I'd get there when I got there, since the road stopped at his house. You couldn't go wrong, the directions said. Hah. If there was one thing I was unusually good at, it was taking wrong turns. Everyone had his or her own little superpower, and that was mine.

I spun the tires a few more times, just to torture myself. It was time to take action. The self-sufficient, proactive, fearless Vivi D'Onofrio could rise to any occasion, I bracingly told myself. Psychopathic kidnappers? Bring 'em on.

A long shudder racked my body. Well. Maybe not so much.

The rain had eased off from a pounding torrent to a regular shower, so I flung open the door of the van, looking around myself in vain for a solid place to put my feet. Edna crawled eagerly over my lap, and I clutched at her harness in alarm. "No way, babe," I said sternly. "All I need is a mud-covered dog. Get back inside. In!"

Edna shrank back, looking reproachful. I rolled my pants up, looked at my cheerful, bright-green high-tops regretfully, and jumped out. At least they were old, like most of my clothes at this point. Maybe a run through a washing machine would salvage them.

Cold, sucking mud swallowed my feet to the ankles. I slogged around the van and assessed the damage.

The tires were half buried. Chilly rain plastered my hair to my scalp and the green t-shirt to my body. I let loose with a stream of explicit profanity, the foul, biting kind I'd learned in the Bronx as a child, and punctuated by kicking a slimy tire. Hard enough to make a bolt of pain shoot up my leg.

Yeah, that's right, Viv. Check me out, yapping like a fishwife at inanimate objects. Very impressive. Very mature.

Farther back, I'd seen what looked like a collapsed shack. Maybe some planks laid down in front of the tires would give them purchase to get out of the muck. Beyond the puddle, the road looked almost drivable.

I would exhaust every possibility before limping to Jack Kendrick's house on foot like a cat left out in the rain. A fine first impression that would be.

Kendrick was still a mystery. I knew only what Duncan had told me. That he was some sort of ex-spy commando who'd been on a top-secret intelligence-gathering task force with Duncan years ago.

Now, unaccountably, he grew flowers. Duncan had been

vague about the details of that career change, his brain being flash-fried from being insanely in love with Nell.

This mysterious Kendrick lived alone in the woods. He evidently had an apartment in his barn. According to Duncan, the man was cool with letting me huddle in this flowery bower like a quivering, nose-twitching bunny until we figured out what to do about our art-hungry, murdering psychopaths. Very nice of him, but it didn't say much for his smarts, or his sense of self-preservation. He must owe Duncan money. Only a true bonehead would take on a hard-luck case like me.

I was still waiting for the other shoe to drop. Duncan had assured me that Kendrick knew the score, that he had agreed to the plan, that he wasn't intimidated by the risks. But come on. No normal person would agree to something that crazy. The guy must have a screw loose. Yeah, sure, invite the unknown girl with the deadly psychopath stalking her to crash in my barn. What could possibly go wrong?

This quiet, bucolic retreat had sounded so perfect, back in New York City. Too perfect, in retrospect. Now that I was pondering it all alone, stuck in the mud.

Ah, yes. There it was, a stack of gray, weathered planks with the odd rusty nails sticking through them at crazy angles. I wrestled and yanked until I'd extricated a few boards, along with some ugly splinters, then negotiated the slippery boards through the fir thickets. By the time I got back to the van, soggy, scratched, and panting, I was spewing a fresh stream of profanity. I hauled out my toolbox, hammered the nails flat, and started wrestling them into place. Mud oozed over the tops of the planks, and I was thoroughly slimed from chest to feet when I heard the deep voice from behind me.

"I don't think that'll work right now."

I jolted up, knocking my head on the bumper. "Who is

that?" I scrambled to my feet, looking frantically around myself. There was no one there that I could see.

I scanned the trees and reached for the tire iron stowed under the seat, groping until my fingers closed over the bar of cold, hard metal.

"Where are you?" I called out. "Say something."

"Over here."

I spun, brandishing the tire iron. A tall man stood there, half hidden in the trees. He was shrouded in a dull-green hooded rain poncho, dripping with rain. I would never have seen him if he had not spoken.

Adrenaline zinged through me. I gave the tire iron an experimental heft. "What do you think you're doing, sneaking up on me like that?" I demanded.

He took a step forward. I raised the tire iron with a menacing face, and he stopped.

"Sorry I scared you," he said.

Edna whined anxiously from the van, sticking her nose outside the door I'd left halfway open. "Stay, Edna," I snapped. "Who the hell are you?"

"I'm not going to attack you," he said, pushing back his hood. "You can relax."

Relax, my ass. Light, silver-gray eyes, cool and unreadable. His face was brown, lean. High cheekbones, a hooked nose. A scar on one temple slashed down into one of his straight, dark eyebrows, leaving a white line. He had a short beard, or maybe longish beard stubble. Dark hair, long and shaggy. He regarded her steadily. Drops of rain beaded his face. He did not look like Snake Eyes, as Nancy and Nell had described him. This guy was not loathsome, swollen, squint-eyed, or malodorous. Not that I could smell him from here. I would have to get much closer. And inhale. Hungrily.

This guy was oh-my-God fine. I tried to breathe. My terror

was transmuting itself into utter embarrassment. An unfortunate development.

"Put it down, please." A small smile crinkled up the skin around his eyes.

"What?" I said, realizing that my mouth had been hanging open.

"The tire iron." He glanced at my white-knuckled hand.

"Oh." I felt foolish, panicked. Acutely conscious of the mud on my clothes, the hair stuck to my face, the way my wet, muddy shirt clung to my tits. Of how incredibly tall he was. Even if he wasn't Snake Eyes John, he was still a stranger, and there was nobody around here for miles. Just me and Edna, the world's friendliest dog.

I looked at the hand that clutched the tire iron. It was shaking.

"The boards aren't going to work," he said. "It was a good idea, but the mud is too deep." He took a step closer. I backed away, then kicked myself for acting like a scared, cringing kitten.

He picked up a stick, walking away from me and heading around the back of the van, prodding at the mud with a stick he held.

Released from the spell of his eyes, I finally managed to exhale. *Get a grip.* He was not going to leap on me like a rabid dog. I had to at least try to be civil. My face felt so hot, raindrops should be skittering on it like water on a griddle. Insane. I never blushed.

"I asked what you were doing here," I said, trying to sound authoritative.

"This is my land," he said.

"Oh." I dropped my gaze, before his bright eyes could catch it and nail it down again. "Do you always walk around in thunderstorms?"

"I do, actually. Rainstorms, at least. The thunder took me by surprise. But I like the rain. I like the way it smells. I really, really wish you'd put that thing down."

"I'll put it down when I'm ready to put it down," I said shakily.

He tossed down his stick. "Whatever. Just don't hit me with it."

"I wouldn't without provocation," I said.

His mouth twitched. "Oh, please," he murmured. "Would you just chill the fuck out, already? You are safe. Completely safe. I swear it. On my immortal soul. Okay?"

That made me feel ridiculous, so I promptly threw the tire iron back into the van in disgust.

"You travel alone?" he asked.

"No. With my dog," I replied.

Edna barked excitedly when her existence was mentioned, taking it as permission to bound out the door. She landed in the mud with a wet plop, shook herself, and trotted over to the stranger. She gave his large brown hand a cautious sniff, then panted up into his face, smiling. Then she stroked her mud-spattered head against his leg.

"Down, Edna," I ordered, startled. Edna had never cozied up to strangers without taking her cue from me first. It made me feel vaguely betrayed. "Get back in here!"

Edna trotted back, panting and smiling. "Sorry about that," I said.

"No problem." A brief smile lit his face. "Nice dog."

"Too nice," I muttered. I started to push back the tangled hair that clung to my face, but stopped short, remembering the mud on my hands.

He gazed at me, projecting a weird, supernatural calm. Maybe hanging out in nature did that to a guy. Look at him, walking through pouring rain because he liked the way it smelled. What was he, a freaking Jedi knight? Give me a break.

It made me feel embarrassed to be myself. Frantic, citified, stressed out, nervous, afraid. A shallow little squeaking hamster racing on a wheel. And the hungry, fanged tomcats were lurking out there, licking their chops. Waiting for lunch.

Oh, for Christ's sake, I needed a vacation. Or at the very least, a night's sleep.

"Your van's not going anywhere today," he remarked.

I suppressed a snarky comment and wiped my hands on the hem of my drenched t-shirt. Good grief. He could see everything through that shirt. I hadn't worn a bra, being all alone, and I wasn't wearing a jacket. And oh, shit, now I was blushing again.

"I figured that out all by myself," I said. "Can you tell me how I might get a tow around here?"

He prodded the mud with his stick once again, looked up at the lowering clouds. "That isn't going to happen for a while," he said calmly. "See how steep that hill is? No one can pull you out until this dries up." He stroked Edna's head. "What possessed you to drive a beat-up old vehicle like this out onto an old logging road in the middle of a thunderstorm?"

"This beat-up old vehicle is the only one I have," I shot back. "It's been my home for years, and it's a perfectly fine machine that's served me very well. It's the damn road that's the problem!"

A frown appeared between the man's brows. "You live in this thing?" His tone was faintly incredulous.

"Yes, actually," I said. "I'm a craftswoman. I work the craft fair circuit, so I often end up living on the road. Up till now, that is."

"Interesting, but this road goes nowhere that's relevant to

you and your crafts fair circuit, so it doesn't explain what you're doing on my land."

Why, that arrogant dickhead. "That's none of your business," I told him.

"It is now," he said. "Since this thing is blocking my road."

I lifted my chin. "Wait a second," I said. "Didn't you just say that nobody's going to be driving on it until it's dry anyhow? Ergo, I'm not blocking anything, buddy."

His eyes looked me thoughtfully up and down. "True enough, I guess," he said. "But it's still my land." He wasn't ogling me, but my body still shivered, as if he were checking me out, inch by inch.

I suppressed an urge to cross my arms across my breasts. I would remain nonchalant or die in the attempt. "Besides, I'm not trespassing," I said, with all the bravado I could muster. "I'm on my way to my new landlord's place. Can you tell me how far it is to Jack Kendrick's house?"

The man's face went blank. His brow furrowed as he stared at me, and then at the mud-splattered, fantastical painting on the side of my van. "Wait," he said slowly. "Hold on. Don't tell me you're Vivien D'Onofrio."

Tension started to tighten, in my belly, my neck. "Why shouldn't I tell you that?"

"You're not what I expected," he said. "I have to talk to Duncan."

"Oh, my God. You mean, *you're* Jack Kendrick?" I was appalled. I'd been expecting a stolid jarhead type, older, thicker, with a paunch, balding graying hair buzzed off. Maybe a long, bushy mountain man kind of beard.

Not a foxy silver-eyed sex god who loved to walk in the rain.

"You're early." There was an accusing note in his voice. "Duncan texted me last night saying you were still in Idaho, so

I expected you late this evening, or tomorrow. Otherwise, I would have texted you alternate directions so you could have avoided driving on this road in the rain. What, did you drive all night?"

"Uh, yes." He didn't need to know what a cowering scaredy-cat I was, so I skipped the explanations, while running our entire conversation through my mind at the same time, trying to assess just how rude and in-his-face I had been to him.

Hmmph. Pretty bad, I concluded. No ruder than he deserved, but still … yikes.

Well, I guess I had to make an effort to fix it now. He was doing me a big, fat favor, after all. If he was still willing to do it at all, at this point.

"So," I said. "Seems like we got off to a weird start." I tried to sound conciliatory.

"Yeah, it does," he said blandly.

I kept my voice carefully light. "What do you mean, not what you expected? What were you expecting?"

"Duncan told me you were a professional designer with a stalker problem who needed to drop out of sight for a while. He did not tell me that you were an itinerant, tattooed, wild child neo-hippy."

All thoughts of conciliation vanished. "That's ridiculous!" I said hotly. "And rude! I'm not a neo-hippy, or a wild child. And I *am* a professional, itinerant or not! Tattoos or not! You owe me an apology!"

"We'll see." Jack's face was blatantly unapologetic.

Wild child? My brain stuck on that like a hook. It was not how I'd describe my muddy, strung-out, sleep-deprived, what-the-cat-dragged-in self, but holy crap, who did this guy think he was? How dare he?

So he was that insufferable kind of man who made snap judgments about a woman solely based on a nose ring and a tie-dyed t-shirt. Though I had, in point of fact, been meaning to take the small, glittering nose ring out before meeting him, just to suss him out first. Military types were sometimes conservative, so I had every intention of stopping at a place with a bathroom, splashing my face, putting on some decent clothes, some deodorant, brushing my hair, maybe even applying a little makeup.

But I hadn't wanted to get wet. Add yet another mistake to the list. Another wrong turn.

I held up my arm, displaying the tattoo of coiled barbed wire that circled my narrow wrist. "You've got a problem with me because of this? For real? In this day and age, when absolutely everyone has ink?"

Kendrick shrugged. "Just calling it how I see it."

I was blushing again. It smarted, to be judged by him. I bit back a babbling flood of explanations that were none of his damn business. Explanations that I owed to nobody.

In truth, that tattoo wasn't one that I had chosen myself. My mom's boyfriend had taken me to his buddy's tattoo parlor when I was ten, to spite my mom. As an attention-getting technique, it had bombed big-time, since my mom had been too focused organizing her next heroin fix to notice. I figured I was probably lucky I hadn't gotten hepatitis or worse from that guy's needle. Or that the boyfriend hadn't decided to put the tattoo on my neck or my face. Talk about a life-defining look.

But I didn't believe in playing the victim, so I'd flaunted that damned tattoo. I'd owned it, accepted it, and gotten plenty more on my own account. Nobody had forced me to get the Celtic knot tramp stamp tattoo over the crack of my ass, or the crescent moon and star on the top of my foot, or the smiling gothic sun face that adorned my shoulderblade, or the flower over my left breast. And Kendrick couldn't even see those.

I'd never felt embarrassed about my funky, alternative

fashion choices before. Usually, I kind of enjoyed getting into the faces of uptight people. I figured it was good for their health to have their assumptions challenged. But for some reason, the self-appointed task of challenging assumptions was no fun at all today.

I just didn't have the juice for it. Not with this guy.

"Would you mind answering my original question?" I asked, my voice tight. "How far is it to your place?"

"By this road, two and a half miles. Cross-country, it's a little over a mile and a half. Why didn't you take the other road?"

"What other road?"

"I had another road put in, from the other side of the property. It's shorter, and newer, and better kept. I texted the directions to Duncan. He should have passed them on to you."

I shoved back my hair, wondering uncomfortably if I'd left a fresh streak of mud across my cheek. "These were the directions he gave me last week, before I took off. He must have forgotten. I wouldn't be surprised. He's been distracted lately. Love, and all."

"I see," he said.

"But just for the record, I'm not a teenager. I'm almost twenty-eight. Nor am I any kind of wild child. Nor am I in any way flaky. On the contrary." I crossed my arms over my chest, and kept my chin up, since I couldn't deny the itinerant or tattooed parts.

Not that I was even minimally embarrassed about them.

He raised an eyebrow, and just waited, silent. I willed myself not to drop my gaze. A raindrop rolled slowly down the sculpted contours of his jaw. I watched it, breathless.

"You don't look twenty-eight," he observed.

I shook myself loose of his spell, and steeled myself to do the grown-up, dignified thing. "Well, I am. But if you've drawn your conclusions about my intrinsic value as a person after just a couple minutes of conversation, then screw it. There's nothing left to be said. I'll just hike back to town and find a motel and someone who can help me pull my van out later on. After that, I'm out of here."

He frowned at me, as if I were the unreasonable one. "That's not necessary. We'll talk logistics later. Get whatever you need out of your van for the time being. You can't walk back to town now."

I drew myself up to my full height, which was only about five foot-three, unfortunately. "I'll do what I damn well please. I don't need your help, or your judgments, or your attitude. I'll just pack a bag to walk to town, and Edna and I will be on our way. I'm sorry about the van being stuck here, but there's nothing I can do about that for the moment. I'll solve that problem as soon as I possibly can."

"You can't do that," he said, looking irritated. "This rain isn't going to stop anytime soon, and it's six miles back to town. You certainly aren't going to find anybody to help you with that van today, and probably not for several days. Get your stuff and I'll take you to my house." He stared at my stiff, stony face and folded arms, sighed, and said, "Okay. I'm sorry. I apologize, already. I was rude and inappropriate. Let me rephrase. Please, get your things. Please, let me show you to the house. It would be my privilege."

I was cautiously mollified, even though he was overdoing it a little. It was a good sign when a guy knew how to apologize. Whether he was sincere was another matter entirely, but just being able to manage the basic form was already promising.

I climbed into the van and shoved clothes into my duffel, too nervous to be methodical about it. I tossed cans of dog food into my backpack, attached my sleeping bag, and jumped out with both bags draped over my shoulder, and found him examining the lurid fantasy mural on the van while he waited. "What's this? A dragon?" he asked.

"No, it's a serpent," I informed him, feeling ridiculously defensive.

He grunted under his breath. "Is that your work?"

I snorted. Asfuckingif. "No," I said crisply. "That's not my style. Actually, I don't really paint at all. I'm a sculptor. An old friend of mine named Rafael painted that. I bought the van from him years ago."

"Hmmm. Whatever. Let's go, if you're ready." He grabbed the heavy duffel from my shoulder, flung it onto his back, and plunged straight into the thickest-looking part of the forest. Edna didn't even wait for me, that bubble-headed so-and-so. She bounded cheerfully after him, thrilled to be released from the van.

I struggled after him with my backpack bouncing as he wove and ducked through evergreens, brambles, and clinging foliage and festoons of lichen with what seemed unearthly grace and ease. I felt so clumsy and heavy with every step, dragging my mud-covered high-tops out of the ground with a wet, squelching sound with every step. Fir boughs slapped my face and snagged my hair.

Kendrick glanced back to make sure I was following and started up a steep incline. The soft mud was extremely slippery. I climbed the hill, half-crawling, grabbing the trunks of little sapling firs for balance. I started sliding downhill and reached for a clump of innocent-looking broad-leafed plants to steady myself, but their tough, leathery stems proved to be covered with thorns, fucking *ouch*. I was so startled, I lost my footing, and stumbled down onto my knee, knocking it against a jagged rock.

Suddenly, Edna was next to me, whining anxiously and licking my face.

"Need a hand?"

Jack Kendrick was looming over me, though to be fair, it wasn't really his fault that he loomed. He was standing above me on the hillside, after all, and he was ridiculously tall to begin with. His silvery eyes were narrowed thoughtfully. "Did you hurt yourself?" he asked me.

"Not a lot. Just, you know. I stuck myself with some thorns." I pointed at the plant, and struggled to rise, cradling my stinging hand.

He helped me to my feet, his big, warm hand under my elbow, cupping it.

"Let me take a look." He turned my hand over, examined it, and began deftly pulling out the tiny pale thorns that were embedded in my palm.

My breath just stopped. My senses were swamped with close-up sensory details. His head bent over mine, drops of rain plopping from the ends of his shaggy, dark hair. Every detail of him was etching itself into my brain. The way the hair grew back from his forehead, the white streak on his temple where the scar disappeared into his hairline. His sensual mouth. Very sensual, when it was relaxed. His lower lip, so cushiony and pink. It looked like it would be hot, soft. Kissable.

I was close enough to smell him. Soap, pine trees, wood smoke, and coffee. I wanted to touch his face, smooth the rain-drenched strands of hair that clung to his forehead.

I recoiled, alarmed at the power of my own crazy impulses. "Let's go on," I said abruptly.

"Okay. But I'll carry this." He pulled my backpack off my shoulders.

I was irritated at the implication that I couldn't handle it. I was small, yes, but I was no weakling. "I'm fine!" I tugged it back.

"Don't be stubborn. You've been driving for God knows

how long. You're exhausted, probably hungry, probably dehydrated. I'll carry it." He plucked it from my hand with an impatient jerk and slung it over his shoulder, along with my duffel. He started back up the hill, and I scrambled after him, knees wobbling. Edna, swiftly reassured that I was fine again, loped off to join Kendrick again. Little traitor.

"A little farther, and the hard part's over," he said over his shoulder.

"I'm not helpless! I was doing fine!" I shouted after him.

He lifted his hand in mute acknowledgement, but his silence made me sound foolish and ineffectual. A dirty trick.

Over the crest of the hill, the forest opened out into a broad sweep of gentle downhill slope. The trees here were taller, with more space between them. Edna pranced around, sniffing at fallen tree trunks. The rain had slackened, and the air was luminous and heavy with fog.

The silent grandeur of the forest worked magic on my jangled nerves as we padded along. Its beauty calmed me. It was magical, the sweet-smelling, pattering rain, the feathery delicacy of pine boughs, the paler green festoons of moss, and tiny star-shaped white flowers that floated ethereally in shiny green clumps of ground cover. It was so shockingly beautiful, I forgot my stinging hand, my mud-slimed shoes, my outraged sensibilities. Even Haupt and Snake Eyes had to retreat before this magnificence.

Twenty minutes later, he led me through a waist-high tangle of blooming wild roses.

Then I saw the house.

Chapter Two

Jack

I watched her as she caught sight of the house, and felt ridiculously gratified at the smile that lit up her face. Yeah, of course she likes it. What wasn't to like? I'd worked my ass off on that place.

Still, it pleased me that she appreciated the grace of the old-fashioned house under the enormous pines. I was proud of how it turned out. The comfortable porch, the huge flower and herb garden that I had meticulously landscaped. After all that work, she damn well ought to appreciate it. Anyone with a functioning brain would.

That, however, did not mean that I would allow some wandering wild child whose wet-t-shirt-clad body made me break out in a feverish sweat to park her lurid van in my driveway and totally fuck my peace of mind.

I'd worked hard for that peace of mind. I wasn't giving it up without a fight.

I'd known in my bones that something was up. Something

about the tone in Duncan's voice, that hidden smile. I knew that sneaky bastard better than he knew himself. Duncan had been keeping something back, and there it was, in all its glory. My job was to babysit a doe-eyed, bra-less, sexpot bombshell. I was supposed to keep her out of trouble. Probably trouble she'd whipped up herself.

Served me right, for letting Duncan jerk me around. It was the God's own truth that I owed Dunc, and would until my dying day, but fuck me.

This, I did not need.

Duncan had said that the girl was in danger. Some muddled, improbable tale about evil Nazis, treasure maps, long-lost art. Christ on a crutch. I'd given up on drama. I wanted peace and quiet. Simplicity. Plants. They didn't talk, or lie, or fuck each other over, or shoot at each other. I respected that. I craved the silence, the calm. I'd decided to dedicate my life to it.

Still, the idea of Vivi D'Onofrio in danger was a disturbing one. She was so small and delicate. Her skin was so pale against that red hair. I wondered if the color was fake. Its brilliance seemed a little exaggerated.

There was one quick, surefire way to find out. I tried to squelch the thought before my dick could swell to maximum capacity once again. Thank God for the rain poncho. Every detail of her figure had been visible in the damp tie-dye t-shirt. Those high, perfect tits, the kind that fit into a champagne cup. That classic, tender, just-enough mouthful. I cursed under my breath.

"You said something?" she asked.

I shook my head. I didn't trust myself to speak.

"Did you build this yourself?" she persisted, waiting for my nod.

"Wow." Her voice sounded almost reverent. We passed

through the riotous array of spring flowers, blooming bushes, lush borders of aromatic herbs, flowers of every type and color. "Is, ah, someone in your family a gardener?" she asked delicately.

"I'm the only one who lives here," I said.

"Ah. I see."

"The barn is around the back." I led her around the building, beyond which stood a large, freshly remodeled and painted barn. The apartment was on the top.

I'd lived in it myself for the time it took me to build my house. I'd been using the bottom floor for a garage and the apartment above it for storage, but last week, after another one of Duncan's epic bullying sessions, I'd finally caved. I dutifully moved my book boxes and gardening supplies out and into the attic space to make room for Duncan's future sister-in-law. I'd pictured her to be some uptight New York artistic type, all in tight black. But I'd never seen anyone as colorful as Vivi D'Onofrio. She glowed, like neon. Even when she was covered with mud, I needed fucking sunglasses.

I led her up the stairs, which I'd built onto the outside of the building, and onto the deck. I slid open the sliding glass doors and stood back to let her enter first. The place was plain, but freshly painted and simply furnished. She gazed at the living room that opened onto the deck, with the views of the river.

She slowly walked into the big bedroom that looked out over the garden, then into the bathroom, looked at the deep sink, the old claw-foot Victorian tub that I'd found at an auction a couple years ago. It had a transparent shower curtain with old-style botanical illustrations of flowers, complete with their Latin names, splashed all over it.

She sidled out the bathroom door past me, careful not to touch me, and walked into the spacious kitchen. She opened the freezer, sighing when she saw the automatic ice maker. She pushed the lever, grabbed a handful of ice, held it to her pink cheek.

"It's perfect," she announced.

She folded her arms in front of her chest, and waited for me to contradict her. Her face was battle ready. There was a streak of mud across one high cheekbone.

"Well?" she asked impatiently. "Spit it out, Kendrick."

"Well, what?" I responded, bemused. "Spit what out?"

Her hair was drying, fluffing up into a fiery mane. "The bottom line," she said. "Have we got a deal? You sounded like you weren't sure, back there. Sounded like my tattoos scared you. Have you decided you have the nerve to endure me after all?"

I exhaled slowly and counted, refusing to rise to the bait. "I have to talk to Duncan," I temporized. "He gave me a false impression."

"I doubt that. I think you just made some stupid assumptions. And clearly, you're still making them. And now, if you'll excuse me, I'm cold, and I really need a hot shower and some dry clothes. Thanks very much for carrying my stuff."

She gestured toward the door with a 'buh-bye!' kind of smile that would have irritated the hell out of me if I weren't already so shaken up.

When I got back to my own kitchen, I tried not to visualize Vivi's body naked in the tub, hot water streaming down her slim legs, her high breasts. Tried and failed. I felt flustered, sweaty, stupid. As unsure of myself as a teenager.

I was usually good at dealing with the unexpected, being flex, turning surprises to my advantage. The trick was to stay calm in my deepest center. That had helped me during those years on the task force with Dunc, back in Afghanistan. And before, in the military, in Iraq, in Africa. It had helped me negotiate my childhood and manage the unpredictable characters who had inhabited it. It had helped me navigate those bleak, lonely months I had spent on the streets of North Portland when I was a teenager.

I'd learned some hard facts back then, and I could never unlearn them. I knew, for example, that nothing lasted forever. That some people couldn't stay in one place even if they wanted to, so there was no point in blaming or judging. Getting uptight about it was like blaming a leaf for being green.

I put on a pot of coffee, just to do something with my hands. A person like Vivi D'Onofrio was liable to climb into her truck, or motorcycle, or van and disappear in a cloud of dust at any time. With no hard feelings, of course. I sensed it on a bone-deep level.

That was not the kind of woman I wanted to be attracted to. I knew how that story ended before it began. I would not do that to myself. I would not be so fucking stupid.

I did not feel calm and still in my center when I looked at her. I wouldn't be able to stay cool and detached. I'd get all wound up, tied in knots. I'd fuck myself up.

But still, I pictured water streaming down over her body, and I wondered. Curly ringlets? Straight swatches? Red pussy hair, or auburn brown? Tightly furled, secretive pale pink pussy lips, or a bright crimson one that burst proudly out of her slit like some sort of exotic flower? Shaved? Pierced? And her flavor?

I had to dangle my head between my knees for a second to manage the head rush just from imagining her flavor.

Chapter Three

Vivi

I tried to relax in the shower, but I was so angry at myself for not stopping to bathe and dress before meeting Kendrick. How sloppy and irresponsible of me. First impressions were so hard to shake. And getting all snotty and all up in his face— what had possessed me?

I'd always been impulsive, hotheaded. Lucia had lectured and scolded and admonished me for years, trying to teach me some class. Turn me into a lady.

With limited success. But it had been a noble effort.

Wow. Amazing water pressure. Fabulous hot water heater. Wonderful deep lovely bathtub. I turned off the faucet and grabbed one of the big, fluffy towels I'd found on the shelf. I'd found some soap and shampoo over the tub, too, and thank God for it, since I hadn't remembered to pack any of my bath stuff into my duffel.

I sorted through my bag, hair dripping, taking inventory. Kendrick's brooding presence outside the van had addled my wits. I had remembered dog food, for instance, but had forgotten the can opener. I was usually extremely organized. Maniacally so. It was an essential survival skill when one lived in a camper van.

I dragged out bits and pieces from the pockets of my purse and duffel. Matches, pocketknife, flashlight. Strange guy, that Jack Kendrick. He seemed so mellow and zen, quiet, soft-spoken, and then suddenly he turned provocative and rude. I hauled out a handful of candles, a pack of my favorite incense, but no pans, dishes, or human food. Which meant that I had to hike back to the van if I wanted to eat.

A bleak, exhausting prospect. My stomach rumbled restlessly.

First things first, though. Edna was waiting patiently, gazing through the glass door from the deck outside in limpid reproach. The pocket-knife would not open a can of dog food. I would have to face the man and beg a can opener off him. There was no avoiding this necessity.

A few careful, anxious primping minutes later, I walked down the stairs, wishing I had a blow-dryer. I needed to fluff myself up, get some volume. With wet hair, I looked even smaller and more insignificant than I already was. Like a wet Persian cat.

I was so angry at my silly self for being so nervous. This man had no power over me. He was nothing to me. He just happened to be good-looking and charismatic, that was all. No biggie. Super normal. I was a hetero female with a regular functioning load of hungry sex hormones, so yeah. I noticed a good-looking man when one came into my field of vision. So sue me.

Although I certainly hadn't thrown out any come-hither glances since the Brian Wilder debacle. That bitter taste in my mouth still lingered. Six years of celibacy. I could hardly believe it myself, but there it was.

And this falling away, weak-in-the-knees feeling? This was absurd. Being afraid of what Kendrick thought of me? Wanting his approval? Yikes. Absolutely not okay.

I could not afford to feel so vulnerable. I'd spent too much energy fighting people's opinions and efforts to control me. Like I had with Brian. I'd paid a high price for that, and the prize had to be worth something. My sense of self was too hard-won.

Just thinking about Brian made me angry, exhausted and sickened.

I'd given up so much to be free artistically. I'd sacrificed a high-profile, lucrative career as a sculptor for that precious freedom. That was why I'd been on the road so long, making the best of the hard choices I'd made. Trying with great energy not to regret them. And working my ass off, too, incidentally, which was nothing to be ashamed of. I'd be damned if I'd let some pinheaded, muscle-bound, small-minded, judgmental doofus make me feel small. No matter how fine he was.

I walked across the luxuriant lawn, up the porch steps, admiring the thickness and variety of the flowers bordering the house and the flagstone walkway. The garden was over-the-top beautiful. Wildly luxuriant.

At the front door, I raised my hand to knock, and my hand stopped in midair as my chest constricted. Oh, please. Enough of this crap. I forced myself to rap boldly.

Bam-bam, here I am.

The door opened after a moment, and there he was. He seemed even bigger, framed by the door. No poncho, so I could finally check out all his assets. Wow.

I was absurdly glad that I'd changed into the green rayon dress. I'd even considered taking out the nose ring. Then I'd concluded that the damage was done. Taking it out now revealed more about my fears and insecurities than leaving it in did.

And as if that wasn't enough to make me feel self-conscious, the dress I'd shoved into the duffel was the very one that dipped down both in the front and the back, showing off the little flower tattoo over my breast, and the sun tattoo on my shoulder.

Just as well. It kept me honest. I'd flaunt 'em. He'd just have to deal with the tattooed, itinerant wild child that I was. Nyah, nyah.

Other than that detail, the dress was quite modest and feminine and pretty. It was ankle length, just skimming my minimal curves, and it looked great with the gold and emerald pendant that Lucia had given me. The last one of our trio. Snake Eyes had stolen both Nancy's and Nell's.

If my hair had only been dry, it would have covered both tattoos, being more than long and thick enough. But not when wet.

His eyes swept over me, and I suffered a burst of agonizing self-consciousness. I hadn't packed a bra into my duffel, and my brights were on, big-time, and not just because of the cold. I'd put on a little bit of makeup, too, just because, and he was noticing it. Maybe he would think I was trying to impress him. Allure him. God forbid.

He was still in his mud-spattered jeans. Without the poncho, I could see how barrel-chested he was. The t-shirt revealed the muscular breadth of his shoulders. The faded jeans affectionately hugged his powerful thighs. *Talk to the man, Viv,* my frozen brain pleaded. *Say something. Anything. Don't just stand there gawking at the man's pecs.*

"Sorry to bother you," I said, kicking myself for my breathless, kittenish tone. None of that fluttery shit was allowed. I had to be an Amazon. A tough broad. Hard as nails.

"No bother. Come on in. I made coffee."

I followed him into a big room with an open kitchen on one

side, banks of windows on all sides, paneled in rosy, fragrant cedar. An old-fashioned woodstove had a couple of soft, battered-looking couches grouped around it, and a stack of cut wood tucked into a recessed space in the wall. There was an old-fashioned braided rug in deep, brilliant colors, on the wood-plank floor. Plants were everywhere: ferns, jades, spider plants, begonias, scores of others I couldn't begin to identify. The deep windowsills were all lined with clay boxes filled with pale sprouts and tender seedlings. It was warm, cheerful, welcoming. Beautiful.

Jack gestured toward an old trestle table in the kitchen area. "Have a seat. How do you like your coffee?"

"Milk, if you have it, and sugar, please."

He poured coffee into a huge earthenware mug, reached into his refrigerator, and held up a carton of half-and-half. "This do?"

"How luxurious," I said. "Nobody I know uses half-and-half anymore. It's always one percent, or skim. Or those vegetable milks."

He grunted. "I eat whatever I like."

A sudden memory of Brian, who had a precision scale in his kitchen and counted every gram of fat he ate, rose up in my mind. I fought back an impulse to giggle and concentrated on stirring a spoonful of glistening, sticky brown sugar into my coffee. I tried not to stare at the way his biceps distended the short sleeves of his shirt.

Tried and failed.

He sat down across from me. I took a cautious sip. The coffee was strong, and delicious. It would have been too strong, but for the shot of cream.

"Great coffee," I offered.

He nodded. I tried to relax by studying the luxuriant house plants, and then noticed that he was staring fixedly at the neckline of my dress. I glanced down, terrified that it was gaping scandalously over a nipple, but no. Nothing out of the ordinary.

"Sorry," he said, looking down. "I, um, was just looking at your eranthis hyemalis."

I blinked at him, perplexed. "My...ah, my *what?*"

He looked embarrassed. "The flower. On your chest. I thought at first that it was *Ranunculus acris,* but then—"

"A what?"

He let out an impatient sigh. "A buttercup. But then I saw the leaves. Definitely *Eranthis hyemalis.* Winter Aconite, I mean."

I looked down at my tattoo. "Oh. Yeah. I like this flower. I noticed it in a friend's garden, blooming in the snow, and that impressed me. I saw it as the perfect combination of toughness and a good attitude."

"Yeah, they're great flowers." He tore his gaze from my body and stared down into his coffee cup as if there were something really interesting at the bottom of it.

I shoved my damp hair behind my ears. "I came down to ask you a favor," I said, taking another sip of the hot, bracing coffee. "I forgot some key things when I left the van. Most I can do without, but the most important is a can opener, so I can feed Edna."

He reached around, pulled open a drawer, and handed me one. "Keep it at your place," he said. "I have another one."

"And some sort of bowl? I forgot her dish, too," I admitted.

He rummaged in a cupboard for a plastic dish. "Anything else?"

"If I could borrow your broom to sweep out the mud I tracked in?"

He gestured behind himself, to a corner where a broom and dustpan were tucked. "Help yourself."

"Thank you. Edna thanks you, too. As only a Labrador

retriever can." I took a final sip of coffee and scooped up the bowl and can opener. "I'll just head on back up to my apartment, then." I grabbed the broom and dustpan, and made for the door.

I'd managed not to giggle or simper. Now, if I could just get out the door without tripping over the rug, I was home free.

"Do you have anything to eat tonight?" he demanded.

"No, but Edna and I might just hike back to the van and grab some stuff. It's no big deal."

"I'll take you into town to do some shopping."

"No, really," I said hastily. "You've gone to enough trouble."

"No trouble. I need groceries anyway. There's just the convenience store here in Silverfish, so I'll take you to the Safeway in Pebble River."

I was still shaking my head, almost desperately. "I don't want to put you to—"

"Look," he said. "This is a necessity for me. I won't be able to eat tonight if I know you've got no food up there."

"Well. That's, uh, sweet of you," I said, flustered.

"No, just practical. If you fast, I have to fast, too. It's the law. And fasting makes me crabby."

That was a new concept for me. I didn't know what to do with it. He took my baffled silence as assent, scooped up my coffee cup, and took it to the sink. "Be ready in half an hour?"

I opened my mouth to argue but stopped when my stomach rumbled. It sounded thunderously loud. He glanced over his shoulder and gave me a smile that dazzled me.

And oh, for God's sake. Whatever.

"Thanks." I mustered all my dignity and still somehow tripped over the rug as I left.

Chapter Four

Jack

To shave or not to shave.

It took me ten minutes to work out that philosophical conundrum. I'd been letting my stubble grow out, figuring what the fuck, but after assessing myself in the bathroom mirror, I decided that I looked scruffy and shabby. I couldn't go into town with her looking like a bum. Not if she was going to wear that green thing.

I should take her out to dinner, I thought, as I lathered up my face. The thought made me as nervous as if I were a teenager, asking a hot girl out to a dance. But it wasn't about that. Not at all. It was just a neighborly gesture.

Right. What the fuck was I going to do with her now?

My dick had some very good ideas, but none of them were smart.

The way she'd talked about the flower she'd seen in the winter garden surprised me. That combination of toughness

35

and a good attitude in the Winter Aconite. She'd seen it. That was rare. Most people saw plants as a commodity, a decoration, a means to an end, if they saw them at all. Not many saw them as entities in their own right.

Yeah, and maybe she was a woo-woo earth-mother type who would want to commune naked with the nature spirits, or something terrifying like that. Jesus. I had to stop shaving for a minute to banish that fleeting image from my mind, or else risk nicking an artery. Pathetic, sex-starved mountain man that I was.

It had been so long for me, I didn't even want to do the math.

I could always make the situation go away by pissing her off until she left in a huff. She was proud, prickly. Shouldn't be too hard. But the idea did not appeal to me.

I wiped off shaving cream as I thought it through. I could make crude sexual advances. Infuriate her into leaving. Duncan would kick my ass, but hey. A man had his limits. And it wasn't like I would be kicking her out. She would do all the heavy lifting herself. All I had to do was be the asshole.

But excitement flooded me at the thought of touching her. Stiff dick, red face, pounding heart. I gripped the sink with both hands and grimly thought it through.

Bad idea. Too volatile. She might press charges against me for sexual harassment, which would be embarrassing and stupid. And absolutely justified. That would suck.

Worse yet, who knew? Maybe she'd reciprocate. God help me then.

And there was the danger issue, too. Entirely aside from the evil Nazi art freaks, it was flat-out insane for a gorgeous woman like that to wander around alone in a fucking van, flaunting her sexy little body right and left. Any ignorant redneck dickhead who saw tattoos and a nose ring would instantly draw his conclusions and make a pass.

Repeat after me, I told myself grimly. Not. My. Problem.

It was the mantra for the day.

Chapter Five

Vivi

I opened to Jack Kendrick's knock. He'd shaved, and combed his wet hair back off his face, which was even more striking now that I could see the stark, lean angles of his jaw, his chin. And those eyebrows, wow.

I suddenly wondered how long I'd been staring.

At the grocery checkout stand in Pebble River, we eyed each other's choices with furtive curiosity. I had gone for the fruits and veggies mostly, stuff from the health food section. He was more classic in his tastes, and definitely a carnivore, but most of his groceries were real food, not empty junk. Which did not surprise me, when I looked at his amazing body. Which I did, at every opportunity.

In the parking lot, he turned to me as soon as he started up the engine. "Let's get some food," he said.

"Didn't we just?"

"I mean a restaurant. You like Mexican?"

"Uh, yes," I admitted, and suddenly, the idea of a plate of

steaming, cheese- smothered enchiladas took me by storm. Oh my God, yes.

The meal went smoothly enough, at first. He started by asking me for a rundown of the security situation, so I munched on the freshly fried tortilla chips with fabulous fresh salsa and *pico de gallo*, and regaled him with the long and harrowing tale of Lucia's death, the gift of the necklaces, the abductions of my two sisters, and the evil Ulf Haupt and his demonic minion, John. Both of whom were convinced that the D'Onofrio sisters could reveal the whereabouts of these mysterious lost sketches, whatever they were, if sufficiently terrified or tortured. I took off my necklace and showed it to him, the last of the trio that Lucia had given to us. He squinted at it for a while, from every angle, and handed it back, shaking his head.

"Un-fucking-believable," was his laconic comment.

"Tell me about it," I agreed, fervently.

Then he started asking questions about me. I told him about studying art in New York, and about my brief and dizzying burst of artistic success when I signed the contract with Brian's gallery. I did not mention my personal relationship with Brian, or why I had broken the contract and run. In fact, I started glossing over more and more details as I went. That cool, assessing look in his eyes shut me up. It was as if he thought he knew something about me. Or rather, like he'd already made up his mind.

"So, you just left everything you built when it was all going so well, and ran off into the sunset to find yourself?" he asked.

My chin went up as I bristled. "I suppose you could say that, if you were being unkind. I didn't like the way the gallery management was pushing me around. I decided I'd do better on the road, on the crafts fair circuit, developing my own designs. With nobody breathing down my neck."

"I guess you must hate that more than anything."

I frowned at him, confused. "Excuse me? Hate what?"

"Having someone breathing down your neck," he specified.

I chewed on that for a thoughtful minute. "Depends on the person," I said. "And what they want from me."

"Doesn't it always," he said. "Did you break any hearts when you ran?"

My belly clenched. Yikes. His hidden agenda was rearing its horned, fanged head, big-time. "That sounds like a trick question," I said. "Extremely personal, too."

"Sorry," he said, sounding anything but. "Just wondering."

I stared down at my half-eaten enchiladas. My appetite was swiftly fading.

"So you did leave someone," he said.

My teeth clenched. "I broke up with the man I was seeing before I left, but I had damn good reason."

"Yeah? What was that?"

Well, actually, I found out that he was the devil, I wanted to say, but didn't, it being none of his damn business. Besides, I didn't want him to think I was a total shit magnet, considering my current problems. "I'm not sure I like your tone," I said.

He lifted his shoulders. "I didn't mean to offend."

"You have no right to judge me, you know," I told him.

"I'm not judging."

The fuck he wasn't. From there, the conversation went swiftly downhill. I did my part, but his responses were terse monosyllables. And his shuttered, glittering stare was starting to unnerve me.

I took a fortifying swallow of my margarita and stared him straight in the eye. "Look, Mr. Kendrick—"

"Call me Jack."

"Okay, Jack. Just tell me what's on your mind, okay?"

His eyebrow tilted up. "What do you mean?"

I shoved my hair back. "I mean, how you seem to be

judging me for things you know nothing about. I mean, how uncomfortable you seem to be with me."

"Is that all?"

I waved my fork. "What else would I be talking about?"

"I thought you might be talking about the fact that I'm attracted to you," he said. "I figured you might have noticed. It's kind of hard to miss."

My fork clattered loudly down onto my plate. "Ah ... actually ..."

"But since you brought it up," he continued, "I might as well just be honest. You're right. I am uncomfortable, for two reasons. The fact that I'm attracted to you is one of those reasons. And the other reason—and I'm sorry if I hurt your feelings—is that you are not the type of woman I want to be attracted to. That puts me in a bad place."

My jaw dropped. "My type?" I repeated. "What type is that? Are you one of those meatheads who think that girls with tattoos are automatically promiscuous?"

He waved that away. "No, that's not the issue. I'm talking about living in a van, moving around all the time, getting bored easily, leaving things half done. I don't want to get involved with someone who's just passing through. It's a waste of time."

Anger burned in my stomach. "Hold on. Did I invite you to get sexually involved with me without me noticing it? Or did you just assume that my type is sexually available to everyone?"

Jack took a slow, swallow of beer, stalling. "No. You didn't. And I don't."

"So, you want to nail me, but you think I'm scum, and you don't want me around lowering your property value."

He frowned. "Don't put words in my mouth. I didn't say 'scum.'"

"I call it how I feel it," I retorted. "You know what? I bet you just want me to get so pissed off, I just pack up and leave, right? And simplify your life. Is that the plan?"

He forked up a bite of his steak fajita. "That would be my plan, if it weren't for this danger issue," he said, reluctantly. "It does sound like you've got one hell of a security problem. But I don't—"

"Let me make a revolutionary suggestion," I announced. "Get this, Kendrick. I know this idea might shock you to your toes, but how about if we just don't have sex?"

He covered his mouth with his napkin to smother a laugh, his eyes darting around the restaurant. "Uh—"

"It's the perfect solution," I went on. "Amazing in its simplicity. You don't have to fuck me, if it would be so upsetting to you. Aren't you relieved? Isn't that just an incredible load off your mind? Just ignore me, okay? It'll be easy. I'll just stay the hell out of your way and do my own thing."

He looked alarmed. "And what exactly is your thing?"

I shrugged. "Living my life. Playing with my dog. Making my art. Duncan mentioned that you have a studio in the barn, but I'll understand if you don't want me to use the space. The apartment will do nicely for now."

Jack rose, bumping the table and knocking over the empty beer bottle. A fork fell to the floor. The restaurant went silent. A waitress froze in position, holding her trays of food. Jack cursed softly. "Let's get out of here."

"Fine." I got up and began digging for my wallet.

"I've got the check," he said.

I swept past him, elbowing him out of my way at the cash register. "I'd rather die than let you pay for my meal," I hissed.

I sat as far from him as possible in the truck. After he pulled into the driveway, I climbed out without a word, slammed the door, and reached for my groceries.

He tried to take the bags from me. I jerked them away.

He yanked them right back. "Let me."

Oh, to hell with it. I followed the crunch of his boots on the gravel through the darkness and followed him up the stairs, still fuming.

He opened my door with his own key, flipped on the lights, and set my shopping bags on the kitchen counter. We gazed at each other as Edna leaped and danced and wagged her enthusiastic greeting.

"Good night," I said to him, pointedly.

"Where are you going to sleep?" he asked.

I opened and closed her mouth. "Wha—what?" I forced out.

"There's no bed here. Where are you going to sleep?"

"Ah," I murmured, blushing.

There was a fleeting hint of a smile in his eyes. "I wasn't suggesting my own bed."

"I didn't think you were," I lied, my blush deepening. "I'm sleeping in my sleeping bag. It was hooked to my backpack. See?"

"Just a sleeping bag? On the bare floor?" He sounded shocked.

"I'm used to roughing it."

He frowned, ruffling Edna's ears. "No one sleeps on a bare floor in my place," he said. "I don't care what you're used to."

"Well, I appreciate the sentiment, but strictly speaking, it's not your place. I'll be paying rent. Which means it's my place. You're not obligated to treat me like a guest."

He turned and stalked out the door, disappearing into the dense darkness. I shut the door behind him, exhaling a deep sigh of relief.

My battle tension dissipated, leaving me exhausted. I opened the sliding doors and let the fragrant night air into the room. Then I put away my groceries in the big, clean kitchen.

That bright, clean, empty fridge just soothed my soul. So much space for everything. It felt strange, after the van, and my sisters' microscopic New York apartments. Their wretched little half-refrigerators.

Though Fate had decreed that both of their new boyfriends have absolute top-shelf, chef's kiss kitchens. That random little detail made me obscurely happy.

Then I lit one of my scented candles and some sandalwood incense, turned out the overhead light, and sat down cross-legged on my sleeping bag. The graceful, empty room flickering with candlelight soothed me. It felt strange and lovely, to have the door open to the night. To let my senses open and soften, to listen to frogs and insects singing their sweet night songs. I'd been so paranoid and wound up tight these last few weeks. But here, oddly, I felt almost safe.

From Snake Eyes and Haupt, anyway. If not from my own sex-starved stupidity.

A sense of his presence jolted my nerves into a state of alert. I jumped to my feet as he pushed open the mosquito screen with his boot and stepped through the sliding glass doors. He carried a rolled-up futon without apparent effort, a feather pillow wedged beneath his muscular arm.

"Knock next time," I said sharply. "I'd appreciate it."

He gazed over the futon, looking aggrieved. "Of course I would, under normal circumstances," he said. "My hands were full." He unfolded it onto the floor, tossed the pillow on top.

"For the record," I persisted, "in the future, I prefer that you not barge in on me like that. Whether your hands are full or not."

The condescending, dismissive gesture he made with his shoulders made me tense. "You're not taking me seriously," I said tightly. "It's bugging me. Do we understand each other?"

"Yes, absolutely. Don't worry, I heard you." His eyes swept

the room until they found my sleeping bag. "Will that keep you warm enough?"

"It always has before," I assured him. "The futon wasn't necessary, but thanks, anyway. It's very kind of you."

"The incense smells good." His eyes followed the thin stream of smoke that undulated sensuously from the tiny bronze censer.

"Yes, it does," I agreed. "It's my favorite scent."

A heavy silence fell. "Ah ... thanks for the futon," I said again. "Very kind of you."

I had intended the words to be a dismissal, but my voice emerged so husky and low and tentative, the phrase sounded almost inviting.

I tried to think of something else to say, but after a couple minutes of strugging, I abandoned the effort. I was too damned tired. It felt false. And this guy wasn't interested in social chatter anyhow. Nor did he seem to be made uncomfortable by silence. He just stood there like a mountain in my bedroom. As dense as granite. An unidentifiable emotion burned from his shadowed eyes. He wasn't leaving this place until he was damned good and ready.

So I just stood there and quietly bore the weight of the silence in the flickering dimness, until it became something more than silence. It was anticipation, taut and aching with things that longed to be said. A breeze wafted through the door and put out a candle, casting the room into deeper shadow.

I took matches from my pocket and turned to relight it ... then froze, realizing that he was right behind me.

"Excuse me. Didn't mean to startle you. I was just looking at this." He gestured at my back with his fingertip, indicating my sun tattoo without touching me. "I caught a glimpse of it while you were paying for your dinner, but I couldn't tell what it was under all your hair." He studied the small circle with radiating lines. "A sun," he said. "Does it have some special meaning? Like the flower?"

"Yes," I said. "It's in memorium. For a friend I lost some years ago."

His hand dropped. "I'm sorry."

I nodded and turned to face him. It took all my nerve to raise my eyes to his, and when I finally managed it, the smoldering hunger in his gaze stole my breath.

"Do you have any other tattoos?" he asked.

I lifted my chin, straightened my spine. He had no right to do this, when I was all alone in the dark with him. Throwing those hot, intense sexual vibes at me, when I felt so vulnerable and tempted. "That's for me to know, and for you to wonder about." I aimed for a crisp, dismissive tone. Insofar as I could, with no breath to back it up.

The breathlessness once again made my words sound flirtatious. God help me.

Sure enough, he didn't look dismissed. He looked like he was wondering what else was written on my naked body, as I had just freely invited him to do. Who could blame him? He was wondering so damn hard, I could feel it against my skin.

If he made a move on me now, I wouldn't have the force of will to push him away. I was gooey to the core. I was sopping wet for him. One featherlight push, and down I would fall, right onto my back. *Take me. Right now.*

After all my uppity pronouncements. All my fighting words.

"Good night." He turned and headed out the door.

I stood for a moment, looking at the black rectangle, wide open to the fragrant, noisy forest outside.

The candlelit room suddenly seemed terribly empty.

Chapter Six

Jack

Ipaced the length of my living room, hands clenched, stopping at each end like a caged beast.

I'd just spent hours on the Internet, researching Vivi D'Onofrio. I'd browsed around on her commercial website, looking at her jewelry designs. It was a kind of rabbit hole I'd never fallen down before. Necklaces, rings, brooches, earrings, nose rings, bracelets, anklets, toe rings, piercings. Little twisted metal frames to decorate perfume bottles, Christmas tree ornaments, mobiles, jewelry boxes. All made of glass, beads, metal, wood, homemade paper, found materials.

The stuff was weirdly beautiful. Unusual. I couldn't put my finger on what it was exactly that I liked about it. I wasn't a jewelry-wearing sort of guy myself, but I liked her prehistoric-meets-steam punk-meets-futuristic vibe. Weird, earthy, ethereal, all at the same time.

I wondered how she dealt with her mail-order business. If I were one of the bad guys, the first thing I would do would be to order a pair of earrings from her site, go to the address they were sent from, and start pushing whoever I found there. Dangerous for everyone involved.

There were also a lot of references regarding a big-shot art gallery in New York City, run by a guy named Brian Wilder. There was a picture of this Brian, one of those stiff, mannered shots, where the subject tries to look smart and deep and thoughtful by holding on to his chin with a hooked finger, as if hiding a zit.

The guy's photo made my prick-o-meter shoot way off the chart.

I had also studied shots of Vivi's artwork from the archived catalogs of the Wilder Gallery, from five or six years ago. They had much the same vibe as the smaller jewelry pieces on her website, but they were much bigger, much bolder and more ambitious, and the prices staggered me. Jesus wept. Even if the gallery took a huge cut, she could have gotten rich, if she'd stayed with it.

But hey. For some people, freedom was more important than wealth. No one knew that better than me. That was the thought that had propelled me into frantic pacing.

The situation was so fucked. I could hardly breathe. Wound up, turned on. The way things were going, I wasn't going to be able to stop myself from tossing her down and having at her like a wild animal. And my instincts whispered the thought to me like a seductive siren song. Angry and proud as she was, I had a feeling that she wouldn't stop me.

There were no checks or balances here. There was nothing to hold me back from this disaster but my own fast eroding self-control. Everything about her pulled me. I was strung out on the fruity, sweet smell of her hair. The outrageous vivid color of it. I couldn't get over those big, brilliant eyes, the exotic shape of them. Her delicate, pointed chin. Her pink, full mouth.

I wondered, uncomfortably, who the friend was, the one she'd gotten the memorial tattoo for. I wondered if this person was a lover who had died. Wondered if she still missed the guy. Or grieved for him. He must have been important, to get his own commemorative tattoo.

Big can of worms. None of my goddamn business.

Her shoulder was so thin and delicate, decorated with that tiny, stylized sun image. Her skin so smooth, her muscles sinuous and strong, despite how slender her small frame was. Small and lithe and well-knit and perfect.

I looked up at the clock and did the math. It was six-thirty AM in Italy, where Duncan was currently wallowing in romantic bliss, in some picturesque B&B in Tuscany. He would be unthrilled to be dragged out of the clasp of his new lady's silken limbs. Good. It served the bastard right for getting me into this.

Duncan's satellite phone rang and rang. Eight times, nine, ten, eleven. I just sat there and waited, grim and relentless.

Duncan finally picked up. "Jack? What the fuck?" His voice was thick with sleep.

"I think that's my line," I said.

"Is Vivi okay?" My friend's voice sharpened.

"She's fine," I said.

"So? What's the problem? Why are you calling me at ass-crack thirty?"

"Think about it," Jack snarled. "Figure it out, Dunc."

A soft, feminine murmur in the background. A questioning tone. "Nah, just Jack," Duncan replied. Another questioning murmur. "He says Vivi's fine. I'll go talk in the other room. Go on back to sleep."

I heard a door click shut, and Duncan's voice got harder. "You woke Nell up. She needs her sleep. She's been through hell lately. Do you have any idea what time it is?"

"You never hesitate to call in the middle of the night when the urge takes you," I reminded him. "Besides, the sun should be up where you are in the world. Why didn't you tell me what to expect?"

Duncan paused, baffled. "I did," he said, his voice blank. "I told you all about those sadistic motherfuckers who are after my fiancée and my soon-to-be sisters-in-law. What else do you need to know about the—"

"No. Not about them. I mean about her."

"Ah ... her? You mean ... Vivi?" he said, in a tone of discovery. "I see. You mean, why didn't I warn you about how cute she was? You're all mad because I didn't fill you in about the long red hair, the big gray eyes, the slender limbs, the rosy lips? Is that what's going on here?"

"Goddamn it, Dunc—"

"You're a sad case, buddy, when you need to be warned about a thing like that. So, did she knock you back a couple of paces? Figured she might. Nice."

"You didn't tell me she was a bouncing tattooed flower child with a fucking dragon painted on her camper van." I felt frustrated, and stupid. I was unable to express exactly why I felt so misled and jerked around. Like I was being set up to be the asshole.

"What the fuck? Her tattoos bug you, huh? Jesus, man, I had no idea your ass was so tight." Duncan clucked his tongue. "Did you see the one over the crack of her ass?"

I jolted upright, as if I'd been stung by a bee. "How the *fuck* do you know that?"

"Saw her in low-rise jeans once," Dunc said laconically. "Nice ink. Looks great."

"You bucket of slime! Aren't you supposed to be in love with her sister?"

"Whoa, aren't we passionate," Duncan observed. "I *am* in

love with the sister. I'm marrying the sister. I'm all over that sister twenty-four-seven, like white on rice. But I still notice a great, mandolin-shaped ass when I see one. So shoot me for sending it your way. God knows, you needed something to get you going, and Vivi's good for giving jolts. The woman's like a walking firecracker."

"You admit it, then? You set me up?" I demanded.

Duncan was silent for a moment. "Hold on here," he said slowly. "You're thinking this is all about you and your deep-frozen dick, aren't you? It's not. Did Vivi tell you what they did to Nell when they took her?"

I rubbed my aching forehead. "We actually never got around to any kind of details like that," I said. "At least not so far. But that's not what I'm—"

"They shot the bodyguard I hired to accompany her. They coerced a little old lady to lure her into a trap, and then they bashed that little old lady in the head. They drugged Nell, and shoved her into the trunk of a car. They tied her to a chair. They beat her. They would have cut her and raped her and killed her if I hadn't gotten there in time. These are the guys who are after Vivi. That's exactly what they'll do to her if they succeed. Think about it, you self-absorbed butthead. I'm doing this for her. Not for you. Are you paying close attention?"

A fierce sigh hissed out from between my clenched teeth. "I don't need a fucking sermon, Dunc."

"Doesn't seem that way," Duncan said. "The reason I'm breaking your balls about this is because this is the only way I can think of to keep Vivi relatively safe. Short of tying her, gagging her, and locking her in a fucking closet. She is not the most reasonable of females. In fact, she's, ah, real independent minded, you might say."

"I noticed that," I said sourly.

"It's a family trait," Duncan confided cheerfully. "Mine is just as bad. It'll drive you bug-fuck. Buckle up, buttercup."

"You need to resolve this before that happens," I said sourly. "Got any leads?"

"Not much yet. Nell and I are renting a car tomorrow to drive down to Castiglione Sant'Angelo and ask around. Nell speaks fluent Italian, you see. Among other things."

The fatuous pride in the guy's voice set my teeth on edge. "Well. How nice for you," I said. "Eat a pizza for me. Isn't that a perfect excuse to run off and leave me holding the bag."

"Dude." Duncan's voice dropped fifty degrees. "That's no bag you've got there. That's Nell's precious little sister. You don't get any further from a bag than that."

I gritted my teeth. "I didn't mean to imply that she was a—"

"Shut up. Just stop being such a stubborn, bad-tempered, contrary dickhead. I send a hot, sexy little red-headed thing your way to liven up your lonesome, monotonous existence, and what do you do? You bitch! You complain! Jesus, Jack! Get the fuck over yourself!"

"Oh, shut up."

"Me, shut up? You're the one who woke us up out of a sound sleep at six-thirty in the morning! Seriously, though, stay frosty, man. Those bastards are looking hard for her, and if they find her, she is meat. And so am I, incidentally, if Vivi doesn't stay okay. You have got to convince her to lay low. Keep quiet. Sculpt stuff. Make earrings. Whatever the hell keeps her busy and out of trouble."

"Yeah, right," I scoffed. "Like I can 'convince her' of anything."

"Come on, man. Sweeten her up. Seduce her. Whatever works for you guys. God knows, you're suffering from testosterone poisoning. Unload some of that energy before you hurt yourself. Get your dick out of the deep freeze and use it for something useful. Melt her brain. Do what you have to do. Find a way to keep her safe. Or else."

I hung up on him, slumped in my chair, dropped my throbbing head into my hands, and shifted uncomfortably in my jeans. I was going to rip out my seams if this bullshit went on much longer.

Sweeten her up. Seduce her. Melt her brain.

Duncan's blunt suggestions had merit, but there was a small but problematic snag.

The brain in question that was melting was my own.

Chapter Seven

John did a drive-by of the Jersey City address stamped on the outside of the mailer. The one with the Vivi D'Onofrio art box in it. Excitement pulsed through him. Finally, a new lead, after these weeks of waiting, listening to Haupt's shrill, repetitive lectures.

Two weeks ago, he'd ordered the gift box from Vivien D'Onofrio's website, for the modest price of $115. Today, it had arrived. Finally, a chunk of meat to throw to the old shit-bag. Finally, something to fucking *do*.

He was trembling with sexual anticipation. Vivien was a skinny little thing compared to her older sisters, with no tits to speak of, but her ass was nice and round, and he liked the fiery hair and the full, pink lips.

He bet she was excellent at sucking cock. She'd have ample opportunity to demonstrate her skill. Girls tried so hard to please when they were motivated. And bad-boy Johnny knew just how to motivate them. Oh, boy, did he ever.

He no longer bothered to ask himself why he hung around to take the abuse from Haupt. John was a skilled professional, at the top of his game, and very highly thought of, in certain, extremely select circles. He didn't need the money. He could retire right now if he wanted to.

But he wouldn't. He'd gladly kill for free, for the fun of it, but he didn't advertise that fact. It was bad for business. Besides, he liked money just fine.

But this job had gone down the tubes weeks ago. It was like he was cursed. At this point, it had gotten under his skin. He'd lost his professional detachment. He'd gotten personally invested in the outcome. That was dangerous. A man had to be able to walk when he reached a point of diminishing returns.

His returns on this job had been diminishing almost from the start, but here he still was. Taking it up the ass, day after day.

He couldn't help but persist until he won, after what he'd been through. He'd been insulted, thwarted, shot at. Stabbed, for God's sake. That sneaky bitch Antonella had practically punctured a kidney. He'd needed internal and external stitches to fix the damage. He was still on antibiotics. It was still bruised. It still hurt.

Those girls were his. All three of them. He wanted to feel their hot blood pumping over his hands. Wanted to feel each of them in turn, flailing desperately in his grip. He wanted to hear them shriek and beg, in vain.

Vivien was the obvious one to target now. Security was too tight around the other two. When the dickheads currently fucking Nell and Nancy were put down like rabid dogs, the situation would be different. Then the way forward would be clear. Simple.

But Vivien had not cooperated. She'd dropped out of sight. She could no longer be found on the crafts fair circuit, nor had she been spotted, on video or in real time, outside her sisters' residences, or their new lovers' residences, either.

Maybe she was hiding here. In any case, whoever lived at this Jersey City address was going to get a long, chatty visit from John about that mail-order business, and where its owner could be found.

A car stopped outside. John slumped, watching. Four large, burly men in dark suits got out and trotted up the steps of the place.

They entered without knocking. The subtle bulges under their jackets were immediately recognizable to a trained eye. Oh. *Shit*.

John's teeth began to grind, and he clicked open his laptop, typed the street address into a search engine, scanned the hits.

Fuck. Braxton Security? He knew the name. It was the security firm that rich prick Burke, Antonella's boy toy, was affiliated with. She'd based her fucking mail-order company out of a goddamn security firm. Swarming with ex-military types, mercenaries, spies, techs.

John was not going to have stimulating chats with anyone today.

Probably cutthroat computer geeks were analyzing all emails that arrived at her site. And the addresses to which her merchandise was sent. He accelerated out into the street and peeled away, infuriated.

Fortunately, he was smarter than that. The addresses he'd used were untraceable. The address at which the package had arrived was a busy post office in Queens. He was sure that he had not been observed.

How dare she. Challenging him. Flipping him off. He drove for a while, until he came to a large chain store with a vast parking lot and pulled into it. His laptop was still open, so he put it on his lap and pulled up his short list of Vivien D'Onofrio favorites.

One was Brian Wilder's art gallery. Her work hadn't been

in the Wilder catalog for years, but John was confident Wilder would remember her. Any guy who had sold pieces of art for fifteen, eighteen, even twenty-five thousand dollars, would remember the artist who had produced them.

He called up Vivien D'Onofrio's own commercial website. Clicked on her bio for the photos. She smiled in the sunshine, hair blowing free, wearing a diaphanous white blouse. In another photo, she was decked out like a pagan bride from the Bronze Age in her own jewelry designs. Necklaces, bracelets, earrings, armlets, chokers, a headdress.

She was smiling that mischievous smile right into the camera. He rubbed his tingling dick as he stared into those big gray eyes.

That little slut was laughing at him from the computer screen. That full, pink mouth wide with mirth. *You idiot*, those eyes said. *You thick, dumb fuck. You just can't get us. You can't get close enough. You 're not smart enough. You never will be. Dumb fuck.*

He could actually hear her shrill, mocking laughter echoing in his mind.

The white mailing box sat on the seat next to him. He wrenched it open and pulled out the gift box. Imagining how her hands had touched it, rubbed it, caressed it. His erection was painfully hard.

The box was made of variously sized chunks of translucent, sand-smoothed bottle glass, both brown and green. Edges lined with strips of copper foil. Soldered together by a webwork of fine silver wire. Her business card was tucked into the bottom of it.

His hand closed over the box in a tight, shaking fist, crushing it. Pieces of glass cracked. Pain stabbed into his hand. Blood dripped out between his fingers. He forced them to open.

The box was mangled, shapeless, poised on his bloody, shaking claw. The business card with Vivien D'Onofrio's name was crumpled, bloodstained. He liked the effect.

He stared at the chunk of garbage. Uppity bitch. She thought she'd won. Thought she was smarter.

She'd see who was boss, in the end.

Chapter Eight

Vivi

I woke up slowly, in a bright patch of morning sunshine that streamed through the curtainless window, straight into my eyes.

I rolled over to find Edna panting right into my face. I stroked the dog's velvety ears. Wow. I felt almost unnaturally comfortable. The futon was so much nicer than the battered old mattress in my van.

But I didn't dare get used to it. I had to find another bed, and fast. No way could I be obligated to Jack Kendrick for anything so intimate as a bed.

I pulled some clothes on, fed Edna, and munched on some of the yogurt and granola that I had bought the evening before. The weather was gorgeous. A great day to hike back to the van, locate someone with a tractor, and stay far, far out of Jack Kendrick's way. But first, I needed to touch base with my sisters. Check my email. I was off any and all social media platforms, as we all were since our troubles began, so I used the deeply encrypted messaging app that Duncan had mandated.

But my phone had no coverage. I looked around the apartment for a phone jack and found one next to the back door in the kitchen, but there was no landline phone attached to it.

Well, that was a pickle. I needed a vehicle to buy myself a phone, and I needed a phone to summon any sort of vehicle, to take me to a car rental place.

Which meant I would have to ask permission to use his phone. Oh God. That thought turned my legs rubbery.

I marched out, and a spasm of doubt stopped me on the steps. Maybe I should give myself just a casual, cursory peek in the bathroom mirror, to make sure there were no crumbs in my eyes or smeared makeup from last night.

I went inside and did a facial-cleansing routine. Toner, moisturizer, the whole shebang. Teeth. I brushed my hair. That made me reflect that the sweatshirt with the sleeves ripped out was shabby as hell. I rummaged through the duffel. Maybe the green tank—no. Too revealing. The green linen blouse, then. With a hint of mascara. And maybe a tiny swipe of gloss on my lips. Barely any.

One last look into the mirror sent me back to my purse to pull out a pair of silver and jade drop earrings. I posed for Edna, who wagged her approval, and out we stepped into the cool morning.

The fragrance was overwhelming: earth, flowers, pine needles, dew, rain. The air itself seemed to sparkle as it went into my lungs. Birds warbled. Pale sunlight sifted through pine needles, in a fluttering, swaying pattern. I looked around, open-mouthed.

I hesitated before his door. It was seven-thirty, after all. Maybe he was a late sleeper. I'd almost decided to come back later when an unfamiliar voice called from across the yard. "Hello, there, missy!"

I whirled around, my heart thudding, like it always did when I was startled these days. I beheld a small, elderly lady with bluish hair, dressed in a rose-spattered dress and carrying a paper bag, making her way up the path with the help of a cane. "Good morning," I replied, smiling at the welcome that creased the old lady's wrinkled face.

"And what's your name, young lady?"

"Vivi D'Onofrio. Pleased to meet you." I extended my hand.

The old lady set down the paper bag and took my proffered hand, squeezing it gently. "My name is Margaret Moffat O'Keefe, but you can call me Margaret. So! My Jack has been a naughty fellow, hmm?"

I was nonplussed for a moment, until I finally grasped the mischievous twinkle in the old lady's eyes. "Oh, no! Not with me, not at all! I barely know the man, to be honest. I'm just a friend of a friend, staying here for a while in the apartment. Up there." I pointed to the barn. "I was just looking for him, to ask if I could use his phone, since my phone has no coverage. But I was afraid he might be sleeping. I didn't want to—"

"Oh, good heavens, no. Jack's no slug-a-bed."

Luckily, her brisk response cut off my nervous babbling. Margaret stumped up the porch steps and rapped smartly with the head of her cane on the front door. "Jack, dear?" she called out. "Are you home?"

There was no response. "Well, his truck is here, so he's probably just gone down to see to his flowers," Margaret said. "Have you seen his flowers yet?"

I shook my head, and Margaret clucked her disapproval. "Young Jack must show you his flowers! They are a sight like you will never see again. That man. Such talent."

"Um ... not these, you mean?" I indicated the flower beds in the yard.

"Oh, no. This is just the front gardens. They're just for fun. I mean the big gardens down by the river. I think he has columbines and lamb's ears and sweet william coming in now. And bachelor buttons, of course, and heaven only knows what else."

I smiled at the beaming old lady. "It sounds magical," I told her, quite sincerely.

"I'd take you down myself, but this arthritis has slowed me down some. You just sit down on the porch and have a cookie, and Jack will be along. I baked some molasses crinkles for Jack. He loves cookies."

"Is he related to you?" I asked.

"Not technically, but I think of Jack as my honorary grandson, since he came here to live with me some twenty-five years ago, or so. In fact, he bought this property from me some years back. Dear boy."

I had to stifle a giggle at the thought of that big block of seasoned manhood being referred to as a "dear boy."

"Well, I'll be running along now. Come have a cup of tea with me one of these mornings when you're settled in. And say hello to Jack for me." She held out the bag. It was heavy and fragrant. "Oh, and tell Jack to show you the hot springs."

"Hot springs?" I was intrigued.

"Oh, my goodness yes, dearie. There are some natural hot pools a couple of miles upriver. Very private. No one ever found out about them. They are just beautiful. Something tells me you would like them, bless your heart." She patted my shoulder.

"Something told you right," I said, with relish. Wow. Cookies. Flowers. Hot springs. I'd hit the motherlode. This place was paradise on earth.

I gazed wistfully after the old lady as she made her slow, careful way down the walk. How incredibly sweet of her. She was not like Lucia in any obvious way—Lucia had been fiercely elegant, a professor, multilingual, a brilliant and cultured expatriate intellectual. But there was something about Margaret's warmth that made me think of Lucia. The pang of longing brought tears to my eyes.

Happily for me, I was distraced by an intoxicating buttery-sweet fragrance that rose from the bag. I peeked inside. Molasses sugar cookies, warm and fresh.

I sat down on the porch steps and reached for one.

Predictably enough, my hand was in the bag when Jack strode around the house, carrying an armful of what looked like columbines, though they were much bigger than any columbines I'd ever seen. I yanked my hand out guiltily, licking my fingers with embarrassed bravado. He stopped in front of me and nodded in silent greeting.

"Hi. I, uh, just met Margaret." I closed the bag and folded down the top. "She brought you cookies."

"So I see," he said.

"She said I could have some," I said, before I could stop myself, and blushed furiously as he began to smile. Lines crinkled up around his eyes, sparking a warm glow somewhere in the vicinity of my navel. That warmth crept inexorably downward.

"Eat all you want," he said. "What kind are they this time?"

"Molasses," I informed him. I wrenched me gaze away from a smile that had now become a grin, complete with shockingly white and beautiful teeth, and focused on his long, work-hardened hands, gently holding those long flowers.

Whew. This guy was loaded up with subtle secret weapons. Every one of them was calculated to lay me low. Columbines, for God's sake. Give me a freaking break.

I struggled to remember what I'd come down to ask him.

"Ah, I need to make a few phone calls, and get online, to check my mail orders. And, ah, my cell has no coverage here. So I was just wondering—"

"Of course. There's a jack in your kitchen, but it's my phone line. I assumed, considering your security problem, you weren't going to want to list a number right now. You mind sharing a line with me? I don't spend much time hanging on the phone."

"Me neither," I said swiftly. "That's fine with me, if it's okay with you."

"If you want to use your cell, hike up to the top of that rise," he

said. "See that stand of spruce? You'll get some coverage up there. But for now, use my phone. Hook your computer up in the kitchen."

"Thanks," she murmured.

"I meant to get you a phone. You weren't supposed to arrive so soon." He gazed at me accusingly through the stalks of columbine.

"Yeah, right. Don't you want to go and put those down somewhere?"

"Yeah, and then I'm going to make coffee. Come in and have a cup."

I watched, fascinated, as he walked across the yard toward a small building. The back view of his jeans was as appealing as the front. I forced myself to exhale slowly.

Inside his cozy kitchen once again, I gazed at trays of seedlings while he put on the coffee. When he sat down at the table across from me, I gave in to my curiosity.

"Duncan said you grow flowers," I ventured. "Margaret, too."

Jack stroked the bottom of a delicate leaf in one of the trays.

It trembled above the forest of thin, delicate pale stems, as if floating there. "Yes. I've got some *Aquilegia flavescens,* and *Delphinium exalta- tum,* and *Dianthus barbatus* coming in right now. I'm taking a load into Portland today."

"What's that in English?" I asked.

"Columbines, larkspurs, and sweet william," he clarified.

I sneaked a quick peek at his somber profile. "Why do you use Latin names?"

"I like how specific it is," he said. "There are hundreds of subgroups for common flower names. Each one has its own totally different personality."

"Wow," I murmured, impressed.

He looked self-conscious. "I don't mean to be a nerd. I got off on studying them when I was in the military. Nothing like staring at flowers when you're sweating in the desert with sand rasping in every crack under your body armor."

"Wow," I said. "Like dreaming of water while you're dying of thirst."

"Yeah, pretty much."

He was standing so close to me now, I could smell the loamy scent of plants and earth on him, although his hands smelled like lemon dish soap. "You're, um, staring at my *Eranthis hylematis,* Jack," I said, in a warning tone. "It's making me nervous."

"Sorry," he murmured. "And it's *Eranthis hyemalis,* not *hylematis.*"

Whoa. That hot, dangerous flirtatious energy was starting to stretch and twist between us, muscular and dangerous and unpredictable.

I had to distract us, before things got weird. "How'd you get into this business?"

"I like plants," he said. "My uncle Freddie was into organic gardening when I was a kid. I studied plant biology on the

Internet when I was in the service, and afterward, too, when I worked overseas."

"In Afghanistan? On that task force with Duncan, right?"

"Right. I've also done some landscaping work for the parks department in Portland and Vancouver, too. Ornamental horticulture, stuff like that. But I prefer to live out here. I've built up a good business. The land down by the river's good for rare specialty stuff, and I know florists who are happy to buy local and get stock that's days fresher than the flowers they fly in over the pole from Holland. I've got a refrigerated truck and a twelve-by-twelve walk-in cooler. I harvest and deliver them myself. Simple, direct, and it works out well for everybody."

"What an awesome way to make a living," I said.

"It's hard work. But I like the flowers." He turned his silver-gray gaze on my face. "Did you sleep well on the futon?"

"Yes, wonderfully. Thank you. That's another thing I want to do, is get myself a mattress so I can get your futon and pillows back to me."

"Don't worry about it," he said. "Use them for as long as you like."

The coffee began to gurgle. He went to the stove, leaving me free to normalize my breathing.

The coffee tasted wonderful washing down Margaret's cookies. Jack finished his cup, got up, and rinsed it briskly. "I'd better get going," he said. "You going to be okay by yourself here with no wheels?"

"I'll be fine," I said. "I've got Edna. We're all set."

"Help yourself to anything you might need, in my cupboards, or the fridge," he said. "There's the phone, as you see. Feel free. Oh, and I called Dwayne Pritchett about your van. He'll be coming over with his tractor as soon as it dries up, but he doesn't want to risk it for a few days yet."

"Great. I appreciate that," I said. "Also, could you tell me how to find the hot springs? Maybe Edna and I will hike up and take a look."

He spun around. "Hot springs?" His eyes had gone cold.

I shrank back, startled at his reaction. "Uh, yeah. Margaret said there were some natural hot springs upriver a couple of miles. Is something wrong?"

He scowled down into the sink. "Shit."

"What's the matter?" I demanded. "Are you pissed because I know about them?"

"Not at you. I'm just irritated with Margaret. We have a long-standing agreement to keep the springs secret. Nobody wants hikers trespassing on our land. Now, out of the blue, Margaret decides to tell a stranger about them."

"I'm hardly a trespassing hiker," I pointed out, insulted.

"No, but it's not as if you're a long-term resident."

"Oh. Does that mean you'll be kicking me out?" I rose to my feet, holding my back as straight as I could. "Please be clear about that, Kendrick. Before I start ordering furniture."

"Don't take it personally," he said impatiently. "It's just that Margaret should've discussed it with me first, that's all. And don't call me Kendrick. It makes me feel like I'm back in boot camp. I'll take you to the springs when I get back from Portland."

I counted to ten, lips pressed flat. "Please, don't trouble yourself." I wished I hadn't asked him at all. Hell, I could probably have found it on my own. A couple of miles upriver, right? How hard could it be?

He read my mind, and fixed me with a stern glare. "Do not go without me," he said forcefully. "The cliffs are dangerous, and the path is washed out."

"Fine." I deposited my coffee cup in the sink.

"I'll be back around four, if you want to go then," he added.

"Like I said, don't go to any trouble. I'm sure I'll be extremely busy."

"It's no trouble. I meant what I said about not going alone."

"I heard you the first time." I let his door slam shut.

Ouch. I'd done it to myself once again. Whenever I let down my guard, zing, pow, he insulted me again.

The second I heard his truck pull out, I went downstairs and into Jack's kitchen and dialed Nell's new cell phone number. My sister picked up promptly. "Hey, you," she said. "Is everything okay?"

"Hey, yourself," I replied. "How's Italy?"

"Amazing," Nell replied. "We were just finishing up a late lunch. Fabulous food and amazing wine, and everything is beautiful. So how's the flower farm?"

"Hmmph. Problematic." I recounted the debacle in the rain and mud. Nell expressed the appropriate horrified sympathy.

"Anyway," I concluded. "So here I am, stuck like a bug on flypaper. But that, I kid you not, is the least of my problems."

"Oh, really? What's going on?" Nell prompted.

I paused, suspicious of the out-of-place cheerfulness in my sister's voice. "Jack Kendrick is my problem, Nell. As I am sure you know."

"Oh? In what sense?" Nell asked, all innocence.

"Nell, what exactly do you know about the guy?"

Nell hemmed and hawed. "More or less what Duncan told you. There's a photograph on Duncan's wall of Jack climbing a sheer rock face, so I knew he was big, with dark hair, nerves of steel, and lots of thick, sinewy muscle. But that's about it."

"He despises me," I announced. "He thinks I'm insignificant fluff. A rootless, brainless tattooed bimbo incapable of making commitments or seeing anything through to the end. And he hates my van."

"Wow." Nell sounded impressed. "That's deep, Viv. You

got all the way to fear of commitment issues? After one single evening's acquaintance?"

"It wasn't my fault!" I wailed.

"I never said it was, honey," Nell soothed. "What's the place like?"

"Out of my wildest dreams," I admitted, staring out the window. "The place is covered with flowers. Edna's having the time of her life chasing something across the field. I hope it's not a skunk."

"So? What's the problem?"

"What do you mean, what's the problem? I told you! The man doesn't want me here! He thinks I'm trash! This is a big, big problem, Nell! Don't play dumb with me!"

"But the van is stuck, right?" Nell prodded.

"Yes, at least until—"

"Well, good, then." Nell sounded satisfied.

"Good?" My voice rose to a squawk. "What do you mean, good? What's good about me being stranded? Grounded?"

"I mean that, at least until your fucking van gets unstuck, I, your sister, and Nancy, too, will be able to breathe easy and sleep at night because for once in your goddamn life, somebody is looking after you!"

The violence in my sister's voice startled me. "Um, okay," I said, cowed.

"I know what these guys are capable of." Nell's voice quivered. "You don't. You have no clue, Viv. And you don't want to. Trust me."

"I do trust you," I assured her swiftly. "And I promise. I'll be careful."

"Hey. Guess what we did this morning?"

I hesitated. The tone in Nell's voice made me wary. "Ah, what might that be?"

"We talked to the domestic staff at the Palazzo de Luca. There was a lady there in her seventies, the daughter of the previous housekeeper. She remembers when Lucia left. And why."

I braced myself. "Yeah? And? Stop teasing."

"It was after finding her father's dead body," Nell said. "In his study, under his writing table. The table we still have. He'd been tortured to death. Cut to pieces. Slowly. Like they threatened to do to me. Like they would have done to Nancy. Or to you, if they get you. Keep it in mind."

It wasn't like it was a big surprise, but still. This evil had deep roots. It was a fresh dose of flesh-creeping, goose-pimpling shivers.

"Be careful, okay?" Nell begged. "Just be very, very careful. Dress down. Don't show the van around town."

"I will," I soothed. "I promise."

Nell sniffled. "Right. At least you're finally attracted to somebody again. Thank goodness for that. It's about freaking time you moved on."

I felt cornered. "You don't get it, Nell. Whether I'm attracted or not, it's a bad scene. He despises me. He sees me as a type, not a person. It's just like when Brian—"

"Viv, stop it," Nell cut in sharply. "It's been years since that scumbag messed with you! Get over it! Stop living like a wandering nun!"

"I'm feeling manipulated," I said tightly.

"Manipulated?" Nell snorted. "Alas, poor Vivi. Trapped in a flowering wilderness paradise with a gorgeous, eligible hunk sworn to protect you from the evil villains. How viciously cruel of us, for doing this to you."

"I'm hanging up," I announced. "I'm too pissed to talk anymore, but I love you. Later, bye." I hung up, my face hot. The mention of Brian's name made me squirm with anger and shame, after six long years.

I was twenty-one when I met Brian Wilder at my student art show. It was during my rebellious period. Wilder was a suave gallery director out scouting for hot new talent. His gallery was affiliated with an art museum specializing in works by emerging artists.

He expressed an interest in my work. Soon after, he expressed an interest in me personally. He was handsome, intelligent. I'd been dazzled, flattered. At first.

Everyone had been so thrilled for me when Brian offered me a contract with his gallery. I remembered the fateful day so clearly. We were sitting in a coffee bar on Bleecker Street. I drank espresso. Brian was sipping a decaf soy latte.

"So? What do you think?" Brian asked, flicking an errant lock of hair out of my eyes.

"I-I don't know," I stammered. "I'm not sure yet what it entails, exactly."

"Let me explain," Brian said, in a patronizing voice. "I see huge potential in your work. Energy, anger, power. But it lacks discipline. Which I can help provide."

"Um." I sipped my espresso, pondering that unwelcome feedback.

"The lack of discipline is a general problem," Brian observed. His eyes flicked down, checking me out. "That skirt and boots you're wearing, for instance." His thin lips twitched. "You have to polish up your image, if you're going to run with me."

I tugged down my purple velvet miniskirt to cover another couple of inches of thigh, wishing I hadn't worn torn-up fishnet stockings. I stared down at my thigh-high lace-up black leather boots, feeling ashamed of my fashion choices, my freckled thighs, the air that I breathed. But he was offering to display my work. Everything had a price. Right?

Brian flicked another lock of my hair back and looked me up and down. "We'll start with a haircut and a new wardrobe."

"I can dress myself," I said.

"Well, if this is the result..." His voice trailed off. His eyes took on a weird, hot glow as he chucked me under the chin. "I've never been intimate with your type before."

I wrenched my chin away from his pinching fingers. "What do you mean, my 'type'?" I demanded, irritated. "What type?"

"You know. The chaotic bad girl with the big innocent eyes. The lost waif. You're like a creature out of a Japanese anime film. All eyes, with that wild mop of hair. It's stimulating." He tilted my chin up again. "So, about the contract. What do you say?"

It was an incredible opportunity. Any of my struggling artist friends would have cheerfully killed for it. But my jaw ached with tension, and my stomach clenched.

I had pulled my face away from his fingers and gulped the rest of my bitter coffee, wondering why I wasn't happier.

"If you sign the contract, it will be with the understanding that you'll accept me as an artistic mentor," Brian said. "And I will expect you to produce. No excuses. I can make you successful, Viv. That's what you want, isn't it?" Brian turned the full force of his cool, assessing gray eyes on me.

My doubts felt vague and foolish and childish. Destiny called. I had to say yes to it.

So I'd done it. I'd signed the contract. I had agreed to let Brian groom me into an artistic sensation. It had been the stupidest move of my life. So far.

I stared at the luxuriant spider plants that hung in Jack Kendrick's kitchen, thinking about the way one's worst mistakes tended to repeat themselves again and again. They dressed themselves in different outfits, but the basic content was always the same.

Here was another man who saw just a type when he looked at me. Another man who made me feel inadequate and embarrassed simply for being what I intrinsically was, in the marrow of my bones.

Except that this time, it was worse. Maybe because my desire to gain Jack Kendrick's good opinion was irrationally strong, and my chances of getting it so small. For fuck's sake, I couldn't even make fat stacks of cash for him with my art to make up for my many personality flaws. I had at least that going for me with Brian.

It was so strange, how I'd considered Brian to be very handsome, in his cold, austere way. But compared to Jack Kendrick, Brian seemed dried up and stringy. Maybe it was that empty, no-calorie crap he ate. But Kendrick, whew. A girl could just sink her teeth into that one. I would never wear that guy out. I would never use him up.

But there was absolutely no excuse for making the same mistake twice.

I grabbed a handful of cookies and marched out of the kitchen, munching them defiantly. Compensating was the only way to go. Grit my teeth. Resist the impulse.

Celibacy hadn't killed me yet.

Chapter Nine

T*ap, tap, tap* on the office door. Interrupted again, Brian Wilder whipped the herbal face pack off his face and waved away the masseuse doing his feet.

"What the fuck is it this time?" he rapped out.

The door to his office cracked open. Damiana, his current assistant, peeked in. Her huge, dark eyes were big in her pale, kittenish face.

"There is a client outside who needs to speak to you," she said, with her faint Italian accent that utterly failed to charm him today.

"Can't you help him? What the hell have I trained you for?"

Damiana shrugged, helplessly. "He says just you. He says it cannot wait. I do not know what to do with him. He is a strange type."

Brian gestured for Coco to wipe off the Ayurvedic oils that were dripping off his feet and to collect the crystals and stones from his body. Looked like his fucking chakras would have to get tuned another time. Another swollen ego to wank.

He shot Damiana an unfriendly look. What was the point of hiring pretty fluff from the local art school if not to have her do the ego wanking? Damiana should be down there, making the guy come in his pants while Brian was left unencumbered to rake in dough. But no. He could not seem to delegate. The ego wanking always fell to him.

Coco and Damiana exchanged commiserating looks as Brian threw on his linen trousers and shirt. He shoved past them, jostling more roughly than he needed to. Punishing them in advance for the whiny cat bitching they were going to do behind his back, on his time, on his payroll, as soon as he was out of earshot. Treacherous twats.

He headed out onto the second level of the gallery, a broad balcony all the way around the room. He took the opportunity to look down and check the guy out. He was currently staring at the Waylan Winthrop bronze that Brian had just placed on display in the center of the gallery. A strong piece, entitled *Teeth*. Price, a modest $38,000. The jaws of the beast reared toward the heavens in a wordless shriek of inchoate rage, its snarl of teeth pointing straight up, like spikes.

The guy looked baffled at the spectacle, but maybe that was the default expression on his thick face. Brian sized him up as he headed toward the stairs. A behemoth. Six four, but an extra eighty pounds on him. Brian brushed his hand over his own washboard abs as he trotted down the stairs. He had only contempt for such a lack of discipline. His own body was buff and toned. Seven days a week in the gym. He watched every bite he ate, made sure it was pure, organic, and calibrated to fine-tune his health and well-being. His body was his prized possession. He honed it.

This guy definitely did not. Brian analyzed the guy's wardrobe, pricing every stitch, as Damiana should have done. Off the rack, bargain basement. Not even particularly clean.

And his breath, dear God. He was going to have to send Damiana around the place with a lemon essential oil spritz bottle, and maybe some burning sage. The sour stench of the man's halitosis was sucking all the prana out of the room.

He extended his hand and smiled. "My assistant said you're looking for me?"

"You're Brian Wilder?"

The man's voice and manner were not cultured. He sounded like he'd come from the wrong side of the tracks in some depressed industrial town upstate. This guy was not walking money. Brian retracted his outstretched hand and gave him another smile, more carefully dosed. Briefer, thinner. "Yes, that would be me. And you are?"

"My name is Craig Wilcox," the man said. "I was told you once handled the work of an artist my client is interested in acquiring."

Brian stuck his fingers into his pockets. "And your client is?"

"My client prefers to stay nameless at this time."

Brian waited. "And the artist? He or she will stay nameless, too?"

The guy's eyes squinched in the puffy fat of his eyelids, not appreciating Brian's quip. His black hair was the wrong color and texture for his face, Brian thought. Wig, or dye job. Strange.

"The artist is Vivien D'Onofrio," the man said.

If Brian had needed anything to convince him that his time was being wasted, hearing that worthless bitch's name was it. "I no longer handle D'Onofrio's work. In fact, I make a point of seeing that none of my professional colleagues handle her work, either. I don't even think she's a working artist anymore. For her sake, I hope not."

The guy blinked, stared with those strange dark gray eyes. Flat, opaque, and metallic, like hematite. "Why?"

"She's unreliable and unprofessional," Brian announced, as he did to anyone who would listen. "And her work is uneven and derivative. Let me suggest some far better investments for your client. There's a new artist I've just taken on who's created a stunning series of—"

"My client's only interested in D'Onofrio's work," the man said.

"I'm the last person you should ask about her," Brian informed him. "I'm not in touch with her. I have no plans to be in the future."

"That's a terrible shame," the man said blandly.

Brian was about to tell the buffoon to stop wasting his time and leave when he caught the man's eyes. Brian's eyes stuck there. As if those hematite eyes were magnets. Sucking at his vital energy, like a vampire.

The fleeting thought gave him an irrational stab of fear. He shook it away. "It's not my problem," he said.

"That's an unhelpful attitude, Mr. Wilder," the man chided. "My client hates to be denied. Price is no object. He likes to indulge himself, especially when things are forbidden. Surely you can relate to that, Mr. Wilder. I think maybe you can. Hmm?"

The fear stabbed deeper. "What do you mean?" he asked, a little too loudly.

The other man lifted his shoulders in a casual shrug. "I make it my business to inform myself about people. I've heard about your late-night assignations from the escort agencies. You like them young, right? No more than fourteen? Slim, small breasts to none, big eyes, no makeup? A different one every time? Fucking perv."

Not possible. Brian stared, transfixed. The man began to

smile. He stepped closer, words coming fast like a concentrated venom. "You like those little lost waifs, hmm? Poor vulnerable creatures, no big strong daddy to protect them. What do you do to them, Wilder? Do you like to make them cry?" He studied Brian's face and let out a muffled crack of laughter. "Hah! You do! I nailed it. You sick, twisted fuck."

"G-g-get out of here," Brian quavered. "Are you threatening me?"

Wilcox laughed. "Threatening? Oh, God, no. My client has so much money, he has no need to threaten."

"Then why are you—"

"Let me reiterate. D'Onofrio is the one my client wants. If you want someone else to sell her pieces to my client, and let that person enjoy my client's good opinion and all that it entails, that would be a big shame ... for you. Think about that, Mr. Wilder. And think fast."

"I don't know where she is," he repeated. Fear was loosening his bowels. He struggled to control his sphincter

The guy's grin looked discolored. "Oh, I bet you could run her down if you really tried. The art world is small. It's worth getting over your differences."

Brian needed to sprint for the bathroom, but he didn't have the nerve to just walk away from Wilcox. "I, um ..."

"Take this." The guy handed him a card, with a cell phone number scribbled on it. "I'll be back to see you, if I don't hear from you first. I know some people are shy about calling. Don't be shy, Wilder." Wilcox walked out.

Brian made his way up the stairs, clenching the banister and his asshole with the same desperation.

Damiana came out of his office, eyes big with curiosity. "What did he want?" she asked. "I am so sorry, but he creeped me out, so I—"

"Go get my electronic organizer. Get on the Internet," he snapped. "I want you to find Vivien D'Onofrio for me. Now."

"Her? But I thought you ... I thought she—"

"Do it!" he bellowed, and she darted away, heels clicking.

He lurched into his office, dismayed to see Coco taking her own sweet time putting away all her oils and colored crystals. "Get out!" he yelled.

She shoved her stuff into her case and scurried.

He got to the bathroom just in time to avoid the unthinkable, and then sat there so long, his ass went numb on the cold ring of porcelain.

How had that man known? No one in his life knew. He kept his dirty little private thing so fucking hidden, it was practically hidden from himself.

He had many lovers. This had nothing to do with his love life. This was a special, secret, private thing. Deep in the night, he sometimes got that secret, nasty itch. To play with a fantasy that had begun with his affair with Vivi D'Onofrio.

She'd been so small, so slender, so young. A lost kitten. She'd been twenty-one when he met her, but she could've easily passed for fifteen. And so talented.

He had secretly hated her for that. All that talent, coming out her fucking pores, and she didn't even know it. So goddamn fucking innocent. The talent was wasted on her.

It had driven him mad with envy.

The next best thing to having talent was controlling talent. And he had tried. God knows, he had tried. But she was like a wild, unbroken horse. Ungrateful, whining, entitled bitch, biting the hand that fed her. They would have made money hand over fist, if she'd just done as he told her. But no.

He'd wanted to play her like an instrument. Wanted it so bad, he lay awake in the dark of the night, grinding his teeth, milking his dick.

After she left, he'd held his nose and done a little digging into the seamy underworld of the New York sex industry and commenced a brand-new secret indulgence. Re-creating a scenario calculated to make himself feel exactly the way he needed to feel. To get off. Explosively.

He didn't do it often. Every couple of months or so. A slender big-eyed girl in a hotel room, lost and scared. Him, controlling her. Using her. Punishing her for what Vivi had done to him. Making her cry.

His heart rate kicked up, hot and jagged, just thinking of it.

This situation with the thug who had come calling was probably Vivi's own fault. She'd behaved badly, got on the wrong side of some criminal badass. The badass was out for payback, and Brian was an innocent bystander. Caught in the crossfire.

Fuck that. He was rolling over on her, the minute he got the chance. He owed Vivi D'Onofrio nothing. She'd stiffed him in every way.

Let her pay the price for her own fuckups.

He was already imagining how he'd respond when the news of her violent, untimely end came to him. He would be shocked and sad but not at all surprised. What a waste, he'd say, his face pale and grave. Shaking his head at the tragedy of it. But he'd seen it coming. Oh, yes, he had. It was just the law of karma in action.

So sad. All that talent wasted.

Chapter Ten

Vivi

I was deeply absorbed in making a list of all the furniture I wanted. A bed, a couch, a coffee table, a bookcase. A nice rug. A dresser, a floor lamp. A spice rack, by God. Such a luxury, to hang clothes in a closet. To stick a fun magnet over a favorite photo onto the fridge.

The knock on the door made me jump. "Who is it?" I called.

"It's me." His deep voice made the entire surface of my skin tingle madly. I braced myself as I opened the door.

Jack stood there, holding a tray of tiny, feathery green seedlings. I gazed at them, utterly confused. Then he just handed the tray to me. "These are for you," he said.

"For me?" I repeated stupidly.

"*Eranthis hyemalis*," he said. "Winter Aconite. I saw some, at the nursery. I thought of you. They're not blooming now, of course, and it's late to plant them, but what the hell, we can give it a try. They like well-drained soil, and lots of shade. We can set them out beneath those big oaks over at the far side of the lawn. If you want."

I closed my open mouth. "Ah ... wow. I, uh—"

"If we get lucky, they'll multiply. Make a floral carpet."

I was so charmed, I felt my face heat up and my throat clutch. "That is so sweet of you," I said.

He shrugged. "I'm sorry. I was a jerk today. And last night."

The heat in my face and throat spread, a soft, warm glow. It felt good.

He stepped in the door as I laid the seedlings on the kitchen counter. "Do you want to go to the hot springs now?"

Hoo, boy. Nothing had changed, even if he had apologized, I reminded myself. Going to a beautiful remote place to sit in a pool of hot water all alone with this man was a dumb idea. And the fact that he was acting sweet was all the more reason to stay away. "I don't know much about plants," I stalled, stroking a tender frond.

"Don't worry about it. I'll show you," he said. "So? Are you coming?"

"Yes," I heard myself say, sealing my own doom.

"Let's go." He started down the stairs, Edna scrambling after him.

"Wait. You mean, right now? This minute? Don't we need towels, bathing suits? Anything?"

"Bring what you want, but be sure to wear jeans. The poison oak is thick."

"One minute." I closed the door, shucked my clothes, and pulled on my battered old one-piece. I yanked my clothes on over it, tossed a towel over my shoulder, marveling at myself. About to bounce off to do the stupidest thing I'd ever deliberately done, and I could barely breathe, I was so freaking excited.

As he had warned me, the path was difficult. We hopped

boulders upstream through the rushing river for about a mile or so, until sheer cliffs began to rise from the swift greenish glacial-melt water. Then I followed Jack up a steep gully and into a thicket of dense bushes, clambering up one steep hill and down another, through a narrow cleft between two towering boulders, under the draped fronds of a blackberry bush.

A tendril snarled into my hair. I was struggling to untangle it when he suddenly appeared beside me. He took the long, thorny vine in his hand. I stared at the hollow at the base of his throat. He was so warm, and he smelled so good. My body ached to know the sensation of leaning against that solid chest.

What would I do if he made a move on me? Flirted with me? Kissed me?

Oh, please. Duh. Like there was any question at all. I would jump all over him. Eat him for lunch. Climb him like a tree. Get real.

He let go of the lock of hair, laying it over my shoulder. He turned without saying a word and started to climb. I scrambled after him, relief warring with disappointment.

The path merged with a smaller streambed from the hillside above that had carved a gully leading down to the river. The walls of the gully were steep, the rocks covered with moss, thick with wild mint and luxuriant, spotted yellow flowers with heavy heads like snapdragons, and tufts of fragrant wild mint. I picked my way from boulder to boulder, Edna splashing ahead of me. At the mouth of the spring, Jack pointed upriver.

"Look there, past that tall rock," he said. "See them?"

My eyes followed his hand, and I saw several pools, sunken into the huge, flat gray rocks of the riverbank. They were surrounded by the nodding yellow flowers and mint.

The last rays of sun that still managed to slant into the river canyon lit up the water, brightening the multicolored pebbles, making the sand glitter like gold. Faint curls of steam rose from the water. The river rushed noisily by a few yards away. He watched my face intently. "Like it?" he asked.

I looked around, enchanted. "Oh, my God. It's superb."

My delight was shattered when I realized that Jack had stripped off his shirt and was unbuckling his belt. Oh, God. Jack Kendrick fully clothed was already too much voltage for me to handle. Jack Kendrick naked would blow my fuses all to hell.

"Hey, you! Just wait a damn second!" I said sharply.

His hands stopped on his waistband. "Yeah?"

"Are you wearing swimming trunks?"

"No. Don't think I even own any. It's not an item that I've ever needed." He waited patiently as I took this in.

"I'm, ah, not comfortable with that," I said, my voice sounding so prissy and prim to my own ears. "Things are already funny between us. I'd rather not, uh ..."

"See me stark naked," he finished.

I blew out a sharp, nervous sigh. "Right on, buddy."

"Do you want me to leave? Can you find your way back alone?"

Ow. That would be so flat. So blah. I absolutely did not want him to leave.

Damn, I didn't know what I wanted. I wanted the situation to be different. I wanted the world to be different. I wanted for him to be different. I wanted ... aw, shit. I wanted something that I could not have.

I wanted him to want me. The real me, Vivi D'Onofrio, in all my glory. The whole damn tattooed, itinerant, wild child, complicated, prickly package.

It was too extravagant a thing to hope for. Besides being inappropriate, silly, and way too soon. For Pete's sake, I'd just met the guy the day before.

I just had so much intense, scary emotion about sex backed

up in my system now. After six years of celibacy, anyone would be climbing the freaking walls.

And I had Brian to thank for that, too. Jerk-off butthead that he was.

"No, don't leave," I murmured, abashed. "Can't you just, um, keep your underwear on?"

His lips twitched, making me feel foolish. "Yeah, whatever," he said. "If it really bothers you."

He pulled off his jeans, revealing simple white cotton briefs. The muscles in his torso were finger-licking delicious. Luxurious curling dark hair tapered down to his belly and turned into a furry mat that disappeared into his underwear. He had incredible glutes, and powerful thighs.

Damn. I might not survive this visual sensory experience even if Kendrick did keep his underwear on.

He stepped into the water, descending until he sat in the pool cross-legged, clouds of glittering sand wafting up from the bottom to swirl and turn in the water, glinting in the sunlight. The water reached to his collarbone. He leaned against the rim of the pool and closed his eyes. A nice show of delicacy while I undressed. He was in perfect gentleman mode now—but I knew his tricks. If I relaxed and let down my guard for so much as one instant, he'd have me in a lathered state in minutes.

I pulled off my jeans and t-shirt, wishing my bathing suit were less thin and worn, and stepped into the water. It was deliciously hot. Like an enormous, full-body kiss. A sprig of mint dangled over my shoulder, brushing my cheek. I was blushing furiously.

"Why are you blushing?" His voice was silky, amused.

"The water is hot," I snapped. "And how did you know that with your eyes closed, anyway? That's sneaky and underhanded. Either they are open or they are closed. Do not peek."

He smiled briefly and made no reply.

We sat, listening to the river rushing by, for a very long time. He kept his eyes closed until it felt almost as if he were trying to hide from me.

I wanted him to reveal something about himself. I'd bared my soul in the restaurant the night before, so he owed me some freaking personal history, too. At least the basics.

"So nudity doesn't embarrass you?" I asked.

"I grew up around people who weren't embarrassed about it. The aftermath of the sexual revolution, I guess. They let it all hang out."

Interesting factoid, that. I pinched off a mint leaf and chewed it, letting the fresh, clean flavor clear my head. Jack dunked his head under the water and smoothed his hair back from his square forehead, and I noticed once again the white streak of the scar that disappeared into his hairline. "How'd you get that scar?" I asked.

He didn't open his eyes. "Long story."

"I'm not in a hurry," I said.

His forehead contracted, and then he wiped his face clean of expression once again. "Another time."

I plucked another mint sprig. "Sorry. Didn't mean to pry."

"It's okay. Talk all you want. Just don't expect me to be scintillating when I respond. Or even coherent."

"Why? Is something wrong?"

He opened his eyes, and looked at me, with that bright, clear, wolfish gaze that made shivers of delicious terror race through me.

"I can't concentrate," he said. "I'm sorry, but I can barely hear you talk. All I can hear is my own heart pounding."

The flat statement hung between us. The force of his gaze burned against my face. I closed my eyes, counted to ten.

I opened them. Looked at him. A lock of hair was clinging to his forehead. A drop of water rolled down his cheek. I leaned forward and touched it with my fingertip. His face was so hot, his wet skin so resiliant, velvety.

He caught my wrist in his hand and pulled, very gently. Enough to make me float effortlessly, inevitably closer to him, unless I put up some resistance. I didn't.

For a few breathless moments, we were face-to-face, staring at each other. My breasts brushed his chest. He touched my lips. Slid his finger into my hair.

And then he kissed me, deeply, hungrily.

It was an explosion of emotions, sensations, bursting into being from deep inside me. Achingly sweet, and tinged with desperation, and there was something fierce mixed in too, something like anger, but brighter, hungrier. Twisting, twining, growing. Demanding. I wound my arms around his neck and hung on, digging my fingers into those thick muscles.

He drew back for a moment, his eyes full of wonder. "You taste like mint," he said huskily, and then that huge vortex sucked us back into another desperate, twining kiss.

Oh, wow. He was so beautiful this close up. His eyes, the incredible length of his wet black eyelashes. Water drops trickling along the crest of the graceful, angled sweep of his eyebrows.

His lips were hot and soft, as wonderful and kissable as I had imagined, and his breath tasted so sweet. His skin was so supple and beautiful, with that delicate rasp of beard shadow over strong, graceful bones and chiseled manly angles. So fine.

I was charged with emotions I did not recognize, but they impelled me to touch him, clutch him. I explored his muscular back with my fingers, wound my arms around his neck, and opened to his kiss. The opening came from somewhere deep inside me, someplace vast and beautiful. A universe of bright, open space full of flowers.

I barely noticed the shoulder straps of my bathing suit

being peeled down. I arched back, abandoning myself to his strong grasp, letting my head fall back and my hair float out in the water like a lily pad. I cried out with pleasure as he hungrily suckled my breasts.

So sweet, so shivering melting hot for him. My nipples felt like points of glowing light. My breasts had always felt so deplorably small, insignificant even, but under his hot mouth, they felt plumper, bigger and swollen with eagerness, alive to pleasure. My whole chest was melting and soft, as if he drank some magic elixir from my body as he licked me, and the more he took, the more I had to give.

The breathless aching pull of wanting between my legs grew keener every moment.

Jack pulled me down onto his lap and slipped his finger under the stretchy fabric of my bathing suit, and made a low, growling sound of pleasure to find me slick and hot beneath it. He slid the tip of his finger slowly inside me, and I squirmed, clenching around him, making a breathless, broken keening sound.

"Oh, wow," he muttered as he caressed my mound with delighted fingers. "You're completely ..."

"Yes," I said. "No hair. I do a Brazilian wax whenever I get the chance. I tried it once on a dare. Realized that I like the way it feels. To be bare. It feels silky."

"Yeah. I like it, too," he said thickly. "Amazing."

I hid my face against his neck, my breath jerking in short, hard sobs. My bathing suit was sinking to the bottom of the pool, forgotten. I had to slow this down.

"Um, Jack?" I faltered. "Wait. Just wait a second."

"For what? I've never felt anyone so ready in my life." He bent his head to my chest again, pulling my nipple into a wet, silken vortex of sensation, his hot tongue rasping, swirling.

"But I ... b-b-but I can't—"

"Don't worry. It'll be amazing." He thrust a finger inside me, penetrating, pressing and swirling deep inside as he licked and lapped, and *ah...*

I cried out, arching back in his grasp as a totally unexpected climax flashed violently through me like a lightning storm.

When I opened my eyes, I was floating in his arms, staring up at the sky. My eyes were awash with tears.

Jack rose to his feet. Water sloshed and slopped as he hoisted me up and set me on the smooth rocks by the edge of the pool. The cool air felt delicious on my pink, overheated flesh. Heat steamed off my wet body. I felt poppy red, feverish, weak in the knees. Shockingly exposed.

He pressed my legs apart and stared down at my pussy. "Oh, yeah." His voice was low and reverent. "I knew it."

"Knew what?"

He pushed me gently back, until my back was pressed to the flat, sun-warmed rock, my legs spread wide. Laid out like a sacrifice on the altar of sexual misbehavior. Wide open to the sky. A warning to foolish, unwary girls.

But at least I wasn't choking up or panicking, like I often had post-Brian, before I gave up on sex. It was magic. I couldn't resist it. I felt so free.

"I knew that your pussy would be like this." He kneeled down in the pool to get closer, and kissed the inside of my thigh. "Those dark red folds, bursting out like the petals of some fabulous hothouse flower. Fucking gorgeous."

I laughed at him, chest jerking shakily. "You've got flowers on the brain, Jack."

"No, actually." His teeth flashed, in one of his rare, gorgeous grins. "I've got your pussy on the brain." He nuzzled my labia, light kisses that promised and teased. "I was half expecting your clit to be pierced."

I jerked up onto my elbows. "Hell, no! You wouldn't ever

catch me sticking a metal pin through the most nerve-dense part of my entire body!" I narrowed my eyes at him. "I bet you're disappointed, right? That I'm not quite as wild and uninhibited as you'd fantasized?"

He played with my inner pussy lips, spreading them tenderly wide like butterfly wings, and the slow, ticklish caresses were driving me mad.

"Actually, no," he said. "I'm relieved, to tell the truth. We're on the same page about how we like to treat those nerve-dense parts of our bodies. That bodes well."

"Yeah? For what?"

"Orgasms," he said, and leaned down, pressed his lips against my clit, gently swirling his tongue, licking, flicking, and oh, God ... he was so *good*.

I jerked helplessly against his face, overcome by the sensations, the wave of heat lifting me, but I wasn't ready. It was too intense. I was scared to death as he kissed his way up over my mons, the tiny swatch of decorative red pubic hair, over my belly, my rib cage, my breasts.

"I want to lick your pussy until you're a lake of lube," he told me.

"Jack." I grabbed his hair to hold him still. "Slow down. I don't know if this is such a good—"

"Of course it's a good idea. The idea makes me practically explode. And besides, it's practical, to make you wet." He unwound my hands and sank down. "It's going to be a tight fit." He slid his tongue boldly between my pussy lips.

The rasp of his plundering tongue, his matter-of-fact words, the thought of him moving inside me, it all nudged me over the top, into a powerful climax. I cried out as my pussy pulsed and clenched around his thrusting fingers, throbbed against his lashing tongue. Long, sweet, echoing ripples went through me, on and on.

He pulled me back down into the pool after the spasms died down, and I rested there on his lap, in his arms as if I had no bones. He held me so that I was floating right over the thick, prominent jut of his erect cock against my thigh.

I lifted myself, trying to catch my breath. "Jack. I hate to say it, but we can't do this now."

He nuzzled her shoulder. "No?"

"No," I said. "We have no latex."

He dragged in a breath between his teeth. "Ah, yes. That."

"I'm not on the pill. I don't have contraception device. And we haven't even discussed our sexual histories yet. I'm sorry. I don't know how I let things go so far." I couldn't stop myself from apologizing, even though the situation was only halfway my fault. "For the record, though, I'm fine, when it comes to that," I offered. "No STDs."

"Same for me," he said.

"No lovers, either. For a really long time," I added.

"I'm not surprised," he replied. "You're so tight. Tiny. Like a virgin."

"But I'm not babyproof," I said. "And I am not prepared to be a mother."

He stared at the river. Wiped water off his face, expressionless. "It's okay. I'll live."

His cool, indifferent tone made me feel punished. "Besides, it's just too soon for going all the way," I went on. "Call me silly and old-fashioned if you want, but I barely know you, and things are weird between us anyway. I just don't want to give it all up to you if you just want to ... ah, I mean, if the relationship has no future."

His eyebrow tilted up. "I should think you would be good at those."

I stiffened, suspicious. "What do you mean? Good at what?"

"Relationships with no future. What other kind could your type possibly have?"

I stared at him, utterly shocked, and then shoved him away from myself, my boneless languor gone. A wave of hot water splashed up into Jack's chest and face.

"Well, fuck you too, Kendrick," I said savagely, standing up.

"I'm sorry," he said. "I didn't mean to insult you."

"Oh, didn't you? Hah! Want to know a fun fact, Kendrick? A couple of minutes ago, I truly, sincerely wanted to suck your dick. But you know what? I don't want to suck your dick anymore. Not even a little bit. Asshole." I yanked my jeans up over my bare ass. I couldn't seem to make my trembling fingers work.

He got out of the pool and moved toward me, but I kept my red face averted. "Don't touch me," I snarled. "Keep your fucking distance."

"Aw, shit," he muttered. "What a mess."

"Yes. Those are my feelings, exactly. I've known you for one single goddamn day, and every time you see me, you insult me, Kendrick. I'm talking big, nasty, mortal insults. And it's ten times worse when you seduce me first. You get me all worked up and loosey goosey, and bam, that's when you really let me have it. Fucking sadist."

"I didn't mean to insult you. Nor did I succeed in seducing you, evidently." He got up out of the pool, and I whipped my gaze swiftly away.

"Keep your back turned," he growled. "I want to take this wet underwear off before I put on my jeans."

"Do whatever the fuck you like," I said. "I'm out of here."

I made my way up the flower-lined, moss-choked streambed, with Edna bounding behind me. I could barely see where I was going. Slowly, the path came back into focus for me, in reverse. The cleft of rock I had to clamber past. The thicket of posion oak to walk carefully around, the tunnel of blackberry brambles to slither through.

Then it was back down to the riverbed, for the rock hopping part of the journey.

I was mortified. He melted me down, turned me into hot, syrupy goop, and then ka-pow, he made me feel cheap and easy for giving in to it.

To hell with him. It was a mistake I would not make again. I was swearing a holy vow to myself this time. That guy could go fuck himself.

My knee-jerk instinct was to gather up my stuff and my dog and get the hell out of there, but my van was still stuck, and Haupt and Snake Eyes were still out there, and besides, I had no place to go, except for all the way back to New York, to park on top of her sisters' lives. Once I had started planning my hideout in Kendrick's flower bower, I had ceased to send in registration fees for upcoming crafts fairs, or to churn out new stock, so I couldn't even do the craft fair circuit, at least not for a while. Working the fairs took a certain amount of lead time and advance planning.

So even if my van was unstuck, if I left it would just be for aimless, money-draining, gas-guzzling wandering out on the road. And I would be too scared to stop. The gas would run out when the money did. And it wouldn't take too damn long.

There I'd be, helpless and broke and alone. A sitting duck.

No. I was a grown-up. I'd already been through hell in my life as a kid, and I had come out battered, but okay, thanks to Lucia and my found sisters. I would not be chased away from this haven like a stray cat. My safety was more important than my poor little hurt feelings.

But neither would I play the nympho sex toy for that arrogant prick. Since that was clearly how he saw me. Thank God I hadn't gone down on him. I'd be feeling ten times worse about everything if I had the taste of his come in my mouth.

I'd come so close, too. My mouth had been watering for it. Bad enough that he'd spent all that time with his face between my legs.

That took all the strength out of my wobbly legs. I sat down heavily on a rock. Clenching my thighs around hot, shuddering pulses of remembered pleasure.

Only the thought of Kendrick finding me there on his way back was scary enough to nudge me up off my ass and get me stumbling home.

Chapter Eleven

Vivi

"Ooh! Your own store, hmm? Lovely idea, honey. Jewelry, pottery, art objects, gift items? Pebble River is just right for a place like that, now that the windsurfers have found it. Tourism has arrived. And windsurfers have money, you see." Margaret poured me another cup of tea out of a rose-spattered teapot and nudged the plate of pecan puffs toward me. "Come on and indulge yourself! Heaven knows you can afford the calories!"

"Margaret, I've eaten five already, and they're not small." I gazed appreciatively at the heap of powdered-sugar-glazed, melt-in-your-mouth cookies. To die for.

"I could help you find a place, you know," Margaret offered. "I ran a cross-stitch shop in Pebble River for thirty-five years. We can get started right away. Why wait?"

"I would, but my van's still stuck," I explained. "Dwayne keeps putting me off because of the rain, but it's been sunny for days, so—"

"Well, now, speak of the devil. Look what's coming up the road!"

I leaned over to peer through the floral print swags of Margaret's window and saw a tractor chugging up the road. A big, round man with a cowboy hat was behind the wheel. "Is that Dwayne?" I asked.

Margaret hobbled to the window and lifted her spectacles. "It is indeed," she said, in tones of satisfaction. "I told him all about you. Dwayne runs the gas station at the exit for Pebble River, you see. Lovely man. Put some cookies in a napkin for him, would you, dear?"

I soon found herself out on the road, reaching up to shake the hand of a youngish bald guy with several chins and a base-ball cap.

"So you're the artist?" he said. "Good to meet you, Ms. D'Onofrio."

"Same here. And call me Vivi." I handed him the cookies with a smile.

"I thought you might be coming by, Dwayne, so I baked your favorite," Margaret said archly. "Vivi, let me know when you want to go to Pebble River. Maybe we should all go together."

"All? All meaning who?" I asked.

"You, me, and Jack," Margaret said, as if it should be obvi-ous. "I'm sure Jack will have some wonderful ideas. He's a very creative young man."

"Oh, no. I don't want to bother Jack," I said hastily.

"Bother me about what?"

My heart jumped up into my throat as I turned around, and ... oh, boy. My reaction to him was as powerful, inappropriate and unwelcome as it ever was. Worse, even.

I'd managed to mostly avoid him since our fight, and I'd been fondly imagining that my feelings and hormones were back under control. Hah. Vivid images of the hot springs incident blazed through my body.

My face turned pink. No, I think that my entire body was turning pink.

"Hi." Jack nodded to Dwayne and Margaret. "Heard the tractor."

"I figured it was dry enough by now," Dwayne said.

"I'll walk down there with you," Jack said.

Oh, God, no. That was all I needed. I swallowed my dismay. "Um. Okay."

Fortunately, the rumble of the tractor chugging ahead of us made our silence less embarrassing on the walk. I'd been using the long, quiet days while the weather dried up to hang up my pictures, write down my goals, make shopping wish lists for some future when I had some money to spend. I'd set up my portable studio on the floor, and I had made several trips back and forth to the van to haul back my work supplies.

It was a new artistic era for me. It was time to beef up my stock, dream up some fresh new designs. Scrounge for new sources of unusual, pretty rubbish. I liked incorporating what most people thought of as garbage into my work. It was part of my artistic philosophy, and my mission. Making garbage beautiful. Using found objects.

Because life was like that. All in the attitude.

My first investment would be a big worktable. Then, I needed to get my hands on some some metalworking equipment. I wanted to get some big pieces of stained glass to play with. I was desperate to spread out. Everything in my life for the past six years had been miniature; from my income to my camper-van home, all the way to my artistic ambitions. But I was sick of being miniature. I wanted to sprawl. I wanted to take up space. Breathe big, greedy breaths. Use up all the oxygen I damn well wanted.

Not that I regretted the choices I'd made. I was proud of what I had accomplished. The traveling jewelry business had been good to me. My jewelry sideline had started one day when Nancy admired a sculpture I was making out of beads, wire, and glass.

"This is beautiful," Nancy had said. "If it were jewelry, I would wear it."

The comment had given me an idea, and for each of my sisters' and Lucia's next birthdays, I had made personalized earrings. Then I made some necklaces to match. Then I had tried a couple of big brooches.

It was fun. Ideas for designs flowed easily.

My art school buddy Rafael had persuaded me to try selling some of them in his booth at the open-air market down on Sixth Avenue, and I had sold several, to my utter surprise, and Rafael's triumphant glee. The profit had almost paid my rent that month.

Brian had been disdainful of my "craftsy little hobby," and resentful of the time it took from the work he demanded from me. But I had kept quietly on with my sideline. And after things exploded with Brian, the jewelry gave me something to fall back on. It wasn't exactly what I'd dreamed of, but it was creative, and it paid for my gas, my car insurance, my food. And it wasn't waitressing or bartending. Not that there was anything wrong with waitressing or bartending, but I was sick to death of them.

I'd been trying to use some of these long, silent days to churn out some more work, but I'd had no luck. I'd chalked it up to exhaustion, worry, and a blazing case of lust. And Haupt, and John the Fiend, of course. There was always that zesty little pinch of mortal dread to liven things up.

I hoped it wasn't artist's block. I'd experienced a very bad period of that, starting a while after I had signed the contract with Brian's gallery.

Working with Brian had been awesome, at first. He had sold a whole bunch of my pieces, the wilder, angrier ones. Money started coming in, and that had been oh, so sweet. I had quit my cocktail-waitressing job and just basked in the thrill of being the hot new thing on the art scene. I spent a lot of the money I had made on clothes, all vetted by Brian, of course.

Then I started experimenting with another style, and things changed. Brian didn't like the new pieces. He demanded that I make more of the old series that sold so well.

"But I'm bored with them," I protested. "That cycle is done. I'm into a new vibe now. They're so angry and negative, and I'm not as pissed off now as I was a year ago."

"I don't care," Brian said. "They sell, babe. The new ones aren't right for our catalog, and they're not right for our clients. I need more pieces like *Scream* and *Howling Skeleton*. You're making your name. Ride the market trend."

I had chosen my words carefully, already afraid of making him angry. "But that's the thing, Brian. Inspiration doesn't depend on market trends. It—"

Slam. Brian's hand slapped down into his desk. "Don't even start with it," he rapped out. "I'm already bored."

I had jumped back, and an ebony goddess figurine on the desk had teetered and almost fell upon her substantial behind. Brian stared at me, his cool gaze menacing. "Don't be an idiot, Viv," he said. "Fulfil your contractual obligations to me. Or else."

I was shocked by his ugly tone. "But ... but I just—"

"You signed that contract. Don't forget that. Your future as an artist depends on it."

My mouth worked helplessly as Brian leaned back in his

chair and leafed casually through a big glossy catalog of Wilder Gallery artwork.

"But ... but what do you mean by that?" I finally forced out.

His smile did not reach his eyes. "We discussed this, remember? Before you signed. You agreed not to play the diva. Not to jerk me around with high-minded bullshit."

"Yes, but I didn't mean that I would be a—"

"I need more pieces like the old series. End of discussion." He slapped the catalog shut. "Oh, and another thing. Our date tonight. I can't make it. Something's come up. Since you now have the evening free, I suggest you get to work. I have clients asking for your work, and I mean to satisfy them."

He got up and stood in front of his desk, hands twitching in the pockets of his tailored suit. He sighed and tilted my face up to his. His cold, hard lips brushed mine.

I flinched from his touch.

Brian sighed, rolling his eyes. "Don't be that way, Viv. I know you're upset, but it'll have to wait," he said, sounding bored. "I'm busy today. Get busy, okay? Chop chop."

I had done as I was told. Tried to, anyway. I had trotted to my studio like a good girl. I had tried to make pieces that would please him. It made me cringe to think of how hard I had tried to satisfy his demands. How pointless all my efforts had been in the end.

Because it hadn't worked. I had run dry immediately. I cranked out a few things, but they were obviously bad, flat, boring. My output ground to a total halt.

Brian had been furious. Convinced that I was doing it on purpose just to spite him. And that was when the sex with him had started to go from tense and problematic to outright scary. Brian used sex to punish. It was subtle, but I felt it.

The only thing I had still been able to work on during that period was the jewelry. It was the one thing that Brian had never tried to control, so I just went with it. I threw myself into it, heart and soul. I had to, since Brian burned all my bridges out of spite.

I cast a covert sideways glance at Jack, walking silently beside me, trying not to envision how he looked naked, and soaking wet. How he tasted. The solidity of his shoulders when I sank my fingernails into them.

Brian might have derailed my artistic career. He might have given me a whole, tedious closetful of stupid sexual complexes. But he also had never driven me out of my freaking mind with breath-stealing, toe-curling lust.

The tractor steadily chugged on until the van came into view. Dwayne and Jack attached the chain, and I got in the van and started the engine.

They pulled and pulled. The van shuddered and strained. Dwayne whooped in triumph when it rolled out of the deep ruts.

I howled in triumph when I felt those wheels turning, bumping over the ruts. I got out and strode over to the tractor with a huge smile of relief. "Thank you so much, Dwayne. How much do I owe you?"

"Ah, nah," Dwayne said bashfully. "It's all right. I'm just being neighborly."

He pushed away the bills I held out, so I folded them back into my wallet, peeking at his hand to make sure he had a wedding ring. "Well, then bring your wife over one of these days to pick out a necklace or a pair of earrings," I offered. "I'd love to meet her."

Dwayne agreed to that plan, and Jack and I watched the tractor chug up the road and disappear around the bend.

I got into the driver's seat. Jack climbed into the passenger's seat. We sat in silence.

"So?" I said finally. "Where do we stand? I'm mobile again,

so what does that mean for you? Do I need to get lost? I could be out of here in twenty minutes. Say the word."

"Please don't be defensive," Jack said.

I made a derisive sound and put the van in gear. It lurched forward, bumping over deep ruts, but it crawled gamely up the hill. "That's hard, under the circumstances," I told him.

"I have an understanding with Duncan. You're welcome to stay for as long as you have this security problem," he said. "If you can stand it, that is. I doubt you'll be staying that long anyway."

"And why is that?"

"Your kind never do," he said.

The van crested the hill. I stared out the windshield with hot eyes. "My kind," I repeated.

"I don't mean that the way you're evidently taking it," he said. "You've decided that I'm insulting you when I'm simply stating an objective fact without a value judgment. But I see from the kind of person you are that you won't settle for long."

The van lurched violently over another washed-out rut, making my teeth jar and rattle painfully in my head. "Is that a fact," I said. "You look at me, and you see that."

"It's a valid lifestyle choice."

"Not when you're talking about it," I said, as we crawled slowly up another steep hill. "I am not trying to prove anything to you, so don't take it that way, please. But I am sick of moving around all the time. Sick of living small, eating road food. I'm going into Pebble River after lunch. I'm going to a furniture store. I'm buying a bed. A table. A bookcase. And I'm going start looking for a place to open my shop."

"Shop?" He turned to her, frowning. "What's this about a shop?"

"Exactly what I said. Pebble River is a perfect place for the kind of business I have in mind—"

"Hold on. Wait a fucking minute. I thought you were in hiding. I thought these bastards were trying to kill you. I thought that was the whole point of being here. Now you're talking about opening a shop? Public records, databases, a Facebook page, some Instagram reels? What the fuck are you thinking? You're out of your mind!"

I exhaled carefully. I'd been going back and forth about this issue into the wee hours every night. "How long can I huddle in a hole and shiver? I can't afford this any longer! I have to support myself somehow, and this is the best—"

"Are you trying to prove something to me?"

"Don't flatter yourself. This isn't about you! I'm just going about my business!"

We had arrived at the house. I pulled the van in next to Jack's truck, got out, and slapped the door shut. I glanced over the painting on the side and my eyes skittered away. Jack was looking at it ... and judging me.

I had always been ambivalent about that painting, but Rafael would have been so hurt if I had painted over his masterpiece. And Rafael had been so sweet and supportive after the Brian debacle, sharing his booth, showing me the crafts fair ropes. The writhing serpent and muscle-bound warrior on my van was an homage to true friendship.

Jack was following me up the stairs. I glared back at him over my shoulder. "Excuse me? Where do you think you're going?"

"I just want to see what you've done with the place," he said blandly.

"I haven't done much of anything, being as how I didn't have a vehicle. It looks about the same. Please excuse me. I want to make myself lunch."

Jack raised an eyebrow and waited. I sighed, fitting the key into the lock. "What the hell. Come on in. I imagine you want lunch, too?"

"Lunch would be nice," he said.

The first thing he did was check the seedlings. I had been watering them, afraid to kill them by planting them incorrectly, but even more afraid of asking for help. But he just stroked the little plants with his fingertip. "We should set these out today," he said.

"Fine. Let's do that." I got to work making the grilled cheese sandwiches, to have an excuse to keep my back to him.

He walked into the living room. I had been doing inventory, and my entire current stock was spread across the green velvet drapes on the floor: earrings; pendants; brooches; my compartmentalized boxes of beads; my stash of chunks of broken hand-blown glass, coils of silver and gold wire, hooks and clasps; my boxes of fun and colorful collected junk. The walls were decorated with hangings, paintings, drawings.

"Did you do these pictures?" Jack asked.

"No," I said. "I've met lots of artists in the past few years, and I collected my favorite pieces. The ones I could afford, anyway. This is the first chance I've ever had to hang them up and look at them properly."

Jack walked slowly around the room. "And your stuff?"

"There's not a lot of my work here," I said, feeling defensive. "Just what's on the floor on the green velvet. My favorite mediums are bronze and blown glass, but you can't do that kind of art in a camper van. I got sidetracked by my jewelry sideline, but I want to get back to sculpture. On a bigger scale."

Jack leaned over the cloth and picked up a fine lacework of antique beads and colored glass. "You sit on the floor to work?"

"I cannot wait to buy a table," I said fervently.

He frowned. "I could have found you something." He

picked up a green bottle adorned with onyx beads and a filigree of silver foil. "These are beautiful."

"Thank you." I was uncommonly flustered by the compliment.

"So, you're tired of making jewelry? That's too bad. Do you get tired of things quickly?" Jack said.

There he went again, poking his stick between the bars of my cage. I suppressed a flare of savage irritation. "No," I said tightly. "I love designing jewelry. What I'm sick of is mass-producing for crafts fairs. That's just assembly-line work."

"Ah," he murmured. "I see."

"I have a good feel for what will sell," I went on. "I study the colors and styles online, and in the women's magazines. I make pieces to match, and they go like hotcakes. It was fine for a while, but I'm burnt out."

"You don't have to prove anything to me," he said.

"Then stop jabbing at me!" I flared. "God, Jack! You're pissing me off!"

He put the bottle down. "Sorry," he murmured. "If you're not a jewelry designer anymore, what exactly are you?"

"I think I'm a sculptor, but ask me again in six months."

"Who knows where you'll be in six months?" He held a pair of malachite earrings up to the light, letting them dangle from his fingers to see them from all sides.

I did not dignify that with a reply. I just stalked back into the kitchen. He was not to be reasoned with. He'd made up his mind about me, and that was that.

I stuck my head around the door when the sandwiches were sizzling in the pan. "Lunch is on. Come get it while the cheese is gooey."

Jack sat opposite me on the kitchen floor. We ate our sandwiches, and then the usual tense, charged silence fell upon us.

I stared at the crumbs on my paper plate. "Would you like a cup of tea?" I asked, with rigid politeness.

"No, thanks," he said.

"Then excuse me while I make one for myself." I put the kettle on and stuffed napkins and paper plates into the garbage.

"You've been talking to Margaret, I take it?" he asked.

"That's right. She's got some good ideas for possible locations for me."

"For your shop. To sell your own designs?"

"Among other things," I said. "I know lots of excellent artisans, after all those years on the circuit. And there's money around here to support a business like mine. A gallery of wearable, usable art."

"And aside from the danger issue, you think that's a good idea?"

"Why wouldn't it be?" I stuck out my chin, crossing my arms over my chest.

"It's a big layout of money," he said. "A big risk."

"Yeah? So?"

"I hope you're not being unrealistic."

"Why?" I demanded. "Lots of people start businesses. Most of them fail. Sure, it's risky. Life is risky. Why do you think it's particularly unrealistic for me?"

I had to ask, even though I was afraid of the answer.

He was silent for a long moment, clearly hesitating. "I think you'll regret it," he said. "That kind of investment requires a huge time commitment. And a long attention span."

I counted to ten, doing careful slow breathing to not react and fly off the handle. "I'm not going to play this game with you anymore, Jack. Cut that shit out."

"It's not a game, Vivi," he said. "Any woman who sleeps in a sleeping bag, eats off paper plates on the floor, and cooks with aluminum campware doesn't impress me with her readiness to put down roots."

I grabbed up the last plate and stuffed it into the garbage. "I've been stranded here for five days with no vehicle," I reminded him, between clenched teeth.

The teakettle began to hiss. I turned it off, reached in the cupboard for a mug and pulled out a plastic travel mug with a sip lid and adhesive plastic on the bottom for sticking to the dashboard of a car. I stared at it, my jaw clenched before I threw in the tea bag, poured the water, mixed in the honey. Every damn thing I looked at felt like a slap, a reproach, a dig. Proof of everything he believed about me.

"Think whatever you like," I said. I grabbed the broom and dustpan and began to sweep up crumbs. "It makes absolutely no difference to me. I'm just going to keep doing my thing."

"Yes, I'm sure your intentions are good."

The detached tone of his voice maddened me. "I can make my business work. I know I can. I have for years." I grabbed a dishcloth from the sink.

"What you're proposing is a very different kind of business, but whatever."

I blocked the bad language that wanted to burst out of my mouth. Lucia had taught me that much, at least. I shook the swept-up crumbs into the garbage and rinsed off my hands at the sink. His sudden presence behind me made me gasp.

"I can't seem to stop making you angry," he said softly. "I'm sorry."

"You're making me crazy." I closed her eyes. "You say, don't go, stay safe. Then you insult me and try to drive me away. Then you flirt with me, mess with me, seduce me. What am I supposed to think?"

"I'm sorr—"

"Shut up." I twisted around, holding up my finger, wagging

it in his face. "Not one more word. You'll just piss me off worse if your lips are moving, so shut it."

He drew in a breath, opened his mouth. I put my finger on it, but when I started to lift my hand away, he just trapped it there, pressing it against his hot, soft lips. His breath tickled my palm.

I snatched my hand away and turned my back again. "Don't. For fuck's sake, Jack. You're making it worse."

The proximity of his body transformed into the pressure of the lightest touch against my back. Then his lips pressed against my nape. He was kissing me. The hell?

The contact was exquisitely soft. A point of warmth, of silent tenderness that spread and grew. Like the sunrise, slowly turning snowy mountains pink.

Oh, no, no, no. This was as bad an idea now as it had ever been, I told myself.

But I felt so soft inside when he touched me. So hungry for the feelings he triggered. For what happened to my body whenever he was close to me.

Like a junkie, craving the poison that was destroying me. I'd watched that drama play out when I was a kid. I had never touched drugs in my life, other than the occasional drink from time to time, but look at me now. Doomed to repeat that nightmarish trap in a different form. People got sucked into their ancient bullshit all the time, in spite of their convictions, their promises to themselves, their deepest fears, their best intentions. They were imprinted. There was no escape.

And I couldn't stop. I could not push his hands away.

He stroked my breast, brushing the tight nipple that poked through my tank top against his palm. He slid his other hand down my spine, his fingers tracing every bump of my backbone until it hit warm skin under the hem of the top—and then delved, ever so slightly, into the waistband of my gauze skirt.

It was hanging a bit loose these days. Ever since Snake Eyes had started circling around my sisters, the stress had been stealing my appetite and shrinking my ass.

He slowly, tenderly petted my hips. Stroking the roundness.

"Why?" I whispered. "Why torture me like this, if you think so little of me? Why not just kick me out? It would be kinder."

"I don't think little of you. On the contrary." He kissed my bare shoulder, lips moving in a caress that left shimmering warmth in its slow wake. "I think you're amazing. Talented, beautiful, fascinating. So amazing, I can't do anything except speak the truth to you. Even when you don't want to hear it. That's respect, Viv. That's the real thing."

"Your truth," I said.

He shrugged. "That's the only one I've got."

"It's not the only one there is," I informed him. "Other people have their own."

Silence was his response to that. Slowly, he lifted his lips from my shoulder. "I know you're scared to leave because of what's happening in your life," he said. "But I also know that once that situation resolves—"

"If it ever resolves," I broke in, my voice bitter.

"Once it is resolved, you'll pack up your van and drive away. As soon as it really sinks in."

I twisted around to stare at him. "As soon as what sinks in?"

"What it means to look at the same damn place, day in and day out. Or the same person." His voice was quiet but utterly convinced. His hand stopped, barely touching the hot glow of excitement between my legs.

"And I can't convince you any different?" I whispered.

He paused for a moment, motionless, and said, "No."

My laugh felt more like a sob. "But you still want to fuck me."

"I still want to be your lover," he corrected. "And I want it respectfully." He pressed his hot face against my shoulder, his hands delving deeper, making me squirm. "I ask it ... respectfully."

I clamped my thighs around his hand, squeezing it. "Oh, yeah? You call that respect?"

"I love to make you feel good," he offered. "That's not disrespect."

I could hardly breathe. I tried to hold his hand motionless with my thighs, but his long, clever fingertips kept delicately caressing me, and it felt ... so ... *good.*

"I don't want to get hurt," I blurted.

"I don't see any way to avoid that." His voice was muffled against my hair. "It already hurts. It'll hurt no matter what we do."

"And we might as well make the best of it?"

He pulled me against him, tightly. "I'll make it the best. I promise."

"One question," I said. "What happens if I just don't leave? Is there a statute of limitations on this notion that I'll run? If I'm still here in five years, ten years, what then? Would you be glad? Disappointed? What?"

He declined to reply, but I could see his answer in his eyes. That door in his mind was closed, locked, barred. Nailed shut.

He would never give himself up to me completely.

And still, I was hungry for what he offered, no matter what was held back. I should be prouder, I should demand more, I knew it. But I wanted every last fragment. Every tiny crumb I could get.

"Yes," I said. "I want you."

Chapter Twelve

Vivi

Jack's eyes flashed, and his fingers tightened on my ass. I waited until I started getting restless and impatient. "So? Jack? Did you hear me?"

"Yes, I heard you. I just couldn't believe it," he said.

"Ah. Well, believe it. So? What now?" I clamped down on my nervous giggles before they could start to turn to tears. "Do we just ... do it?"

His grin flashed, but his face was wary. "Sounds fine to me."

I groped for a tissue in my skirt pocket and blew my nose. "I'm so embarrassed," I muttered. "It's been so long. I don't even know where to start."

"I do," he said swiftly. "I could absolutely help you with that."

I snorted with laughter, covered my face with my hands. "I just bet you could," I said. "So? What's the plan?"

"We'll start here, definitely." He sank promptly to his knees in front of me and pressed his face against my mound through the thin fabric of my gauze skirt.

"Oh, God," I said weakly. "That, again? You're obsessed!"

He lifted up the yards of fabric, seeking his prize. "God, yes. Your pussy is so pink and salty sweet. I want to make it puffy and slick and hot pink. I want to lick you like candy. Until you melt into hot slippery girl juice. Then we'll work out what comes next. We'll take it slowly. One step at a time."

I could barely speak. He shoved the wad of skirt into my hands and murmured with approval at the skimpy white lace thong. "Behold me, on my knees," he continued, flashing me a mischievous grin. "Your desperate supplicant."

"Oh, stop. As if." I shook with a fresh attack of nervous giggles.

He wasn't put off by them at all. He was extremely focused. He pulled aside the gusset of my panties and tucked it to the side. My legs buckled when he pressed his mouth to my naked flesh.

"I can't handle it," I whispered. I had no experience at receiving oral sex. Brian had been entirely uninterested in it. In performing it, at least. He'd been more than happy to receive it. Had considered it his God-given right, in fact.

The fierce glow in Jack's eyes transfixed me. "You'll handle it," he assured me. "You did at the pools. And you're so small. I'm going to take my sweet time with you. You taste amazing."

My legs trembled. Jack looked around for a chair, saw none, and hoisted me up onto the kitchen counter. He tugged the tiny wisp of stretch-lace panties off my legs and tossed it away. I balanced there, clutching his head and trembling, skirt wadded against my chest. I was so aroused, the feeling bordered on terror.

"I love your taste," he murmured. "I could lick you for hours."

"I wouldn't survive it," I said, and he laughed, pleased.

He knew instinctively just how to touch me, how deep, how hard, how soft. Voluptuous thrusts of his tongue, lapping up and down, plunging deep. His long fingers opening, stroking, while he suckled, insisted, pushing me to that screaming point of no return ... and oh ... yes. *Yes.*

Pleasure jolted heavily through me, deeper and wider and sweeter every time.

I floated back and found myself draped over him. He'd caught me, held me as I came.

He lifted me up so that I straddled him, and braced me against the wall, reaching down to fumble with his belt—

And the shimmering warmth inside me flash-froze. My heart skipped, bumped. Panic flashed through me. Faintness, suffocation.

Shit. It was happening again. That sickening black fog rising. The memory of those last awful times with Brian. They haunted me.

Brian had liked that position, especially when he was snorting coke. On his feet, pinning me to the wall. Or else holding me down, immobilized. His face, a taut, stiff mask of lust. Eyes fixed, staring. A million miles away. Not listening when I told him that it hurt. Not caring.

I hadn't been able to be intimate with a man since that. I had tried a few times, but nothing wrecked the mood faster than a stress flashback.

Finally I had just let it go. I figured it was simpler to learn to do without sex.

But goddammit, I wasn't going to do without this.

I grabbed his shoulders. "Just a minute," I said, gasping for breath. "Just ... let me get myself together. Don't go away."

I could hear him talking, from far away. His tone was

urgent, anxious, but I couldn't make out the words over the roar in my ears. The frantic, deafening gallop of my heart.

Breathe, silly. It's now, not then. It's Jack, not Brian. Get a grip.

"... okay? Jesus, Viv! What did I do?"

"It wasn't you," I said, through shaking lips. "I'm sorry."

"What the fuck? What happened?"

"It was that position," I admitted, my voice small. "It just triggered some bad memories, that's all. No big deal. I'm okay now. Really. Totally fine."

"What do you mean, that's all?" His face was pale with alarm.

Crap. I had been so close to getting through this stone wall in my own head, and I had to have a meltdown right now, just when I got to the good part. So freaking typical.

"... memories? Can you talk about it?"

The look on his face told me that he wasn't going to let this slide. I gave in to the inevitable with a sigh. "It was a bad boyfriend I had once, years ago," I explained. "The relationship went sour. So did the sex. It took a while for me to pry myself out of the situation, and in the meantime, well. It left me hung up. He was, well. Heavy into control, let's just say, and leave it at that."

I was afraid to look at Jack's face. Pity would make me cringe. But when I finally looked, it wasn't pity I saw. It was fury. A blaze of anger that made my heart do a weird galloping skip of primitive fear.

"Tell me his name, and where he lives," Jack said. "I'll rip that filthy piece of shit to pieces and grind him into the fucking dirt for you."

I blinked at him stupidly. "Ah, well. Um, thank you," I said, flustered. "That's a very kind offer, but I'm okay with it now."

"You didn't look okay two minutes ago," he said grimly.

"I'm sorry I—"

"Stop apologizing!"

The harshness of his voice startled me, and he looked away, shaking his head. "Fuck," he muttered. "Sorry. I didn't mean to yell at you."

"We can't seem to stop apologizing to each other." I kept my nails dug into the muscles of his shoulders, as if I was afraid that he would run away from me, but he didn't. Not at all. His hands crept up, crossing his chest, to cover mine. Enveloping mine. Flooding my body with reassurance.

"Do you want to, uh, just leave it for now?" he suggested gently.

"No!" I yelled. "I will not let him fuck this up for me, too! He has taken enough from me already, goddammit!"

"You don't know how happy I am to hear you say that," he said fervently. "Thank God. Just tell me what I need to do. Or, uh, not do."

"It's not that complicated. Just do what you do. You're fabulous. Just not shoved up against the wall. And don't pin down my hands. Or press on my throat. Or pull on my hair. And we'll be fine. I think."

That tightly leashed fury flashed again in his wolfish eyes. "That sick, filthy fuckhead," he said.

"Yeah, maybe he is, but starting now, he leaves the scene," I said sternly. "No more airtime for the sick, filthy fuckhead. It's just us now. Just Jack and Vivi, *capisci?*"

He nodded. The silence grew so long, we both started to laugh.

"I feel really shy, now," Jack admitted. "I think you're going to have to choreograph this one. I'll just follow your lead."

"But I don't know where I'm going," I protested. "That is to say, I have a rough idea, but I might drive us into the swamp, you know?"

"So we'll lead each other. Like hands on a Ouija board," he said. "I'll give you a tip to get you started. Take my hand and lead me into the bedroom. That'll get us going."

I lifted my hands from his shoulders and grabbed his hand, pulling him into the adjoining room. It was practically empty but for the futon with my sleeping bag and my suitcase tucked in the corner.

The walls were alive with shifting green shadows from sunlight sifting through oak and maple leaves. I longed for the cover of dusk, or night, but no. It was all going to be so visible. So terribly deliberate.

I gave him a questioning look. "Next tip?"

"Take off your clothes," he said.

I giggled nervously as I began, but I put all my bravura into it. Kicking off my sandals. Peeling off my top. I stretched and preened as I pulled pins out of my hair and tossed them to the floor. The tinkle as they fell was loud in the flickering silence.

He watched me uncoil the long, twisted tail of red hair, shaking it down into loose waves over my shoulder, my breasts. I began to circle him, and he followed me with his eyes. The movement felt ancient. Like a ceremony, a spiral dance, an invitation. A sacred rite that would braid their male and female energies into a rope of pure magic.

"The skirt," he reminded me. "Lose the skirt."

I loosened the drawstring and let the skirt drop. Now I was naked, but for Lucia's Renaissance pendant. The one thing that I never took off.

I scooped my hair up over my head, arching my back, tossing my hair. Turning, in front of the raw hunger in his beautiful silver eyes. Not a single nervous thought for my itty-bitty boobs, or my not-so-little ass, or my in-your-face tattoos.

Flaunting myself, and absolutely sure that I would please him.

"Now my clothes," he told me, kicking off his sandals.

Wow. Even his feet were sexy, and I'd never given a thought to feet before, as long as they smelled okay. His were beautiful: long and brown, with graceful toes, square nails, elegant bones.

I attacked his clothes. A goofy grin wasn't the right heavy-eyed, sensual temptress expression that I had wanted to assume for the occassion, but I was having too much fun to pretend to act serious.

I peeled his t-shirt off inch by inch, taking the opportunity to explore his torso with my fingertips. Feeling the grain of his hair, those lean, cut muscles. Every detail fabulously lickable.

I flung the shirt away and attacked his belt, but as I started to shove his jeans down, he stilled my hand, dug into his pocket, and fished out a string of condoms. A long string. He flung them onto the futon.

Ah. Well and good that he was prepared, but the calculated gesture struck me as a provocation. He shoved his jeans and briefs down, stepped out of them, and kicked them away.

Oh, yes. He was perfect. His huge cock thrust out, thick and high, bobbing with its own swollen weight. "Touch me," he directed.

My hands rejoiced as they closed around that velvety supple rod, his vital pulsing heat, his velvety skin, his steely hardness and heat. He more than filled my hand.

I loved his gasps as I stroked and twirled my hand, pulling him, milking him. It made me feel like a goddess, handling storm clouds, thunderbolts. Fearlessly playing with devastating power as if it were my own personal toy, made for my amusement.

"I know this thing of me leading started out as a precaution to keep me from freaking out on you," I said. "But it's changed. It's turned into a kinky power game."

"Maybe," he admitted. "But if a woman as proud and strong as you plays along with my kinky power game without telling me to fuck off, it means she really wants me, right?"

I swirled my hands around his cockhead, making him gasp. "It turns you on," I challenged. "Telling me what to do. Admit it."

He grinned. "Busted. But in my own defense, everything about you turns me on."

"Aw, cute. You think you're so smart, huh?"

He gave her a rueful smile. "Not at the moment."

"I know your tricks," I said breathlessly. "You're showing me how completely you're in control of the situation, right?"

His eyes went thoughtful. "Not exactly," he corrected. "I'm showing you how completely I'm in control of myself. I think you need to be reminded." He gathered up a hank of my hair and kissed it, with that lovely, secret smile glowing in his eyes.

He was so sweet, it made tears well into my eyes, for no reason I could understand.

"I don't know how you do it," I said, my voice wondering. "You have a split personality, Jack. Either you say the exact wrong thing that makes me want to smack you, or you say the exact right thing."

"Yeah?" he prompted. "Which makes you want to …?"

"Um, grab you," I said primly.

His grin flashed. "Go for it, then. Grab me. I love it."

I took him at his word, caressing him with slow, sensual pulls. His hands clenched, flexed, trembled. "So I never say anything neutral, like please pass the peas?"

"What peas have we eaten? We haven't gotten that far in our relationship."

And we never will. According to you.

I shoved the bleak thought away. I would not let anything

screw this up. Not my fears, not the Brian fallout. Not even the plain, undecorated truth.

To hell with the plain truth. Who needed it. I would just live the fantasy for now.

It was time to change the vibe and distract us both, so I kneeled down and unzipped my bright purple down sleeping bag with the lavender nylon lining, spreading it out over the futon mattress.

I curled up, tits stuck out, hair wild and touseled, and looked up seductively through my eyelashes at him. "So? And now?"

He sank down, his face still cautious. "Do you need to be on top?"

I thought about it for a moment. "I think I'm shaking too hard," I confessed. "I don't think I'd even be able to stay upright. I'm melting."

He looked worried. "But I'm big. I wouldn't want you to—"

"Uh-uh," I said, shaking my finger at him. "Don't you worry. I won't flip out on you. I know where I am, and whom I'm with."

He smiled, cautiously relieved. "You're sure?"

"Oh, God, yes," I assured him. "And I love it that you're big. It's hot. Bring it on." I twisted my hand appreciatively over his cockhead, spreading around the slick precome.

His face and neck went rigid. "Oh, God," he muttered. "You're laying all the responsibility onto me, huh?"

"You can take it," I informed him cheerfully. "I have faith."

He put his hand on my belly, stroking me with a light hand. As if I were some delicate, exotic creature that he didn't want to frighten.

I stared at his hand, blinking at another rush of tears. Moved by how worried he was. Tender and gentle. Big, yummy, succulent. And he needed to get on with it. *Now.*

I grabbed the hand that was petting me and gave it a yank. "Get down here," I ordered him. "I want to feel you. On top. All over me."

He allowed himself to be dragged down. I opened my legs and tried to roll him over on top of myself, but he pulled away from me.

"Wait. Hold on." He groped for the condoms. "Let me deal with the practical details before I completely lose my mind."

He fumbled the latex on one-handed, and finally, I managed to pull him down on top of me. I twined my arms and legs around him and squeezed. The sweet shock of his hot body against mine opened the leaky tear faucet again, and off I went.

Jack looked into my wet eyes, alarmed. "Vivi? Are you okay?"

"Fine, great, fabulous," I assured him. "You just feel wonderful. It makes me weepy, but don't worry about it. Not a problem. It's all good."

He stared into my face, his eyes soft, and kissed the tears away from my cheekbones and my temples. Oh, Lord, he felt so good. My hands were going crazy with so much to choose from: his thick shoulders; his powerful back; his taut, muscular ass; that dark, shaggy mane of silky hair tickling my neck. The urgent prod of his cock against my thigh. He wasn't hurrying me at all, but I felt it, eager and stiff, throbbing hopefully while he kissed my neck, my breasts. Caressing my pussy, spreading my lube all around to ease his way.

The wild fluttering anticipation kept rising. This was really happening.

He lifted his head, unexpectedly and gave me his now familiar master-and-commander stare. "Tell me what you want me to do."

I tried not to giggle. It was too frivolous for the vibe. "Isn't it obvious?"

"Doesn't matter," he said. "I want to hear the words."

I reached down and gripped his cock, squeezing it through the thin barrier of latex. "This is another kinky power game, right?"

"Yes. Absolutely."

I writhed beneath his weight, arching until I could press the thick bulb of his penis against the slick opening of my pussy, and with some breathless wiggling, forced him inside. He felt huge, unyielding.

"Please," I whispered. "Put your cock into me."

He stared into my eyes, shifted his weight, pressed deeper.

I gasped and bit my lip. "Oh, wow."

"Relax," he murmured, his voice strangled. "I'll go really slow. It'll be good."

He did, and it was. I had braced myself for a sting, but he barely moved, just hovered over me, rocking gently, kissing me with all his incredible skill, melting me while he caressed my clit with his thumb.

His kisses were a silent language that some deep part of me understood. Something inside him, coaxing and pulling at something inside me. Beseeching me to soften, bend, and melt for him, then demanding it. And there was no way not to give him what he wanted when I wanted it myself so badly.

He made me come again, deep and hard and wrenching, and when I opened my eyes and remembered who I was, his cock was deep inside me. Huge and hard and throbbing. I could barely move.

But he was in no hurry. He rolled me onto my side, draping my leg over his, and we kissed, embraced, hips pulsing lazily together. Slowly, gently rocking.

Time stretched, creating a magical space around us. The room with its flickering leaf shadow was a verdant bower. Colors seemed unnaturally strong. The sleeping bag was the splayed petals of some voluptuous, sexual flower, and the two of us writhed and undulated inside its glowing, silky depths, utterly lost to pleasure.

At some point, I realized with some surprise that I was not uncomfortable at all anymore. My body had relaxed around him. He was easing in and out of me in slow, teasing thrusts, with a skillful swivel and slide that tenderly stroked over every wonderful, throbbing hot spot inside me. I jerked and shuddered with each plunge.

He was so attentive, so sensitive, feeling his way with unerring instincts. His passionate attention unlocked every closed, fearful place inside me and sparked an endless string of delicious explosions. We were fused, a single moving, surging glow. I could not stop the tears in my eyes from slipping out and rolling down, tickling my face, but he just kept tirelessly kissing them away.

It took me a long and delicious interval to convince him to let himself come. To persuade him that he would not hurt me or scare me if he did. He finally picked up the pace, and I clawed him into action, inciting, demanding. Sinking my nails into his ass, pulling him deeper.

He finally gathered me up tightly against him and gave it to me harder than I would ever have dreamed I would want it, but I did. I was transformed. There were no walls or locked doors inside my mind to slam up against. He'd gotten past them all. I was all softness, eagerness, pleasure. It was so good. I loved it all, his fierceness, his strength, his vigor, his size, jarring me, ramming into me as the energy gathered, and then, his hoarse shout. That hot blaze of explosive energy, pumping out of him

...

I couldn't get enough of it. I loved it. I loved ... *him.*

The terrifying thought reverberated through me as our mutual climax wiped us out. When I opened her eyes, we were side by side, limp and damp and spent. Arms and legs entwined. Still panting.

He gazed into my face, touched my cheek with the tip of his finger. "I can't believe how soft your skin is," he said.

I grabbed his hand, and kissed it impulsively, my terrifying realization shining inside me. Part pleasure, part a keen, stabbing pain. It wanted so badly to be shared. But I couldn't. It was premature, stupid, ill-considered. It would ruin everything.

I snuggled up to him, hiding my face against his chest, and we stayed that way until the afternoon sun began to lengthen and turn a warm gold.

Finally, he brushed my hair off my face. "Want to go and plant that *Eranthis hyemalis* with me?" he asked.

I was taken aback. "Right now?"

"I don't know how much of a chance they have to root now, but we could give it a shot," he said. "What the hell, right? I'd hate to see them just wither away without even giving it a try. Doesn't seem right."

I thought about that for a moment. What an ironic choice of words. And he had no clue. I could tell from his face. He was just talking about flowers. His mind was hardwired that way. Straightforward and literal. Calling a flower a flower.

I didn't know how much of a chance the two of us had to root. Not much, maybe. But I was going to give it a shot, by God.

I sat up. "Yes," I said, reaching for my clothes. "Let's go plant those little guys right this very minute. They deserve their shot."

Chapter Thirteen

Jack

I patted the earth down after setting out the last seedling and rose to my feet. "There you go," I said. "Now we just watch, and hope."

Vivi's smile made me feel so strange and good. Charged with energy.

"Would you show me your other flowers?" she asked, hesitantly. "Margaret told me they were beautiful."

"Sure." I brushed earth off my hands, looked at them in a moment of doubt. I wanted to hold her hand, but it didn't seem right, with all that dirt.

She resolved my dilemma by grabbing my hand herself.

We set out toward the river, through a clearing on the hillside that glowed with wildflowers lit from the side by the setting sun. They seemed to dance and flicker like flames. She hardly seemed real, wafting next to me in that floating skirt. Something from a dream. So pretty, she hurt my eyes, with that fiery hair streaming, cheeks so pink, lips so red. Eyes that bright, glowing gray. Already, I felt the hot tingle of a brand-new erection coming on.

We hadn't bothered to shower, just pulled on our clothing. Vivi seemed urgent about the planting, as if something bad would happen if we lost any time, and I had seen no reason not to indulge her.

I kept ogling, marveling. It was official. My brain was slop. I had never even dreamed of sex like that.

After we got past the scary stuff, of course. My free hand clenched at the thought of her evil ex. How a man could hurt any woman was beyond me, let alone one like Vivi. So beautiful and scrappy and strong.

She'd probably scared the shit out of the cowardly bastard. Given him a huge inferiority complex so that the dickhead felt compelled to use the one advantage he had: his greater size. That was a classic. The standard playbook of asshole men.

Not that it was an excuse. He would pay. I intended to see to the matter personally.

Vivi stared up at the trees, the rays of sunlight slanting through them. I gazed hungrily at the perfect curve of her arched neck, the angle of her jaw.

Then we stepped out of the pine thicket, into another world.

The floor of the little valley was covered with spires, buds, blossoms of wildly contrasting colors. Edna yelped and readied herself to plunge into a bank of *Kniphofia.*

Vivi caught her collar and held her fast. "No way, girl. You stay right here. Sit!"

A branch snapped in the forest, and Edna twisted out of Vivi's grasp and bounded off into the woods to investigate.

"Come out into the field," I offered. "I'll show you around."

I led her out into the field, between the beds, and pointed. "These are *Kniphofia,* otherwise known as red hot pokers. The

Lilium auratum on the other side are almost ready. Down there are Oriental poppies, and *Anthoxanthum odoratum*, which is a type of ornamental grass. There's some *Centaurea cyanus* and *Stachys byzantina* on that rise over there. Bachelor's buttons and lamb's ears, in common English. And see those white and blue ones? *Campanula aurita*. Bellflowers. And columbine, at the far end."

She looked enchanted. "Who taught you to grow flowers?"

I hesitated, and then just owned up. "My uncle Freddy," I admitted. "I lived with him for a while. Until I was fourteen. He was heavy into organic gardening."

"He grew flowers, too?"

"You could say that," I answered.

She lifted an eyebrow. "What do you mean? He did or he didn't."

"Uncle Freddy specialized in cannabis. Various strains of specialty marijuana. Very profitable for him, for a while. It was a different era."

"Oh." Vivi looked startled, but not unduly so.

"The principles are the same," I said. "He loved plants. He knew how to give them what they needed."

"Oh," she said again.

"I prefer flowers myself," I went on. "More color. Less stress."

"Is your uncle still ... um, never mind."

"It's okay. I doubt if he's still in business. It's a very different game, now that it's legal. And he had to leave the country one night twenty-some years ago. Haven't seen him since. Don't even know if he's still alive. He'd be over seventy by now." I kept my gaze averted and stroked a *Campanula aurita* bud. They were getting ready to bloom at any minute. I always liked that moment of suspense, leading up to the big explosion.

"That was when you were fourteen, you say?"

"I'm thirty-seven now," I said. "That would make it twenty-three years ago."

"Were you there when he left? Was it a drug bust?"

My discomfort surged up. "Yeah."

"How awful," I said. "What happened to you afterward?"

I walked into an aisle between two rows of fluttering poppies, turning my back to her. "Nothing happened to me," I said.

"Did he just vanish?" she persisted, following me.

"I'm fine now. Let's leave it."

"Excuse me," she said. "Never mind. I know it's none of my business."

Fuck. I felt like shit, but I did not want to talk about it. I was dick-for-brains stupid for bringing it up and ruining their excellent mood.

A distressed yelping came from the trees. Vivi picked her way hastily through the flower beds toward the pine thicket. I caught up with her as she plunged into the trees. Her dog was whining and pawing anxiously at her muzzle.

Vivi grabbed her collar and crouched down, holding the trembling dog still. "Easy, girl," she soothed. "Oh, God. Oh, no."

Porcupine quills stuck out of Edna's nose and jaw, like long, crazy whiskers.

I crouched down and took the dog's shivering head in my hands, examining it. "There are only twelve," I said. "I've seen worse."

Vivi bit her lip, searching through Edna's coat for more quills.

"Let's go to the house," I suggested. "I've got scissors. Pliers."

"I don't want to bother you with this," she murmured, not

meeting my eyes. "I've got pliers in my jewelry toolbox. I'll deal with it."

I gave her a horrified look. "Get real."

Edna slunk between them, tail down, through the woods as they went back toward the house. Our camaraderie, that perfect elusive glow of joy, was gone.

It was so elusive. Such a fucking mystery. I wished I knew how to hang on to it.

Once at the house, I led her and her dog into my front room. I got the scissors and the pliers out and kneeled down beside them on the floor. "Hold her," I said.

Vivi held her dog firmly as I snipped off the ends of the quills. Edna made high-pitched whining noises in the back of her throat.

"Why are you doing that?" she asked. "What's the point of it?"

"I've been told that if you trim the end of the quills, the vacuum inside collapses and the barbs should let go more easi-ly," I explained. "Theoretically, at least. I haven't tested the theory personally."

Vivi blinked, and swallowed. "Oh," she whispered.

We powered through the painful job. It didn't really take all that long to pull out the quills, but it felt like forever. Vivi winced with each shrill yelp and jerk, although her low voice never stopped murmuring low encouragement.

I tried to be brisk and matter-of-fact, but by the time we were done, Jesus. I sagged back against the side of my sofa, limp as a wet rag. Inflicting pain on an innocent animal was fucking horrible, whether it was for the animal's own good or not. Thank God I worked with plants. I needed a drink after that ordeal.

Edna curled up in Vivi's lap, still trembling. Vivi was bent over her, her face hidden against the dog's silky brown shoulder.

Leaving me all alone, with memories flooding back, weirdly sharp and clear. Taking over my whole goddamn mind. I couldn't stop seeing it. Hearing it in my mind's eye. That June night when a wild-eyed Uncle Freddy had slapped me on the shoulder.

"Sorry, kid, but I've got to run. They got Pete, and Pete's such an airhead, he'll give me up for sure. I gotta leave the country."

I remember my stomach heaving. "Where are you going?"

"I'm not gonna tell you where. It's safer that way. Here." He thrust a handful of limp, grimy bills into my grubby, nerveless hand. "Take this. I wish it was more, but it's all I can spare."

"Can't I come with you?" I asked.

"I wish you could, Jackie, but you don't have a passport. Shit, I don't even think you have a birth certificate. I'll be an outlaw, see? I can't have a kid. Keep your head low and your mouth shut, okay?"

"Okay," I said dully, pocketing the money.

"We shoulda drilled for this, but it was going so well. I got sloppy." Freddy gripped my skinny shoulders in his big, work-stained hands. "Lemme give you some advice. Don't mix it up with the police, the social workers. Hit the road. Go out and seek your fortune. You can do better for yourself outside the system."

"Like you did?" I said bitterly.

"Hey, don't hold this against me. Come on, chin up. You're, what, sixteen? Seventeen? You'll be fine. You'll land on your feet."

"Fourteen," I corrected him, my voice toneless.

"Fourteen? Jesus, kid. I thought you were older." Freddy tugged on his beard, looking distressed that I was not older.

"Tavia's number is on the fridge, okay? And your mom—where is your mom, again?"

"The ashram. In India," I reminded him.

"Oh, yeah. The ashram. Damn. I guess Tavia is your best bet, kid. Oh, hey. You could always call Mrs. Margaret Moffat. Your mom and Tavia and I stayed with her one summer when we were kids, in Silverfish. Dad was working the carnival, and Mom had to go into the TB hospital, so she took us in for a couple of months. Nice lady. Baked great cookies. Call her if you get in a tight spot. But try Tavia first."

I stared at my feet, mouth trembling. Uncle Freddy tousled my hair. "Sorry, Jackie. But you know how it is."

"Yeah," I said. I knew exactly how it was. I knew better than anyone.

And after a flurry of packing and a rough, sweaty hug, I had stood in the driveway and watched Freddy's taillights disappear into the dark.

I'd tried calling Aunt Tavia in L.A. A guy answered, and said she hadn't lived there in four months, and no, he didn't know where she was. He'd heard somebody say she'd gone to Baja. But it might have been Boulder. Or Bali. Then the guy told me that I seemed stressed and should practice "letting go." "Hanging on" caused all

the suffering in life. In fact, if I would tell him the date and hour of my birth, he would be happy to provide me, for a small fee, with a mantra calibrated to attain the serenity of non-attachment, and also—

I hung up on that babbling prick. Then I took the tattered envelope off the fridge, and dialed the long string of numbers written on it for the ashram.

The guy who answered spoke only Hindi, and had then passed the phone to someone else who must have been speaking German. I struggled with that for a while, repeating my mother's name, and then hung up on that guy, too.

I stared at the phone. Finally, I picked up the receiver, dialed information for Silverfish, and asked for Margaret Moffat.

"I have an M. Moffat in Silverfish," the operator had said. "Do you want the number?"

"Sure." I wrote the number down, folded it, stuck it into my jeans.

I had no idea what to do next. I had wandered around the empty house as night deepened. The quiet terrified me. I wondered when the police would come, and what could happen to me if they found me there. If they would put me in jail, too.

At dawn, I had filled my knapsack with as much stuff as I could carry, tied a rolled blanket onto the top, and headed out onto the road.

"... okay?" I jolted out of my memories. Vivi's face was close to mine, her gray eyes wide with worry. She patted my shoulder.

She tried again, louder. "Are you okay, Jack?"

I focused on the faint pattern of freckles on her perfect, narrow little nose. Like a constellation of stars. "Uh, yeah," I said. "Sorry. I was someplace else for a while."

She touched my cheek with her knuckles, a shy, tender stroke. "No place good," she said. "You had that look on your face."

I shook myself to alertness, embarrassed. "What look is that?"

"Sad," she said simply. "Can I make you some tea?"

"Coffee," I said, rousing myself. "Tea doesn't do it for me. Sit down. Stay with your dog. I'll make it."

"No, no. I'll do it." She pushed me back down. "It's the

least I can do. Thanks so much for helping. It would have been a lot worse alone."

"It's nothing," I muttered.

"Not to me and Edna it's not." Her smile was so warm and bright.

I followed her into the kitchen, just to stay close. Taking every sneaky opportunity to touch her, brush against her, sniff her scent as we put the coffee on together.

When it was done and poured, we sat across the table from each other. I reached out and grabbed her hand. They'd hit another smooth patch, and I was going to ride it for as long as I could. "I'm sorry for what I said in the—"

"Don't," Vivi broke in. "You apologized the last time you insulted me, and the time before that. Every time, I let down my guard and let you do it again. Let's establish a rule. No insults. No apologies. Okay?"

"You misunderstood. I never insulted you," I said.

"No? Me, the itinerant sexpot neo-hippy?"

I narrowly avoided spluttering my coffee. "That doesn't count," I protested. "You took me by surprise. In a wet t-shirt, no less."

"Oh?" She gazed at me over the rim of her mug, eyes sparkling.

"Yes! Give me a fucking break! There you were, soaking wet in the forest, nipples poking through your shirt, looking like something out of a *Penthouse* centerfold—"

"It's not my fault it was raining! I looked like a freaking mudslide!"

"Yeah, and it's not my fault all the blood in my body got instantly rerouted to my dick," I muttered. "You expect me to be rational when a gorgeous woman tricked out like that waves a tire iron at me?"

Her eyebrows went up. "Did the tire iron turn you on, Jack?"

"I'll tell you what turns me on," I told her. "A proud, beautiful, self-reliant woman who takes no shit off anybody. That absolutely yanks my chain. Big time."

Her eyes fell, but she was smiling now. Maybe I'd manage to navigate this one without going off the rails. "I never insulted you," I went on. "I made a rational assessment of the situation based on the information I gathered. You read it as an insult, but I was not judging you."

"Wrong," Vivi said sternly. "Your assessment is faulty."

"I don't think so," I said. "I've had lots of practice."

"Whoever you've been practicing on isn't me. But let's not talk about it, or we'll just crash and burn all over again."

She tried to tug her hand back, but I hung on to it, stubbornly. "That wasn't what I was apologizing for," I confessed. "I meant when we were out in the field. You asked about my uncle. And I got all uptight. I closed you off." I blew out a careful, measured sigh, trying to relax my clenched insides.

Her eyes softened. She set down her coffee and reached across the table. "There's a reason I was asking those questions about the bust, you know," she said.

"Yeah?" I asked warily. "And what's that?"

"I just wondered if it was something that we had in common," she said. "I was in the middle in a big drug bust once, too. When I was a kid."

I stared at her, my mouth stupidly open. "Huh? You?"

"Me," she said. "It sucked. As you are highly qualified to agree."

"But aren't you ... didn't you ..." I racked my brains for the details that Duncan had given me about Vivi D'Onofrio's background. Italian nobility. Priceless art. And now drug busts? What the fuck? This did not compute. Not at all.

"My two sisters and I were all adopted," she said, answering my silent confusion. "Lucia took us in as foster kids. I went to her when I was eleven. I was lucky. Nancy and Nell had to plow through years of bad placements before they found Lucia. I hit pay dirt right off the bat, on my first go. Lucia was amazing. And I got two kick-ass, readymade sisters in the bargain. They were the best. I hit the jackpot."

"And before?" I prompted.

Her face clouded. "Ah. Before. Well, my mom was a junkie. And the men she took up with were all dealers."

"Jesus," I said under my breath.

"I got used as a sentry," she said. "Deliveries, too."

"No fucking shit!" I was aghast. "How old were you?"

She shrugged. "Eight, nine. Red pigtails, freckles, ruffles. Who would suspect what was in my Hello Kitty knapsack? I liked it, at the time. It made me feel important, grown up. Useful."

"Used," I corrected, harshly. "Anything could have happened to you! A little kid, for drug deliveries? That's fucking insane!"

She made a dismissive gesture. "Duh. But anyway, the shit came down. There was a shoot-out. My mom's boyfriend, Randy, got killed in the bust. My mom went to prison."

I winced. "Tell me you weren't there when it happened."

"I wasn't," she assured me. "I was at school. And I didn't cry for Randy. He was a real prick. I have him to thank for this." She held up her wrist, with its barbed-wire tattoo. "This was his idea of a joke."

I stared at the fuzzy, faded tattoo around her slender wrist, anger simmering inside me. "All I can say is, the list of people whom I want to dismember and grind into the dirt on your behalf is growing," I said.

"Thank you, but it's ancient history now. So, how did the

bust shake out for you? Did you end up with Child Protective Services, too?"

I shook my head. "No. I just took off."

Her eyes widened. "Alone? At fourteen? How did you live?"

I hesitated for a moment before replying. "Barely," I said. "So what about your mom? Is she out of prison?"

Vivi shook her head. "She OD'd in prison. Eight months after she went inside."

I felt sucker-punched. That was what I got for trying to distract her from my own story. "Aw, shit. I'm sorry," I said, helplessly.

She gazed intently into her coffee mug. "It was a long time ago," she said. "And I was as lucky with my second family as I was unlucky with my first. I'm okay. You can relax, Jack."

We listened to the wind in the trees. I reached out until I touched the flower tattooed on her chest. "The perfect combination of toughness and a good attitude," I said.

She blushed. "You're doing it again, Jack. Saying all the right things."

"Is it working? You want to grab me again?"

Her devastating secret smile turned dazzling. She got up, came around the table and sat down on my lap.

My arms encircled her. Emotion made me speechless. My dick was stone hard against the pressure of her ass, but it wasn't just that. I just couldn't believe she was there, draping herself over me, holding me, trusting me. She was so beautiful, so special, so shining. Like a unicorn, laying its head in my lap. Me, breathless with the wonder of it. So turned on, I could barely suck in a chestful of air.

She gasped as I stood up and swept her into my arms, heading up the stairs. "Jack! What the hell do you think you're doing?"

"Being masterful," I said. "Stop giggling like that. Get into the vibe."

"Hail, oh conquering hero," she gasped out, between giggles. "Do with me as you will, my wild warrior lover. How's that?"

"Great. Works for me." I shoved open the door to my bedroom with my foot and set her on her feet. We faced off, breathing hard. Her color was high, her eyes were shining. I tossed off my shirt. Vivi whipped off her tank. Call and response. I jerked open my belt, popped open my jeans buttons. She yanked loose the drawstring of her skirt, let the garment puddle around her ankles. Her beauty unraveled me.

"Turn around," I said hoarsely. "Let me see your ass."

She obliged me. I came up behind her and knelt, my hands sliding down over her ribs, her waist, to clasp her hips. I pressed my lips against the tribal looking mandala tattoo at the small of her back. "What's the story with this one?"

"Oh." She shivered as I licked her there, my hand sliding up between her legs. "That was a celebratory tattoo. To mark the occasion of getting away from Bri—from that crappy ex that I mentioned before. I called my buddy Rafael on the day that the shit hit the fan, and he whisked me away in his van, which is now my van. Drove me to my first crafts fair, in upstate New York. I had a good day, sold a bunch of stuff. After, we celebrated with buffalo wings and beer and a tattoo. Rafael got a dragon tattooed on his butt that night, if I remember correctly. I was a little more conservative."

I turned her to face me, my eyes level with the perfect contours and sweet downy hollows of her groin. Breathing in the hot, heady smell of sex. My cock ached with eagerness. I placed her hand on my shoulder to steady her and lifted her delicate foot. She teetered, giggling, as I touched the tattooed images of the crescent moon and star on top of her foot. "And this one?"

"There's no real story with that one," she admitted. "I just thought it was pretty."

"It is," I said. All of them were. Fit embellishments for her vivid beauty. Even the barbed wire around her wrist had its own poignant grace.

I gazed up at her pink face, her dilated eyes, the whole perfect length of her sweet body. Her pussy, still shiny and flushed, poking proudly out of her labia. "What an incredible view," I muttered.

I rose to my feet, moving behind her, my cock prodding the back of her thighs, and slid my hands around her waist, sliding one hand down between her legs. The tender seam of her pussy was slick and damp beneath my fingers.

"I want to take you from behind," I said. "Is that a problem for you?"

A fine tremor went through her, but I couldn't tell if it was fear or desire. I nuzzled and petted, waiting until she gave me a clearer answer. Several breathless minutes went by as I caressed her. She began to writhe and make keening sounds in her throat as my hands grew bolder.

"It's okay," she whispered, finally.

I let go of her, stepped back. "Show me, then."

She shot a puzzled look over her shoulder. "Show you what?"

"That it's okay," I said. And just waited.

It worked again, just as it had before. She thought about it for a moment, her full, rosy lip caught seductively between her teeth.

Then she straightened her spine, tossed her hair back, and sauntered over to my bed. Taking her time. She climbed on, positioning herself on her hands and knees, presenting her perfect ass. She looked back, with that secret, alluring smile, and parted her thighs, undulating. "Convinced?"

I didn't bother to reply. Seconds later, I was in position, condom in place. My fingers rejoiced at her flawless skin, her lithe muscles, her sweet curves. I teased the secret shadows of her pussy while I kissed the mandala tattoo, playing with her sensitive clit.

She squirmed and moaned and lunged back against me, wet and hot, but I took my own sweet time easing inside her. The tight, hot clutch of her was sweet torture on my cock. She clung to me, her pussy flushed and full. A juicy, suckling kiss.

I let her rock back to take me deeper, a little more with each stroke, until I was buried deep. Then some gasping, panting minutes of stroking and petting, licking her back, working her clit, and she started to make catlike sounds, pressing back. Demanding that he move Deeper. Harder.

Yes. Now she was ready.

I thrust, hypnotized by the shiny pink lips of her pussy clinging to my flushed, gleaming shaft. I withdrew and drove in again, again, seeking the strokes that made her soften and yield and shiver, using that subtle, inner awareness I'd never really brought into focus until I was making love to her. Now that I'd discovered it, I was strung out on it. Life was going to be so flat, so flavorless, without her.

That thought stabbed into me like a blade. My hands tightened on her hips. And something inside me cracked wide open.

I lost control. Moved inside her with the energy of a lifetime of unsatisfied need, seeking that blinding moment where I wouldn't have to think, or fear.

It hit me, and I exploded into blinding nothingness.

When I finally surfaced again, Vivi was wiggling beneath me on the quilt, kicking at my ankles. "Roll over," she said tartly. "I can't breathe."

I rolled over, and she pulled away, sitting up. Her eyes were very wide. "That was, um, intense," she said, her voice small.

"I'm sorry," I said, alarmed. "Did I hurt you?"

"A little, but it was really exciting. I came, of course. You always make me come. But you weren't with me anymore. At the end. I felt, well ... alone."

I didn't know what to say. I felt her withdrawal like a cold wind. I reached out, but she shrank back, and I let my hand drop.

"I'm sorry," I said, feeling helpless.

"I told you. It's okay. I'm not mad."

"Wait for me while I go take this thing off, okay?" I asked.

"Okay." She didn't move. I waited, watching her until she rolled her eyes and obliged me. She slid between the sheets.

"You won't go?" I asked. "Promise?"

"No," she said. "I promise I won't go."

I smoothed the quilt over her, my face reddening. I was acting like a little kid. Afraid she would disappear like a puff of smoke. Damn. I was a goner.

"The sooner you go, the sooner you'll come back," she said, waving for me to go.

I stared at myself in the bathroom mirror and turned on the cold water. I splashed my face, tried to think clearly, and abandoned the effort, after about five seconds.

All I wanted in the world was to hold her again. Wrap myself around her in a grip that she could not even hope to break.

I wiped off my face and grabbed the little wastebasket from under the sink, since it was stupid to run back and forth every time.

She was still there when I got back. Holding the covers open. I slid into bed and embraced her.

She smiled at me, and something tight and fearful in my

chest uncoiled. I resisted the sensation, automatically, and then yielded to it with a shudder of nameless emotion.

I arranged her so that her head was cradled on my shoulder, her arm resting on my chest, her leg flung over mine. I stroked her back, and felt her heart beating under my hand, until she fell asleep.

So soft. I stared at the swirls of red hair tickling my nose, my chin. Her slender shoulder. I loved her scent, the soft moist bloom of warmth of her breath against my shoulder. I memorized the curve of her spine. If I concentrated on these details, and thought of nothing else, I could cling to this emotion that was vibrating inside me like a tightly strung instrument. Part of me wanted to shove it back down into the darkness, but the feeling sang on, a fragile, stubborn thread.

I clung to it, counting the rise and fall of her breaths. Keeping the rest of the universe at bay. Let there be nothing but her, and her breath. In. Out.

Late afternoon eased with the smoothness of a sigh into twilight. I barely noticed the change. I could lie there forever, feeling her heartbeat. Letting that strange feeling vibrate inside me. That faraway, mysterious melody.

Contentment? No. I rejected the word. I was familiar with contentment. I was contented with my house, my work. I counted myself lucky to spend my days with the smell of the earth and rain, the sun, the colors of flowers. That was contentment.

This feeling was new. It was a long, quiet hour before I dared to put a name to it.

It felt almost like happiness.

That scared me. There were pitfalls there, fatal traps. Behind that word were doors in my mind that had been locked for years. Like when Randy left, when I was eight. Deborah, who always insisted that I call her Deborah instead of Mom, told me that Randy had to go and find himself. "I gotta have space," I remembered him saying, very loudly. I remembered also thinking that was really dumb. It was the Oregon desert. There was so much space, it gave me the willies.

But Randy evidently needed more. He took down his teepee, threw it in his truck, and drove away. I remembered standing there, bewildered, while Randy's truck got smaller. I had wondered sometimes if Randy was my father, but Deborah had been somewhat vague on that point.

Then we'd stayed with Jim and Consuela in the Yakima Valley, until Deborah met Manuel. We moved into Manuel's trailer in the peach orchards. Manuel taught me Spanish, how to fight, how to change the oil in a car. Then Manuel got in trouble because he didn't have a green card. He had to go back to Mexico.

After a while, Deborah decided that she had to follow her heart and go to Mexico, too. Which had freaked me right the fuck out.

"You'll stay with Tavia," she told me.

"But why can't I come?"

"Oh, it's complicated, baby. But I'll write you letters, and I'll send for you real soon. You'll love it with Aunt Tavia. Her commune has lots of kids, and a swimming hole, and a tree house and everything."

So off I went, to Tavia's commune, near Olympia. I got some letters, but they started coming less and less frequently. I was just starting to get used to the place when Tavia fell in love with Mick, a guy from Oakland, and decided to move down to California to be with him. But Mick didn't want me to come. "The family thing is just not my scene," Mick said firmly.

So off I went to Uncle Freddy's place in southern Oregon. And in the meantime, Deborah broke up with Manuel, who was "too enmeshed in his culture," the letter said. She had decided to go to India to study yoga with a guru, "to get her head straightened out and recover her sense of self." Shortly after that, Tavia broke up with Mick, left Oakland, and moved to Los Angeles with a guy named Mike.

I had trouble keeping it all straight. But I had liked the benevolent Uncle Freddy. I had liked the garden, the farm, the mountains. I had almost begun to allow myself to think of the place as home when the bust went down.

That was the time I most hated to remember. I hadn't thought of it in years.

I stared at the barbed-wire tattoo around Vivi's slender wrist, tracing it, and suddenly realized that her eyes were open. She was studying me.

She scrambled on top of me, folding her arms over my chest and resting her chin on them. There were questions in her eyes. She wanted to talk.

It terrified me. Too much reality would chase away that feeling I liked so much. But even so, I wanted to know her. Her history, her dreams, her hopes, her plans.

No, on second thought, maybe I didn't want to know her plans.

Chapter Fourteen

Vivi

I felt so relaxed, sprawled on top of Jack. My body just couldn't get enough contact with him.

"So?" I prompted him. "Shouldn't we talk?"

"Probably," he said cautiously. "I'm not feeling very articulate."

"Hmm." I shifted, breasts brushing his chest, my crotch rubbing against his thigh. He hardened beneath me instantly. Already up for more. Wow. The man was tireless.

"You just wait a goddamn minute," I said with a teasing smile. "We should talk before we make love again. This is too easy!"

"What's wrong with easy?" He groped for a condom and ripped the package open. "We can talk if I'm inside you, can't we? Nothing's stopping us."

"Right," I said. "Like I'm supposed to chitchat while a two-hundred-and-thirty- pound sex god is nailing me to his bed with his enormous thing, giving me multiple orgasms? Puh-leeze."

"Consider it a challenge," he suggested, rolling the condom on. "I won't move. I just want to be inside you. Please?"

He nudged himself inside me, and stared into my eyes for the whole, long, tight slide. I felt like I fit over his broad, pulsing shaft like a skintight glove. I was blushing again, from my chest on up. And I was the one who started to move over him. I just couldn't help herself. Manipulative bastard. He knew I couldn't get enough of him.

I would have felt embarrassed, if I hadn't been so busy working myself up to another climax. I flung the covers back and rode him, chest heaving, back arched.

He touched my breasts, held me, playing skillfully with my clit until I collapsed over him, gasping and sobbing, in spasms of pleasure.

After, I lifted myself up onto my elbows, hazy with residual pleasure, and realized that he was still hot and huge and hard inside me, staring into my eyes.

"Ah, Jack?" I ventured. "What about you?"

"What about me?" he said. "I'm fine. Didn't you want to talk?"

"But don't you need to come?"

He gave her a swift grin. "It'll wait. No hurry. I just want to hang out, miles inside you. My dick is in heaven. It wants to take up residence."

I buried my laughter against his silky mat of dark chest hair. "If you say so." I pushed myself up, pulsing my quivering pussy around him, and tried to compose myself. Here went nothing. "I was wondering if you'd go with me into Pebble River, like Margaret suggested," I said. "To look at rentals. For my gallery."

His face stiffened. "You know what I think of that idea."

"Yes, but it's what I plan to do," I told him. "I know you

think I'm married to the road, but I took that path by necessity. Not by choice."

"Please. Don't make promises you can't keep."

I sighed in frustration. "They're not promises. I'm just telling you my plans. Why won't you listen to me, Jack?"

He shook his head. "Duncan will kill me if I let you do this."

I jerked up onto my elbows. "Duncan does not make my decisions for me. I am almost broke, and I cannot hide forever."

He let out a heavy sigh. "I see that."

"And you can't say there's nothing between us," I said, resolutely. "Not anymore."

"I'm not saying that. But please, let's just stay in the moment. Let's not look at it too closely. If we do ..." His voice trailed off.

"It'll disappear?" I finished. "You really think that about me?"

His silence was my answer. I drooped back down onto his chest, downhearted, feeling him shift and pulse. Reminding me of his presence inside my body.

"So we can't talk about the future," I said. "What can we talk about?"

"We don't have to talk at all," he suggested.

I laughed at him. "Nice try, buddy. No, we're talking right now. So buck up."

"Okay, then," he said. "The past. Tell me about your past."

I blew a wisp of hair out of my eyes. "Wow, Jack. Big topic. Want to break it down a little for me?"

"Tell me how you became an artist," he suggested.

"Ah. Okay. Well, it was a challenge. Lucia sweated for years, trying to turn me into a civilized human. I was a wild animal, even though I loved her to pieces from the start. Hyperactive, hot tempered, foul-mouthed. I got bad grades. I had impulse control issues. I got into fights."

"I'm not surprised," he said. "You have a certain uncompromising quality."

I ignored that and went on. "Lucia was determined to make me respectable. She wanted me to study something that would make me good money, turn me into a pillar of the community. She loved art, but she liked classics. She didn't understand wild experimental art. We had a hell of a time fighting it out."

"And you won?" He twirled a lock of my hair around his finger.

"No, not at first. I compromised. I agreed to study graphic design. I tried, I really did, but I was miserable, and my grades sucked, and I ended up losing my scholarship. Lucia was furious with me."

"And? What did you do then?"

I shrugged. "I mostly waitressed and tended bar. I was a bike messenger for a while. I saved enough to reenroll in art school, one semester at a time. I survived on art show openings for a couple of years."

He looked puzzled. "How's that?"

"You know those wine-and-cheese receptions at art galleries when a new exhibit opens? You can find one every night in New York, if you inform yourself. Cheese, crackers, grapes, strawberries, mini-quiches, puff pastries. If you're too broke to buy groceries, they're great. You can choff a day's worth of calories all in one go."

He stirred uncomfortably. "You were that desperate?"

"Oh, it wasn't so bad," I assured him. "I saw a lot of art. It did me good. And then I met this gallery owner, Brian. I signed a contract with him. And he started to sell some of my stuff. My brief artistic golden age."

He lifted his head. "Brian? He's the filthy fuckhead ex, isn't he?"

I went utterly still on top of him. "Ah ... what if he is?"

"Brian Wilder, right? Wilder Galleries, in Soho?"

I was shocked. "How in the holy *hell* do you know that?"

"It's the age of information," he said innocently. "Shouldn't be hard to find out where the prick lives."

"You wouldn't!" I felt panicked, as if that poisonous toxic waste from my past could reach out and somehow contaminate this delicate, shining thing I had discovered with Jack. "Don't you dare! Leave him alone! Promise me!"

He stroked my back. "Shhh. Don't worry about it."

I hissed at him, anything but reassured. "If you mess with Brian, I'll take you apart! I will deconstruct you and sell you for scrap!"

He pressed my ass, pulsing his cock inside me. Reminding me he was the man, no doubt. Hah. "I hear you," he soothed. "So, back to your story. The fuckhead started selling your work, and then? What kind of work was it?"

"Well, I met him during my barbed-wire and broken-beer-bottle period."

His eyes widened. "Your *what?*"

"I was rebellious at the time," I explained. "I felt very put upon because of my tragic childhood. I was mad at my birth mother for going to jail and killing herself. I was mad at Lucia for trying to control me, et cetera, et cetera. And I was drinking way, way too much espresso. I put all of that wild mojo into my work."

"I see." His voice was guarded.

"Anyway, Brian discovered me, you might say," I went on. "Decided to clean me up. Make me marketable."

"And you got involved with him?" He cupped my breast in his hands.

"Yes," I said, my voice catching breathlessly. "It was a disaster. On every level, not just a personal one."

"What happened?" He began to rock his pelvis up against me, pressing his pubic bone against my clit in a slow, circular movement.

I pushed against his chest until I was upright, glaring sternly down at him. "Don't distract me," I lectured. "This is hard stuff to talk about. You're cheating!"

His hips surged, making me undulate helplessly on top of him. "Sorry," he murmured. "You're just so sexy. I forgot myself. And then?"

"What happened was that he turned out to be an art vampire, in addition to being an evil fuckhead. All he wanted was to make me into his money-grubbing zombie slave."

"I see," he said.

"And ... well, I couldn't. I tried to be a zombie slave, but nothing came out. He got really angry. And you know the rest."

"Yeah," he said. "I do."

He stared up into my hot, flushed face. The deep rocking slide of his cock inside me was impossible to resist. He held me firmly, thrusting up, stirring me around, making me gasp and bite my lip, trembling with wild excitement.

"I destroyed his office, at the end," I said. "I was so angry. Freaked out. Out of my head. I think I smashed probably thirty thousand dollars' worth of art."

"Good." He thrust harder, jarring a whimper from my throat. "Did he say, 'You'll never work in this town again,' et cetera?"

"Yes," I said, bleakly.

"And you believed him?"

I braced myself against his chest. "Of course I believed him!" I said tartly. "It was true! He blacklisted me, Jack! The guy has clout!"

He stopped moving, petting my hair. "Okay," he murmured. "Sorry."

"I thought I was finished," I went on. "Then Rafael stepped in."

"Who's this Rafael, anyhow?" Jack frowned. "Another boyfriend?"

"Rafael? Good God, no. Rafael's just my buddy, and besides, he likes boys."

"So you drove off with Rafael and left the whole mess behind you."

The finality of his voice made tension grip my chest. "Hey. Don't you dare blame me for—"

"I'm not blaming you," he said. "You did the right thing."

I was startled. "I ... you really think so?"

He pulled me back down on top of him. "Yeah. I do."

I relaxed against his solid warmth. His quiet statement soothed something deep inside me. "I think you're the only person who's ever said that, except for Rafael," I said. "Lucia thought I was giving up. My sisters, too. It's hard to go against everyone's advice."

He stroked my back without replying, warm and comforting.

"Poor Lucia," I murmured. "I was a heartbreak to her. I defied her in every way. From my clothes to my ill-fated career choices."

"Were you one of those girls with spiked hair and safety pins?"

I snorted. "Not quite. I did have thigh-high lace-up black leather boots, though."

"Really?"

"Oh, yeah. They were the centerpiece of my wardrobe. I wore them with ripped fishnet stockings and a purple velvet miniskirt."

"My God," he said, with feeling. He reached down to slide his thumb tenderly into the top of my labia, circling around my clit. "Do you still have them?"

I writhed against him, gasping with pleasure, eyes shut. "Have what?"

"The boots."

My eyes popped open, and I started to laugh. "Ah...I don't think so," I said. "Maybe in a box in Lucia's attic. It was a long time ago."

I giggled at the wistful look on his face, and he frowned at me. "What's so funny?"

"You," I said. "I thought you would disapprove of my slutty boots. Brian hated them with a passion. You surprise me, that's all."

"Brian was a sick, evil fuckhead. Don't compare me to him. Of course I want to see you in those boots. I'm a normal guy, okay?"

"You're not a normal guy, Jack."

He kissed me fiercely into silence, and lifted his head some time later, when I was dazed with lust. "Besides. You're a fine one to talk about normal. Barbed wire and broken beer bottles, for God's sake."

"Oh, shut up," I murmured, and kissed him back hungrily.

A moment later, I reached up to touch his cheek. "Jack?" I asked, tentatively. "Would you do something for me?"

He froze, eyes guarded. "If I can," he hedged.

"I want to try something," I said hesitantly. "I want for you to, ah ... hold my hands down."

He jerked up onto his elbows, rocking me back. "Why, for fuck's sake? After what he did? Why would you do that to yourself? Or me?"

"Shhh," I soothed. "Nothing sick about it. I really think that it would be okay, with you. Hot, even. But I can't know until I try."

"But I'm the one who feels like dogshit if it doesn't work out!"

"Please, don't get mad," I pleaded. "You don't have to, if it makes you upset. I just thought, well, I don't want all these dead zones and 'danger, keep out' signs in my head. I want to feel free. And if anyone in the world could do that for me, it would be you. Believe me. I would never ask such a thing of you if I didn't trust you."

Even though you don't trust me back. I held the thought at bay with great difficulty.

He stared into my face for a long time, as if trying to read my mind. "You're sure about this," he said carefully.

I nodded, swallowing hard.

"And you won't blame me if—"

"Not in the least. I swear it."

In one swift surge, he rolled us both over, pinning me beneath his weight. He folded my legs up high, hooking them over his shoulders, and grabbed my hands, pinning them beside my head.

He waited, staring fiercely into my face. Gauging my reaction.

I gave him a tremulous smile. "I'm okay," I whispered, stretching luxuriously against the ballast of his hands. Undulating beneath him. "Feels good."

He leaned down and kissed me, deeply, possessively. His tongue thrusting and twining boldly with mine. "Look into my eyes," he said. "The entire goddamn time. Or else I stop. Got it?"

I nodded. My throat was quivering, and my heart felt full as I stared into his face, but I wasn't panicking. No stabs of fear, no numbing black fog, no clench of tension. My heart was pounding from pure excitement, not from fear.

He was not gentle, nor did I want him to be. His body challenged mine, pounding deep and hard, and his face looked angry, eyes burning, mouth grim.

Except that I knew him now. I could feel his concern, his tension, his need. His intense awareness of me.

And I was aware of him, too, on levels I'd never known before. I sensed that the conquering, dominant pose excited him, and his excitement fed mine in a confused, muddled, delicious feedback loop of emotion, sensation. There was no play-acting. My surrender was as real as his conquest.

I gasped for breath, jerking up to meet his thrusts. Staring with wide, tear-blinded eyes into his face. Struggling voluptuously against the implacable strength of his beautiful body, his steely arms, his gripping hands.

I could go there with him. All the way. I could go anyplace I wanted with him, as far as I could dream of going, always knowing that he would carry me back, completely safe, all in one happy, sated piece.

Afterward, we lay tangled together, limp and damp. We roused ourselves at last to take a long, lazy shower, washing each other. Jack's tireless cock rose to full salute, but I just laughed at him. "Dream on, big boy," I said. "I'm all done for the night."

He toweled me off, with his usual passionate attention to detail and herded me toward the stairs. "Food, then," he said, resigned.

We made sandwiches in his kitchen. Devoured the rest of Margaret's latest batch of cookies. When we could find nothing else that was quick and easy to eat, we went back up the stairs into Jack's bed to twine our naked bodies as closely together as we could.

We talked, carefully. Long, tentative, groping conversations about our pasts, our histories. Circling delicately around forbidden topics.

But I didn't want dead zones and "danger keep out" signs in our conversations, either. I sat up, pushing his hands away when he reached to pull me close again.

"I have a question, Jack," I told him.

"Ask away," he said, his face now hidden in the shadows.

"What happened after the bust?" I let my hair curtain my face.

Jack took my hand, squeezing it. "We're having a beautiful time," he said, his voice halting. "Don't ruin it by asking me questions like that."

"I'm not picking a fight," I said gently. "I just need to know. Did you go to one of your other family members?"

He shook his head. "I couldn't reach any of them. My mother was in India, meditating with some guru. My aunt had moved on to some other boyfriend. They hadn't stayed in touch."

"You just took off all alone?"

"It wasn't so bad at first. It was summer, and there was fruit and corn to steal. I ate a lot of hot dogs. And became an excellent shoplifter."

I laughed, incredulous. "You?"

"Yep, me. I was unbeatable. I told you, remember? Fasting makes me crabby."

He fell silent, and I reached out to stroke his shoulder. It was rigid. "And then?"

"I lasted about eight months," he said flatly. "I found the places where the runaways crashed. But the winters get cold. One night, I was in this flophouse in North Portland. Some guys picked a fight with me. It ended badly." He touched the scar on his forehead. "That's where I got this."

I leaned down, and kissed his eyebrow, his forehead.

"That was it for me. I found a phone. Called Margaret, collect."

"Margaret? You mean, you knew her then?"

"No. But Freddy knew her," he corrected. "From when he was a kid. He'd told me about her. So I gave her a try. The operator asked if she'd take a call from Freddy Kendrick's nephew, and she accepted the charges."

"Wow," she whispered. "So you went to live with her?"

"For a while," he said. "She was good to me. I was lucky to have landed with her. I joined the military as soon as I was old enough. Didn't want to be a burden to her."

I ran my fingers through the sable texture of his hair as I thought about it all. "You think I'm like them, right?" I said softly. "Like your family? That I'll run out on you?"

He rolled over, clapping his hand over his eyes. "Oh, fuck, Viv. Don't." He sounded exhausted. "It's so beautiful. Don't wreck it for me. Just let it be what it is. Please."

"But I just want you to—"

"Let me have this, okay?" He sounded angry again. "For however long as it lasts. Can't we just stay in the moment?"

I hid from the revealing shaft of moonlight that illuminated the quilt. There was something to be said for staying in the moment, hard though it was. But I was a normal, flesh-and-blood woman. I craved the usual reassurances, promises, declarations of trust, faith, love. And I wasn't going to get them from him. Period.

But so what? That did not mean that what he gave me instead was not precious. Or that I shouldn't cherish it anyway.

After all. Suppose we stayed in the moment, for, say, thirty years? Forty? Fifty? Maybe when he was a grizzled old man, he would give in and laugh at himself. And finally admit that it had been love all along.

I slipped back between the sheets and into his embrace. The idea made me smile, but my eyes were wet.

Chapter Fifteen

Vivi

I stepped back from the wall I was painting and surveyed the warm ivory tone with satisfaction. I pictured the elegant earthenware vases that I planned to showcase there, and stood back to imagine the effect. Classy.

My store was shaping up. My crafts fair friends were coming in from all over the West Coast to bring consignments. Stock was pouring in. Just that morning, Betty and Nanette had left an assortment of handblown bottles and stemware. Yesterday, Rockerick brought some of his leather work. Brigid left a pile of jewel-toned handwoven silk shawls and throws. Miraben brought teapots, vases, jugs, dishes. With my own stuff, the shop would be a gallery of gorgeous, wearable, usable art.

The bells over the door tinkled and Jack walked in. A smile spread over my face. His gorgeous answering grin made my toes curl in helpless delight.

He looked around with his usual cautious reservation. He

had disapproved of my decision to open my shop. Vociferously. Tirelessly.

"Looking good," he said, grudgingly.

Well, my-oh-my. That was unusually positive, for him. I gazed at him, savoring the glow of sensual energy that hummed between us.

"You look incredible," he said, leaning toward me.

I pulled back. "Hold on, you. Let me wash my hands. Paint cramps my style."

"Hurry," he said.

I ran to the bathroom and scrubbed paint off my hands. I stripped off my t-shirt and cutoffs, threw my green dress over my head, shook my hair down. We had been lovers for weeks now, and I still got swirling flutters in my stomach when I saw him.

Jack gazed at the snowy bulk of Mount Adams when I emerged. "Great view," he commented, as I stood on tiptoe to kiss him.

"It's a great location," I said. "Ten days, and I'll be ready for my grand opening. So what brings you here, Jack? I thought you were taking those larkspurs and veronica into Portland today."

"I did. The truck overheated on the way back. It has a broken fan belt. I left it at the shop."

"Oh? You mean, you're bumming a ride home? You're sure you can endure being seen in public in my disreputable van?"

"I'll wear a Lone Ranger mask," he said. "I found out that there's a blues concert tonight, at the riverfront park. Want to go dancing?"

"Dancing? Wow! Yes!"

He cupped my head in his hand, kissed me again, and began sneakily maneuvering me toward the privacy of the little office in the back. I giggled, and pulled away. We'd gotten up to hours of juicy, delicious mischief back there on my secondhand desk almost every time he came to the shop, but not today. "Don't get any ideas," I protested. "I have a lot to do before I can fling myself into the abyss of rampant sensuality."

"I'll be back in a couple of hours, then." A brief, dazzling grin, and the bells tinkled again as he walked out.

Breath escaped slowly from my lungs.

I was absolutely terrified at how happy I was, but the feeling was marred by a keen edge of uncertainty. I was trying to get used to uncertainty, but it still rattled me.

The last few weeks were like a dream. The two of us spent every waking moment that we weren't working together. I was sleeping in his bed, eating with him, living in his house. The apartment in the barn had turned into my studio, when I worked at all. I'd never been so distracted, so knocked off track. I was drinking too much of his powerful coffee, soaking in his big tub, eating his excellent cooking, wearing his huge shirts around. It was delicious.

Our hungry, intense lovemaking left me drained, shivering, empty of thought. When I was in that condition, I could stay in the moment, as he'd begged me to do.

And I found myself in that enviable condition a lot of the time.

I'd gone on with my plan of opening a shop, in spite of Jack's anger and protests, and the frantic objections of my sisters. If I wanted to put down roots, I had to get on with it.

I tried to protect myself emotionally, the same way Jack tried to shield himself from me, but he was intensely sensitive to my moods. When he sensed me withdrawing, he just seduced me again, and rendered me mindless and whimpering with helpless pleasure. But he never let down his own guard. Not completely.

Patience. We belonged together. We couldn't keep our

hands off each other. Things looked promising. For God's sake, we were going dancing tonight. How very normal of us. Like a real couple. That was progress.

Everything else was perfect. The trendy location I'd found for my shop in Pebble River was ideal. A local woodworking shop was making a carved hanging sign that read "Vivi's Treasure Box." Glass-fronted cabinets were ordered and on their way. I'd organized wholesale accounts with the most talented artists I knew. My credit was maxed to the limit, but hey, life was risk.

I could stand it. All I had to do was persuade Jack that we had a future together. That was the biggest risk I'd ever taken. The highest stakes. All or nothing.

But I had no idea what I would do with myself if I lost.

The breeze was warm at the riverfront park. The sensual blues tunes of the band from Portland pulsed through the evening air. A slow romantic song began, and the two of us merged without a word, swaying like a single body.

It was really happening, I thought, in a haze of unbelieving happiness. We were going to let our fears and hesitations go. Together, we formed something greater than the sum of our parts. The music throbbed around us, and his body was the core of my spinning universe. I would never find another man so right for me, one who moved me so deeply, and now was the time to say it. He was ready to listen. I could sense it.

I was so enthralled as I stretched up to whisper into his ear, I barely noticed the large hand tapping on my shoulder.

A big, booming voice intruded on my consciousness. "Vivi? Viv D'Onofrio? Sweet thing, is it really you?"

I turned. A stocky blond man with a goatee, a waxed moustache, and a purple silk shirt stood smiling at me. A narrow tie dotted with suns and moons adorned his shirt.

He grinned widely, revealing his trademark golden eyeteeth.

"Rafael!" I cried out, as he enveloped me in a bear hug. "Is it you? What happened to the beard, the dreadlocks, the tie-dye?"

"And this is my disheveled pixie Vivi? You look stunning. That long, long hair! I could just eat you up with a spoon! Give me another hug!"

"Put her down." Jack's voice was quiet, but authoritative.

Rafael swiveled his head, leaving my feet dangling a foot off the ground. He took one look at Jack, and let go abruptly. I thudded heavily to the ground.

Rafael's widened eyes traveled the length and breadth of Jack's body. "Vivi!" he exclaimed. "You naughty little minx! Where did you find this one?"

"Jack, this is Rafael, my buddy from art school, the guy I told you about. Rafael, this is Jack Kendrick. My van got stuck in his mud."

"How provocative," Rafael murmured. "The van clued me in that you were here. I saw it in the parking lot, and I've been prowling the grounds looking for you. And what does this Jack Kendrick do?"

Jack blinked at him, quizzically. "Uh ..."

"He grows flowers," I supplied.

"Oh, my God. How picturesque." Rafael's golden teeth flashed. "What are you doing in these parts, angel? Apart from, ah ... the obvious." His gaze flashed toward Jack, eyebrows waggling wildly.

"I'm starting a business in Pebble River," I said.

Rafael's eyebrows shot up. "Oh, really? Putting down roots, are we?"

God, I hoped so. "I'm burnt on the crafts fairs," I told him.

"But enough about me. Tell me about your incredible transformation. Are you respectable now?"

"Prosperous, my dear. Different from respectable," he said, fingering a diamond that glinted discreetly in his ear. "Remember Rudolfo, the promoter of the show we did in Monterey? He made me his site manager, and one thing led to another, and now I'm a promoter! And making quite a killing at it, if I do say so myself."

"That's great, Rafael! I'm so happy for you!"

Rafael twirled a diamond solitaire ring on his finger, batting his eyes. "Thank you. I was so ready to change my lifestyle, and my image. You should see me in full regalia! Armani, Prada. I look like a million bucks."

I tugged at his tie affectionately. "That makes me happy. What brings you here?"

"Business," he said. "I was in San Francisco, setting up a gallery show. And I'm heading back to New York tomorrow, because some clients are flying in from London on Saturday—"

"Whoa, you're riding high!" I was impressed. "The last time I saw you, we were roasting hot dogs around a campfire!"

"I know, but life marches on! The art in my New York gallery can be seen by appointment only, I'll have you know," Rafael informed me proudly. "Artists would kill to show me their work. I act disgustingly self-important. You'd laugh your head off if you saw how I behave. Anyway, this band is a fave of mine, so I popped over from Portland to see the concert before I fly back to New York, and am I ever glad that I did! I've been desperate to get in touch with you, but you have dropped completely off the grid, girlfriend! I have the perfect job for you. Which is to say ... mine!"

I gazed at him in total confusion. "What? Yours? How?"

"You heard me. My clientele is growing, and I'm putting together high-end shows that travel, but with my gallery in

New York, I can't always be on the move. I need a curator and site manager. You could do for me what I did for Rudolfo. I'm talking invitational shows, darling. Where you handpick the artists, jury the art, curate the show, plan the tour, choose galleries, lofts, ballrooms, hotels. The money is extremely good. And it is a very canny career move for a developing artist, if I may advise you."

"Wow," I said thoughtfully. "It's a very generous offer, but—"

"Don't make a snap decision!" Rafael admonished. "This job has been good to me. I want to pass on the good fortune! Think about it!"

"It's an incredible offer," I said, touched. "It's kind of you to think of me, but the truth is, my life is complicated right now. And I'm kind of in the middle of something here."

"I can see that!" Rafael swung his gaze back to Jack and looked him over with blatant approval. "But let me just explain how perfect my job is for you."

I abruptly became aware of the quality of Jack's fierce, silent attention. "Um, Rafael, do you suppose we could meet for coffee and talk about this tomorrow? Now is not the best time for—"

"What better time? We arranged this time in the astral plane, sweetheart! There's no time to lose. I'm catching a plane tomorrow from Portland. Seize the moment!" Rafael took my arm and led me away from the crowd.

I glanced uncomfortably back at Jack. He followed closely, his face impassive.

"Listen carefully," Rafael began earnestly. "A sample month in the life of Vivi D'Onofrio, art promoter. One week in San Francisco, eating sushi and going to the opera. The next week in Berkeley, taking in wild experimental theater. A tour of the wine country in between. On to Los Angeles, San Diego,

Santa Fe, always a different view. No fleabag motels, no moldy campground showers. You eat in award-winning restaurants, you sleep in five-star hotels, and you deal in outrageously expensive art. It's fun, stimulating, challenging. What do you say?"

"You know money has never been a big priority for me—"

"Oh, I know that." Rafael patted my shoulder. "But just try making lots of money for a while, and see how fast you get used to it, angel girl."

"The real reason is not the money," I plodded on. "I'm—"

"This job is your way back into the high-end art world! Everything that bastard Wilder took from you, you can have again! I'm not suggesting you be a site manager or curator forever. I'm thinking about your long-term artistic career! If you go this road, with the contacts you develop, you can write your own ticket!"

"But my shop is already organized, and I—"

"A little shop in a little town has its charm, but just think about it for a while. Work with me, and in no time, that scumbag Wilder will be eating your exhaust. Imagine the satisfaction."

I imagined it. Then I twisted gently out of Rafael's grip and wrapped my arms across my chest. I was shivering, although the night was warm. The crowd swirled around us, but the music faded to the background as I pondered Rafael's offer.

The big-time art world. Success, fame, money. The life I'd dreamed of as a struggling young artist. Odd, how it didn't make my heartbeat quicken anymore.

I lifted my gaze past my friend's hopeful, expectant face, to where Jack stood, behind him. His stance rigid. Eyes fixed on her.

That life absolutely didn't include Jack. The finality of that fact sent a stab of nervous panic through her. "Ah ... ah, it's tempting, but—"

"And you could play fairy godmother to your artist friends! You'd have the power to bring their stuff to the attention of the high-end buyers! You could change their lives! Wouldn't that be grand?"

I took a slow breath. "It sounds great, but I found a perfect location for my shop. I'm content with that. I'm staying put."

I twisted to see if Jack was still listening. He was close behind, but when I tried to meet his eyes, he just looked straight ahead.

Rafael's gaze shifted, from Vivi to Jack, back again. "Ah. I understand, angel. You just think about it for a while. I won't push."

I turned to Jack and reached to take his hand. "The band is starting another song. Let's go back near the stage, okay?"

Jack's hand was stiff. "I'm ready to leave," he said.

Rafael's smile faded. He looked at Jack fingering the waxed ends of his moustache. "Oh dear," he said in a low voice. "I hope I haven't put you in a tight spot, love. But will you think about it, at least?"

"Certainly, I'll think about it," I told him. "And thank you. It's a beautiful offer, and you're a wonderful friend. I'm so glad to be back in touch."

Rafael gave me an impulsive hug. "Give me your cell number. Promise me you'll give it some serious thought. I'll walk you out to the van."

I pulled out my phone. "I don't get much mobile coverage out where I live," I told him. "I'll give you the landline number at my shop, and at Jack's house, too."

We exchanged numbers as we strolled. Rafael's eyes grew nostalgic as we stopped at the van. He turned to Jack. "Did Viv tell you that I—"

"Yeah," Jack said dourly. "You painted the serpent."

Rafael's eyes turned dreamy. "This was my best van painting. I'd be more than willing to paint the other side for you, love. How about a portrait of the two of you? Chain-mail bathing suits, shreds of fur, a flaming sword? You can be hugging his leg. I love it when the girl hugs the guy's leg." His gaze flicked to Jack's muscular thigh.

"Oh, no, no. That's okay," I said quickly. "I like just having the one."

"I had such wild times in that van," Rafael reminisced. "One night Billy and Ronnie and I got some tequila and limes and salt, and we—"

"You told me that story," I interrupted hastily.

"I painted that scene after I broke up with Ronnie," Rafael said, wistfully. "That was my 'man-alone-battling-his-demons' period."

"Yeah, that about sums up the last few years of my life, too," I said ruefully.

I dug my keys out of my purse and gave Rafael a tight hug. "It was great to see you, Rafael. I'm happy to see you doing so well."

"Thank you, angel. Let me know what you decide. Contact me on the astral plane, by all means, but call my cell phone, too, okay?"

"I'll do that. Thanks."

Jack climbed into the van and slammed his door shut. Rafael waved exuberantly as I backed out of the parking spot.

The silence was unbearable. Jack sat like a graven image in the dark, not responding to any of my attempts to speak. We got to the toll bridge, and I scrabbled in the dark for quarters. He handed me the change. The small contact gave me courage.

I flung them into the basket and let the van surge forward. "Jack," I began.

"Don't start." He was using his cool, detached voice again, the one that I had not heard for weeks. Not since before we had become lovers.

"You have the wrong idea. Rafael is a good friend, but he talks too much, and he has no idea where my head is right now—"

"Shut up and drive, Vivi," Jack said.

I closed my mouth with a snap, stung into silence. When I pulled into the driveway at home and killed the engine, he got out without a word and headed toward the house.

I stared after him, wondering if I was even still welcome in there.

Edna leaped and bounded at his heels, licking at his hand as he unlocked the front door and shoving her way in when the door opened. In any case, I had to retrieve my rambunctious dog, so I walked slowly up onto the porch and stepped inside, shutting the door. It was dark inside the big room, but he had not turned on any lights, so I didn't either. The dark made it easier. I didn't really want him to see my face.

"I don't want Rafael's job, if that's what you're thinking," I told him. "It's a fabulous offer, but it's not for me."

"That's not how it looked." Jack's voice was bleak. "You looked tempted. And you should be. That job's a road back to the career you always wanted. All your hopes and dreams and training. Do what you have to do. Don't let me hold you back."

I shook my head. "No. I have everything I need right here. Rafael was trying to help me, but I don't need any help. His timing just sucked, that's all."

"No, his timing was perfect," Jack said. "I was starting to delude myself. I owe him for bringing me back to earth."

That drove me right over the top. I took a step closer to him and whacked at his chest with the heels of my hands. "You were not deluding yourself! You were starting to trust me, and

I deserve to be trusted! We have something special!" I whacked him again, trying to shove him back toward the couch. "Thick-brained lug! Would you just take a goddamn chance on me?"

He trapped both of my wrists in one hand. "Don't get in a wresting match with me, Vivi."

"Why the hell not? What's the point of controlling myself? Why bother?"

"Because I'll win." He dragged me close and cupped my ass so I could feel his erection. "Is that what you want? I'll give it to you like that right now, if it is."

We stared at each other, grim and furious. Angry as I was, he always aroused me. And I couldn't back down with this guy. Something inside me just wouldn't allow it.

My heart pounded when he pushed me back onto the couch and shoved up my skirt. His fingers parted my folds, slid inside me, found me already wet and yielding.

I clenched around his delving fingers. Ashamed, to have made it so goddamn easy for him. It wasn't right to be so compromised. So helplessly strung out on him. I shoved at his chest, scratching at him, but I was trembling, melting down.

Wondering, too, if sex might make him more mellow and receptive.

"You like it like this?" He wrenched open his belt.

"What if I do?" I responded, my voice shaking. "And besides. It's not 'it' that I love. It's you. Get that through your thick head!"

"Shut up and let me focus on the one thing we've got going for us." He slid the thick bulb of his cockhead up and down my pussy.

"Don't shush me, you son of a bitch—"

His kiss cut off my protests. It was angry and fierce, but so was mine. I clawed at him, clutched him, cursed at him. Wound my fingers into his hair and kissed him as he spread my legs and nudged his cock heavily inside me.

He thrust hard. It was an intense sensation, excited though I was. I cried out, and he stopped instantly, lifting his panting mouth from mine. Staring into my eyes. Waiting to understand whether or not he should stop.

I jerked him closer with a furious yank. I was in it now, and there was nothing to do but ride it out to the end.

He let loose. Every plunging stroke of his cock was a licking lash of guilty delight. His hands on my breasts, his hot mouth on me, his big body, pumping hard ... *yes.*

I came intensely, shuddering and wailing. He was still driving hard toward his own pleasure when I realized that he hadn't used any latex, but I couldn't stop or even speak. Just whimper, at each wet, desperate slap of contact.

His breath hissed with each jolt, gaining momentum, and he flung back his head and came. Hot jets spurted inside me.

He collapsed over me, panting.

I stared up at the dark ceiling, pushed far beyond any recognizable emotion. My fingers were still wound into his hair, as if I could hold on to him somehow. Keep him close to me. But already I could feel him slipping away. Receding into the distance.

And there wasn't a goddamn thing I could do about it.

The sweat on our bodies was cool before either of us dared to move. He lifted his head, cleared his throat. "I, ah ... I didn't ..."

"Yes," I said. "I noticed that."

He pulled himself out, stuffed himself back into his jeans, keeping his back turned to me. "Is it a dangerous time?"

"Hard to say. I'm pretty irregular." I got up, smoothed my skirt down. His sperm trickled hotly down my leg. "I wish I knew what you were trying to prove with this demonstration.

That I'm a weak slut who can't say no? That you're stronger than me? What's the message here, Jack?"

"No message. I just couldn't stop myself. It's that simple."

I laughed, bitterly, and pressed my hand to my leaky nose, longing for a tissue. "Simple, my ass. You're anything but simple."

He sighed. "Jesus, Viv. This is hell. What do you want from me?"

"I want you to believe me when I say I love you," I told him. "That's all I want."

He was silent for a moment. "Fine," he said. "Marry me, then."

I stared at him, dumbfounded. "What did you say?"

"You heard me."

I examined his inscrutable silhouette, then got up and turned on the lamp on the table by the couch. His face was hard, tense. As if he were bracing himself for a blow.

I exhaled, slowly. "Jack," I said.

"We're already working on making a baby, right? So let's go all the way. Tomorrow, we go to town. Get our documents in order."

"You bastard," I whispered.

"Yes or no, Vivi. It's a simple question."

I chose my words carefully. "It's not a simple question," I said. "Because it's not a real marriage proposal. It's a rocket grenade attack. You're setting me up. And jerking me around."

He grunted. "Huh. That sounds suspiciously like a no."

"That sounds like an 'it depends,'" I said. "Besides, if I said yes now, you wouldn't believe me anyway. Not in the state you're in." I put my hand against his chest.

He stepped back. My hand dropped. "But since you haven't said yes, we'll never know, will we?"

Dread twisted in my belly. "Oh, God, Jack. I need for you

to believe me," I said miserably. "I can't keep trying to convince you. You're exhausting me."

"So get it over with. Dump me. I can't stand the suspense any longer."

I pressed my hand against my trembling mouth. "Dump you? How could I do that? That would imply that we were involved in a relationship. But we never have been. At least not according to you. You never let me get that close. You just wanted to fuck me, remember? And stay in the moment. So that's where I've been living, Jack. For weeks, now. The moment."

"Maybe. Looks like the moment has ended."

"I figured that out all by myself." I mopped angrily at my eyes with the backs of my hands. "Party's over, huh? Everybody out of the pool."

"Time for you to move on to the next big adventure," he said. "No regrets."

I turned away, so I wouldn't have to see the look on his face. Struggling to control my own.

"Stay up in the apartment for as long as you need to, of course," he added. "I'm not throwing you out to the wolves."

A derisive laugh jerked out of me. "Hah. As if I would. Don't worry. I'm absolutely convinced. I'll be gone as soon as I can pack."

I started toward the door as if I were walking the plank. One sign from him, the slightest softening, and I'd fall over backward. I'd marry him in a heartbeat. I'd have his children. I'd weld myself to him.

I stopped moving when I passed in front of him, still hoping.

"Better sooner than later," was all he had to say.

Well, then. No dice. I kept on going. Walked outside, as stiff as a robot.

I headed up to the apartment and began to pack. I hadn't bought much stuff since I'd been here, just a set of Miraben's plates. I'd been sprawled all over Jack's life, so there had been no need. I'd been eating off his dishes, using his soap, sleeping in his bed. Too busy madly boinking to think of how I was going to feel when it all came crashing down on my head. As I had known that it would. Goddamn it, I'd *known*. I was so pissed at myself, on top of the heartbreak.

I filled my arms with shopping bags and staggered out to the van. *Soldier on,* I told myself. *You've been through worse.* But I didn't feel strong. Why bother soldiering on? To where? I was going nowhere. My life sucked. Snake Eyes was welcome to it.

Well, then again. Maybe I wouldn't go quite that far.

Several of my new Miraben dishes broke as I tossed the box down onto the floor of the van. I didn't bother to check how many.

Chapter Sixteen

John waited until the last few people came out of the Wilder Gallery. An hour or so ago there had been an exodus of well-dressed buttheads flooding out of the big opening for some hotshot new artist. The ones trickling out now were the employees of the gallery itself.

He shrank back into the shadows behind a dumpster as the skinny foreign slut he remembered from before came out. Her tits were shoved up into a glittering silver tube dress, her lips shiny with hot-red lipstick, and her black hair was freshly bobbed with cruelly short bangs, like a dominatrix. Wilder's assistant, Damiana.

She was usually the last one to go, apart from Wilder himself. Probably stayed behind to suck the boss's dick.

And there was Wilder, a few minutes later, stepping out the door. Last one to go. Bastard didn't trust anyone else to close for him. First, he armed the alarm with his remote, punching in a code. Then he got to work on all the locks and bolts. After came the rolldown metal door.

John sauntered over while he was still working on the locks. "Evening, Mr. Wilder."

Wilder jerked back, hit the door, and dropped his keys. "What?"

John smiled, toothily. "Good evening," he repeated.

"What are you doing here?" Wilder's forehead was already shiny.

"I'm here to discuss the phone call we had a couple of hours ago."

"What's there to discuss? I did exactly as you asked, okay? I already told you everything I managed to learn in our phone conversation. Rafael Siebling was here tonight at the opening. He ran into D'Onofrio yesterday, in Oregon. Some place called Pebble River. She's opening a shop there. That's what I was told, and that's absolutely all I know. I did not speak with her, nor did I get her number, or her address. I cannot help you any more than that. So, uh, good night." Wilder gave him a bright, toothy smile that said, *Alrighty, then, you big inconvenient asshole, you're dismissed.*

John waited until that smile started to quiver and unravel into the raw components of pure fear.

"How about Rafael Siebling's address?" John asked softly.

"I'm sorry, but I don't have it. We are not colleagues. We don't travel in the same circles. But it shouldn't be all that hard to find. His gallery is very hot these days, though I can't imagine why. He has no taste. All flash, no content. I don't have his number in my cell phone because he's the last person I would ever call. I don't even know why he came in here tonight. To gloat, I suppose."

"Gloat?" John cut off the guy's babbling. "Why would he gloat?"

Wilder made an impatient sound. "Oh, he and Viv are old friends," he said. "I think Siebling wanted to rub it in about her new boyfriend. As if I gave a shit who that stupid, no-talent bitch fucks. She could do dogs and pigs for all I care."

New boyfriend? Fucking dogs and pigs? A hot, red glow began to obscure John's vision. His hands clenched. Boyfriend. So, it was true. Vivien, too. A slut, just like her slut sisters. He pictured her writhing and begging, taking it in every hole. And, all the while, laughing at him. Mocking him.

Brian had shrunk back against the door, hands up, and his voice was a breathless babble that John cut off. "What's the name of the new boyfriend?"

"Like I know, or care," Wilder said. "Some big redneck farmer clod."

John immediately pictured the raw-boned, thick-necked guy, naked but for a John Deere cap, fucking Vivien from behind. She was bent over a bale of hay, squealing with delight at each savage poke, and looking up at John, that pink mouth open and panting, eyes bright with lust and malicious glee. Calling John a tub of lard. A big, dumb fuck.

Punish. He had to punish someone. Had to calm the screaming inside him. The wild hurricane wind. It wanted something. Tidal waves, atom bombs rigged to blow, hammers crushing. Had to be appeased.

Punish. *Now.*

"You must have Siebling's number in your office files," he said. Wilder looked blank. "I, ah, don't think so."

"But you're not sure, hmm?" John picked up the bunch of keys and shoved them into Wilder's limp hand. "Let's go check."

"I really ... uh ... I don't think that would be a good—"

"Let's ... go ... *check!*" John hissed the last word, a sharp, silibant punch that made Wilder cringe against the door.

"Ah, um, whatever." Wilder unlocked the door with hands that shook. "But I'm sure it's useless."

"We'll see," John said. Blood roared in his ears.

The place was dark, but Wilder flipped an all the big hanging banks of lights that hung from the high ceiling. He muttered as John followed him through the main gallery. They passed tables, one of which had several bottles half full of white and red wine, and trays of food with silver brocade cloth napkins flung over them.

Wilder's nervous prattle came briefly into focus, like a radio tuning into an elusive frequency. "... useless cunt didn't even finish cleaning up the food," he said. "I'm kicking her scrawny little Italian ass tomorrow. If we get rats, it's her fault."

He started up the staircase, shooting nervous little looks over his shoulder. As if he thought John was going to play grab-ass with him.

But Wilder's ass did not appeal to him. And it would take a lot more than that to calm the screaming, the pounding, the roar inside him. It was like a hurricane.

He followed Wilder all the way around the upper balcony level of the gallery, to the lavish office in the back. Wilder unlocked the door, and pushed it open, blocking the door with his body. "Ah, one moment," he said. "Wait here. I'll check that address for you."

Not in this universe, you little squeaking shitbird. John smiled and followed him in.

Wilder rolled his eyes and scurried to his desk. He clicked and tapped on the laptop and shook his head. Too quickly.

"Sorry, no Rafael Siebling here," he said. "Can't help you."

"Look again," John said.

The guy looked miffed. As if he were way too important to perform such a basic, simple favor for John as looking in an address file. As if he were better than John.

He was giving him that look. The look that said, "You big, dumb fuck."

John began walking toward the desk. Wilder turned gray. Then he scrambled to punch Siebling's name into the search engine.

"Ah! Here it is!" His voice sounded passionately relieved. "I don't have his personal number, but here is his gallery's home site. I'll just print out this page for you."

The printer's buttons lit up. It hummed and then spat out a sheet of paper. Wilder grabbed it and handed it to John with a teeth-clenched smile. "See? Address, phone number, email, and website address. So glad to be of help. And now, if you'll excuse me, I have another appointment that I'm already late for."

John glanced at his watch. 2:39 A.M. "At this hour? No shit."

Wilder yanked the door open. "Don't want to keep her waiting. You know. Women." That genial tone, that world-weary smile irritated the shit out of John. Condescending to him. *You big, dumb fuck.*

The mocking words echoed in his head as he followed Wilder out the door onto the gallery walkway. Wilder began walking faster. John lengthened his stride, closed the gap. Wilder began to trot.

Enough. John leaped, took him down. Wilder's shoulder hit, with a brutal crunch, against the iron balcony rail. He started to scream.

It hurt John's head. There was already too much screaming inside, that constant screaming, driving him crazy. He grabbed the guy by his collar and his belt, lifted, swung, heaved him over the rail ...

The screaming stopped abruptly.

Ah. Now he could breathe again, in the sweet, calm silence.

John panted for a moment, enjoying a sensation of intense relief, and then began to stroll the entire perimeter of the balcony. It gave him an opportunity to enjoy the effect of his handiwork from every angle.

He was feeling much better now. His vision had cleared, his breathing deepened, his heartbeat normalized. He was even feeling a bit nibblish.

He stopped at the table next to the enormous Waylan Winthrop bronze that held pride of place in the center of the gallery. The one he'd been so fascinated with a few weeks before. The one entitled *Teeth*.

He grabbed one of the napkins, and loaded it up with water crackers, mini caviar sandwiches, chunks of cheese, artichoke tarts. A couple of juicy pineapple chunks from the remains of the fruit bowl. He'd be wise to tank up on food right here. There would be no time for a meal tonight. He'd need to race to whatever airport had the earliest flight to Portland, Oregon. That old turd Haupt would insist on going, too, but at least John had gotten a lead at last. Maybe it would earn a break from the scolding.

It was lucky, that he'd been able to unload some bad energy. He could function now.

He stuffed his face with some more tasty tidbits as he gazed up at the new, revised version of *Teeth*. Dark drops of blood plopped heavily down, dangerously close to his shoes. He moved his feet out of range and ate another couple of juicy chunks of pineapple as he gazed up, admiring the effect.

He dug out his cell, framed the shot, snapped a few pictures. Very nice.

He'd gotten a feeling, weeks ago, when he first saw those sharp, spiky teeth pointing straight up into the air, that the sculpture was missing something. It lacked that extra little thing, some color, some interest, that would really make it pop.

It was perfect now.

Chapter Seventeen

Jack

The gophers were eating the Asiatic lilies again. I was going to have to rotate the bulbs to another field. The idea exhausted me.

I rocked back on my heels and stared at the big, spotted orange lilies, struggling to remember what the fuck I was doing at all. Bucket. Lilies. Clippers, in my hand. Yes, it would seem that I was cutting them. Then, I had to haul them to the cooler. Before dawn, I had to drive them into Portland. Right.

I grabbed the bucket, pushed my way listlessly through the towering stalks of *Aconitum columbianum*. The royal blue blossoms were just about to open. The vivid pink of the *Campanula medium* hurt my eyes. The *Penstemon azureus* was about ready, too. The *Crocosmia 'Lucifer'*. The gladioli, too.

I was behind. Slacking off. I'd been too busy rolling around in bed to keep up with my flowers. I was going to lose money if I didn't haul ass.

That idea exhausted me even more.

I hauled the bucket across the field and squatted in front of the *Physostegia*, staring stupidly at the white blossoms. Snip. Put the cut stalk upright into the bucket. Mind on what I was doing. Second by second. Better to get used to it all at once. Much better than just to procrastinate and then have it ripped away again.

I'd be okay. I always had been before.

But goddamn, this was different. Vivi was everywhere. The cosmos flower reminded me of her posture. Colored yarrow, crimson bee balm made me think of her hair, her lips. My bed seemed as wide as a football field without her curled up in it. And her freckles. Faint constellations on her shoulders and throat. I knew them the way an astronomer knew the night sky.

I stared at a ladybug clambering into the glowing white cavity of a half-open *Physostegia* blossom, and thought of her skin, her throat. Her red hair, vivid against my pillows.

I had never even told her that I loved her. I hadn't wanted to confuse things, complicate things. Set up expectations that I would then have to dash when reality finally hit us. Like a train.

It was raining. I had hunkered on my haunches so long, my feet had fallen asleep. I staggered to a tree and leaned against it, waiting for the pins and needles to die down. Rain pattering on the pine needles made me think of the first time I had seen her. The way her wet green shirt clung lovingly to her body.

I slogged toward the house, with the vague notion of making coffee, maybe some lunch, though it was late for lunch. I hadn't eaten any breakfast. I'd have coffee. See if there was anything edible in the fridge. I didn't really care if there wasn't. Fuck it.

In my kitchen, I was as confused and slow as I had been in the field. Coffee. Right. I unscrewed the pot, moving like an arthritic old man. Grabbed the half-and-half out of the fridge. The carton was empty.

I stared at it, wondering what I must have been thinking, putting an empty carton back into the fridge. So I'd drink it black. Fuck it.

It took a long time to realize that the phone was ringing. Even longer to decide whether or not I cared enough to answer. Whoever was calling was stubborn to the point of insanity. My brain kept count. Twenty-two rings, twenty-three, twenty-four.

Then, blessed silence. I had just breathed a sigh of relief and slumped back down again when the fucking thing began to ring again.

I leaped to my feet with a filthy epithet, and grabbed the thing off the wall. "Who the hell is this?"

There was a nervous pause. "Uh, this is Rafael Siebling. Remember the guy you met at the blues festival a few nights ago? Is Vivi there? Because I really need to—"

"No, she's not here, and she's not going to be in the future, ever. Delete this number from your phone and call her fucking cell if you want to talk to her."

I slammed the phone down, suppressing my natural guilt at having been needlessly rude. Margaret would have lectured me if she heard that outburst. The guilt evaporated in an instant when the phone rang again. I snatched it up. "What?" I bellowed.

"I will overlook what a flaming pig-dog asshole you are because this is so important," Rafael said, his voice frigid. "I have to talk to Vivi, and I—"

"I told you! She's moved out! Call her cell!"

"I did, you cretin!" Rafael yelled back. "Her cell phone's not working! And I have to get in touch with her, like, now! It's a matter of life or death! Literally, you get me?"

I finally registered the fear in the man's voice. Life or death? A chill gripped me. "What's going on?" I asked.

"Well, since you're so monumentally uninterested in anything having to do with Vivi, I won't bore you with—"

"Cut the shit." My voice slashed across the other man's nervous bitching. "Just tell me now."

"It's a creepy coincidence." The other man's voice shook. "I went to an opening at Brian Wilder's gallery last night. The man is evil incarnate, but I thought it would be fun to do a little networking at Wilder's expense and let that nasty dickhead in on the fact that Vivi's happy and thriving, since he tried so hard to destroy her. But of course he didn't succeed, because she's a goddess with more talent in one of her pinkie fingers than he has in his entire—"

"And the creepy coincidence?" My guts were twisting nastily.

"It's horrible." Rafael's voice rose in pitch. "The prick deserved it, if anyone ever could, but even so, it gives me the shudders that I was actually talking to him just hours before it happened, and he just—"

"What happened to him?" I bellowed.

"He ... well, his assistant found him this morning when she came in to work. He was impaled on the spikes of a big Waylan Winthrop bronze sculpture, like a hot dog on a stick. Someone must have flung him down from the walkway above. They say the sculpture was completely drenched with blood. Wilder's assistant is in the hospital, having a total breakdown."

My body was electrified with fear. Thrumming with the excess voltage. "And Vivi won't answer her phone now?"

"Ah, no. I've been calling for over several hours. As soon as I found out."

I ran it through my head. "Did you tell Wilder where Viv was?"

"Uh, well, yes. I did mention that I saw her at a concert in Pebble River night before last," Rafael faltered. "And ... but why should that ..." His voice choked off for a moment, and then he gasped, as it finally sank in. "Oh, my God," he whispered. "Oh, my sweet God. Did I ... what the *fuck* is going on?"

"Are you at home now?" I demanded.

"No, actually. I left this morning to meet a friend up in East Hampton. Why?"

"Stay there," I told him. "Don't go home. Under any circumstances."

"Oh, Jesus," Rafael moaned. "What have I done? What in holy hell is she mixed up in?"

"It's bad," I said. "But it's not her fault. And you're mixed up in it too, now, so watch yourself. Look, Rafael. Gotta go."

"But I ... but no! Wait! Tell me what this is all—"

"No time. I have to go find Viv. If they found out where she was late last night, then they could already be here by now. Or they could call someone in the area to go after her. Call this number." I rattled off Duncan's cell to the other man. "That's Viv's future brother-in-law. He knows everything. Nell can talk to you, too. He'll tell you what to do. But do not go home. Promise me. You got that straight?"

"Got it," Rafael echoed faintly.

"Good." I hung up on him and dialed Vivi's cell from my landline. The recording told me it was off, or out of area.

Then the stench of burning rubber assailed my nose. The coffee had all boiled away, and the heat had melted the rubber ring while I was on the phone.

I flipped off the gas, turned my back on the mess, and ran toward my gun safe.

Chapter Eighteen

Vivi

I locked up my shop and headed toward my van. I had finally finished painting the place, and I was a rumpled, snarled, ivory-spattered mess. I caught sight of myself in the rearview mirror as I started up the ignition, and winced at the spectacle. Yikes. Eyes red and puffy, face paper white, mouth blurry and dry.

But who cared how I looked? Hell with it.

I pointed the van in the direction of Evergreen Acres. I'd asked around yesterday, and that was the one place I could afford that would accept my dog. It also bordered on a creek and had a little forested area nearby for Edna to run and catch sticks and do her doggie business. The downside was, it was a pathetic dump. It was clear that the creek had overflowed its bounds and flooded the rental units more than once. The number of discolored waterlines and the rotting carpet were my first clues to that. Besides the overwhelming stench of mold, of course.

The cinder-block cube they'd assigned to me was the last in the row. It was tiny and cramped, and it stank of cigarettes, damp, and just a faint touch of urine to blend with the scent of toxic mold. The ceiling was so splotchy, it looked like it would fall down right on top of me. The curtains were full of cigarette holes. It was a tableau of misery.

Spot-on perfect for my mood.

I pulled into the Acres, parked my van next to my wretched little abode, and stared at it, dispirited. Back to roughing it. Back to making do. I'd gotten so spoiled.

Feeling sorry for myself would not help. I had learned that lesson so many times, in so many ways in my life, it still amazed me when the "poor-little-me's" took me by storm. Like, who the fuck cared how I felt? No one. Deal with it.

I let Edna out of the van, and we headed down to the creek so Edna could stretch her legs. After that, I would clean up, change, organize my stuff, and get motivated for some tight-assed, dollar-a-day grocery shopping. Not that I had any appetite, but I needed to act like a grown-up. Starving myself would not help matters.

I flung the stick for Edna until my arm felt like it was about to fall off, and finally decided to stop procrastinating. I walked back to the cabin. Staring at the flimsy door with the knob lock that a credit card could swipe open in one pass. At the single-paned windows with the warped, swollen wood sills that I hadn't been able to wrench closed.

I hadn't known how safe Jack's infrared alarm, and more than that, his tough, stalwart presence at my side, had made me feel until now. I'd been so relaxed, soft and open inside, for weeks now. Now that it was taken away from me, I felt like a snail with no shell. Fear was my constant backdrop.

I shoved the key into the lock. Edna stopped at the threshold and shrank back, whining, but I was trying so hard to be tough, I didn't register the dog's gesture until I'd stepped in, flipped on the light—

And found the two men lurking in the dark on either side of the door.

Their two pistols were pointed straight at me.

Chapter Nineteen

Jack

I drove by the highway interchange for the third time, scoping out the parking lots of the budget hotels clustered there, scanning for Vivi's van. Her shop was locked up, at four p.m. Usually, she stayed there working until dark or later.

I could hardly breathe, I was so shit-scared. And furious at myself, too. I'd gotten so wound up in my own self-pitying bull-shit, I'd lost sight of the danger that stalked her.

I should have known that a guy like Rafael would spew Vivi's location to the four winds. I should have said something to the guy, taken steps, been thinking clearly.

About her. Not myself. Dick-brained *asshole*.

I pointed my truck back up the hill to Pebble River Heights, where the commercial district and Vivi's shop were located. It was still possible that this was just a paranoid freak-out. But the image of Wilder spitted like a hot dog on a stick jangled my nerves. Could be the fuckhead had other enemies, of course. But an enemy like that was rare and special. And felt familiar.

I jerked the truck to a stop in front of Vivi's store, deciding to make the rounds of all the shops. I got lucky on my eighth stop, at the Bakitchen lunch counter. Myra, the proprietor, gave me a smile.

"Hi, Jack. Coffee?"

"Not now. Quick question, Myra. Do you know where Vivi D'Onofrio is staying?"

"Thought she was staying with you, honey. Had a fight?"

I clenched my jaw. The older woman crossed her arms over her chest.

"Well, she was in here yesterday morning," Myra conceded, after an uncomfortable moment. "Asking about an inexpensive place that would let her keep her dog. The only thing I could think of off the top of my head was Evergreen Acres, but it's such a dive, it should be condemned. I hope she didn't go there."

I tensed up, horrified. Evergreen Acres? I hadn't even checked that place, it was so unthinkable to me that Vivi could have landed there. The Acres was an end-of-the-line dump, frequented by bums, drunks, addicts, down-and-outs, prostitutes and their clients. It was visited often by police cars in the middle of the night. Jesus. Of all places to go.

"Love problems. Well. That would explain why she looked like she was coming down with the flu," Myra said knowingly. "Come to think of it, you don't look so hot yourself, honey. Hope you guys work it out."

I barely heard her words. "Later, Myra," I said, turning for the door.

"Nice girl, that Vivi. Sweet little shop she's got. Makes friends fast, too. She sure is popular today. You're the second one come in asking for her in the last two hours."

I spun on his heels. "Who? Who was looking for her?"

Myra smiled, archly. "A man. Which is not surprising.

She's a dish. If you're not careful, some other guy's going to snatch her right up and—"

"What guy?" I bellowed. "What does he look like?"

Myra looked affronted. "Do not yell at me, Jack Kendrick!"

My teeth ground. "Sorry, Myra. Please. It's important."

Myra grunted. "Well, he was no looker, I'll tell you that much," she said, mollified. "Big, heavy guy with squinchy little eyes. He said he'd heard she was opening a shop, and would I tell him where it was."

"And did you?"

"Of course I told him! She can't afford to lose any business! She's just starting out."

Panic swept up, threatening to engulf me. "Myra, do something for me." I couldn't control the shake in my voice. "Call the cops. Send them down to Evergreen Acres."

"But why?" Myra shouted after me as I ran back to my truck. "What do I tell them?"

I leaped in, started the engine. "Whatever the fuck you want! Just tell them quick!"

The truck surged forward with a roar. The urgency inside me was building so fast, I felt like my chest was going to explode.

Chapter Twenty

Vivi

I felt strangely calm. Numb, even.

Finally, the other shoe had dropped. There was a sense of colossal inevitability to it all. Like continental drift, this moment had been coming my way all my life. All the anxious hiding and scrambling and scurrying in the world could not have stopped it.

"I was wondering when you two gentlemen were going to pay me a visit," I said evenly. "I was starting to feel left out."

I was proud that my voice did not shake. Not yet, anyway. I'd get there eventually.

Edna was growling, fangs bared, head down. What a strange spectacle that was. I had never seen my bouncy lab retriever in defense mode. I hadn't known that she possessed one.

"Take the animal. Put it in the bathroom," said the old guy with the accent. Ulf Haupt, I presumed. He was exactly as Nell had described him.

I hesitated, and the big, stocky younger guy pointed his gun at Edna. "Now," he snarled. "Or I shoot the dog."

That broke my paralysis. I gripped Edna's collar and dragged the growling, barking dog toward the tiny bathroom in the corner. I closed the door. Edna whined and pawed at the door, her nails rattling and scraping.

"Come back to the center of the room," Haupt ordered.

I did as I was told. "How did you find me?"

"With difficulty. But we prevailed at last." John gave her a wide, manic grin. "We found the shop through your old boyfriend, Wilder."

"Brian?" That astonished me. "But how did Brian know where—"

"Your friend Siebling ratted you out," John taunted. "He went to Wilder's gallery. To needle him, I think. Told him all about this big, randy stud who's been servicing you. That you were all pink and juicy, getting it left, right, and sideways ten times a day, huh? Filthy slut. Dirty little cocksucking whore—"

"Enough!" Haupt's voice was shrill. "You exhaust me, John. Do not get distracted. Excuse him, my dear. John is very single-minded when he gets worked up. I must constantly remind him, work before play, no? Vivien, your cell phone is in your purse, I presume. Take it out and give it to John."

I picked up my purse from where it had fallen and passed it over. I had turned the thing off the previous day, not wanting to deal with any calls from my sisters. I was too raw to face even them. Another crazy, childish mistake, on top of all my others.

John cracked open the shell and ripped the various components apart. He dropped the pieces and crushed them beneath his boot heel.

"Rafael?" I repeated. "You hurt Rafael?"

"Not quite yet, but we have someone on it," John told her.

"We've hired an army for the endgame. Men are waiting for him in his condo. I can arrange for them to film the event. Popcorn, beer, arterial gouts, detached body parts. Big party."

Sick faintness came over me. Oh God. Rafael.

"That asswipe Wilder's dead, too," he went on. "You should've seen him when I was through. A work of art, quite literally. I took a few pictures. Want to see?"

John held out the cell. I flinched away in revulsion.

"Focus, John," Haupt reminded him sternly as he stumped heavily over to me, his watery, pink-rimmed eyes shiny with mad cheerfulness. "I think this one might be my favorite of all the sisters," he said. "So pretty. So vivid."

"Her tits are too small, but other than that, yeah." John licked his lips, his eyes hot. "I like the feisty ones who spit and squirm."

"I am seldom tempted at my age," the shambling old horror whispered. He lifted the silenced barrel of his pistol, petted my cheek with it. "But you inspire me. Perhaps I will indulge, in my own special way." He used the silencer to tug down the neckline of my shirt, revealing the tattoo. "How pretty," he commented. "A buttercup."

"No, actually." I cleared my throat. "It's *Eranthis hyemalis.*"

The gun jabbed my breastbone. "Are you contradicting me?"

Fear was starting to poke through my fatalistic numbness, big-time. "Um, no."

He petted the flower tattoo with the gun barrel. "I heard that you have tattoos. My father kept a collection of tattoos, you know. He gathered them during the war. I inherited his secret album when he died. There must be fifteen or twenty of them. Papa did love his trophies, but he had so few people to share them with. People are squeamish, you see. Not me. I treasure it." He chuckled. "Perhaps I'll follow my father's example and take your tattoos for mementos. I can start my own album. Never too late, hmm?"

I'd started shuddering violently. "What do you want from me?"

Haupt sighed. "The usual, my dear. For you to tell me something useful that I don't already know about the Conte de Luca's hidden treasure."

I squeezed my eyes shut. "Oh, shit," I whispered.

"Yes, yes. I understand the drill. You're as ignorant and useless as your two sisters. But the Contessa's letter suggested that the three of you together had a chance. And if Lucia de Luca was convinced of this, then I continue to be optimistic."

"You'll never get my sisters," I said, with conviction.

"No? I'm already planning hits on your inconvenient future brothers-in-law. As soon as they're out of the way, we'll have no problem with your sisters. Particularly after we send them the recording of John having his naughty fun with you. That should flush them out." He leaned so close, I could not avoid his sour smell, and pushed my chin up with the gun. He twisted his hand around my emerald pendant until the chain snapped, and stared at it intently, then let out a snort of disgust. "Just like the other two. A cheap reproduction. A worthless gaud."

He opened a briefcase and flung it carelessly inside. I saw the gleam of gold, a snarl of chains. Nell's and Nancy's necklaces were in there too.

Haupt jerked my chin back up. "This is you last chance, Vivien. Do you wish to spare yourself pain and disfigurement? We can be reasonable, if you are."

"Of course," I said.

"Very well. Then tell me something interesting." His tone was coaxing, as if I were the one being tiresome and difficult, refusing to cooperate out of spite and pique.

Tears of frustration leaked from my eyes. "I don't know anything," I said bleakly. "Not a damn thing. Believe me. I would tell you if I did."

Haupt let out a sharp sigh of annoyance. "Well, John, your dream has come true. It appears that have to play out this whole bloody, noisy drama right here and now. Set up the video and aim it at the bed. You brought in the tripod? And your mask?"

John set up the scene as Haupt held the gun and barked orders. The barrel was pressed painfully hard against my jugular. I could feel the quick throb of my heart against the pressure of the metal. Beating stubbornly on. For a little longer, at least.

"How will you get all of us together if you kill me?" I asked.

"We won't kill you. Not yet. John will be careful. He's a specialist, you see. He can inflict excruciating pain without causing mortal injury, particularly if the subject is healthy and strong-willed. As I can see that you are." He chucked me under the chin with the gun. "You may not be all that pretty by the time your sisters join you, but never fear. You'll still be able to contribute to the brainstorming."

"Another thing," John said, fiddling with the camera. "This guy you're fucking. I don't want any surprises. Who is he? And where is he?"

I swallowed, hard. "He's no one. And nowhere."

John slow clapped sarcastically. "Brave words. But we'll get it out of you. Or maybe Siebling. Whoever cracks first."

"John, go do a final check," Haupt directed. "We were going to take you to a different location, but I've decided that this atmospheric place is even better for our purposes. It looks like the unit next to yours is not occupied, and I doubt the other inhabitants of this establishment will call the police even if they do hear you screaming. Chances are, they've got problems of their own." He stroked her hair. "What an amazing color. Perhaps I'll keep the hair, too. But later for that. Let's get on with it. John, tie her."

Chapter Twenty-One

Jack

My heart thudded like a jackhammer when I saw the van parked at the end of the Evergreen Acres complex. I killed the engine and let the truck roll silently down the downward grade toward the parking lot. There was a black SUV with tinted windows parked a few units up from the battered van. Shiny and new. Worth a hundred and forty thousand bucks. Glaringly out of place.

I pulled up the emergency brake, wondered for a split second if it would be smarter to wait for reinforcements.

Hah. Definitely smarter, but who cared? Waiting was not an option.

I left the door open and slunk along the row of dingy, scarred doors in the long, gray-painted cinder-block complex.

I came to the last window. Edna was barking inside, shrilly and desperately. I heard men's voices, talking. A man laughing, nastily. The smart *crack* of a blow, a feminine cry of pain, bravely choked off. *Vivi.*

I had years of experience, training. I knew better than to let rage control me, but the force that moved me felt more like demonic possession. I whipped up the H&K and squeezed off a shot through the window toward the ceiling. Glass shattered. Shouts, frantic yelling. I flung myself at the door full force and took the fucker right off its hinges. I swung the gun around wildly as my eyes adjusted to the dim interior.

The *thunk* of a silenced pistol, and a bullet rustled my hair, punching into the cement blocks behind me. Dust and debris flew, stinging the back of my neck.

I returned fire. The bearded hulk of a guy dove behind the bed, where Vivi lay hog-tied, twisted into a knot on her side. Her eyes were on me, wide and terrified. The muzzle of the silenced gun rested on her ribs.

The guy peeked up over her body. He squeezed off a shot, and I dropped, noticing with eerie clarity how the carpet was disintegrating into stinking chunks. I peered beneath the bed. Shot from below, right underneath it.

A squeal, like a stuck pig. A hit. *Yes.* I followed up my advantage, scrambling up to my knees and waiting for the big scowling guy to peep up over Vivi's body.

He crawled out, clutching his bloody right arm, howling something unintelligible. Bullets sang by my shoulder and punched into the easy chair. Stuffing flew. One of them slammed into a plasterboard armoire, splintering it.

I somersaulted, rolled up to my feet, and whipped my leg up, knocking the gun from the man's hands. It hit the wall, then the floor. My gun swung up, took aim—

"One more move, and her head explodes," a cracked voice rasped.

My head jerked around. A hideous, goblin-like man clutched Vivi's trussed body against his. His pistol was shoved under her chin. Her breath hitched. Her bright eyes were fixed on mine, wide and desperate.

The old man giggled shrilly. "Drop the gun. Or I'll kill her."

I doubted that was true. Whatever these fucker's kinky plans were, they involved live D'Onofrio women, not dead ones.

But I could be wrong. And my whole universe hung on that yes-or-no question.

I preferred to die rather than get it wrong.

The old guy edged along the wall, dragging Vivi's slight body for a shield. "Drop the gun!" he shrilled. "I will kill her! I swear it!" He jabbed the barrel against Vivi's soft, white throat. She made a desperate, choking sound.

My hands opened. The H&K dropped to the floor.

"Cut her hands and feet free," the old guy ordered curtly.

The burly younger man, clutching his bleeding arm, gave the old guy a stupid, confused look. "Huh? What the fuck?"

"She must drive the van, you moron!" the old man shrieked.

I watched, paralyzed, as the burly man sliced the ropes near Vivi's wrists. She winced as he slashed the rope between her ankles.

"Kick the gun to me," the big guy growled at me.

In the seconds that followed, every detail was printed and burned into my mind. As I stared into Vivi's eyes, trying to scream through the silent realms of timeless eternity that I loved her. Hoping she'd hear me. Forgive me for being a stupid dick.

Suddenly, she wrenched out of the old guy's grip, and headbutted the bastard.

The old man screamed and stumbled back. The burly guy swung a savage backhand blow that knocked her sprawling. The old man took a shot at me, and then another. Both shots went wild. The decrepit asshole didn't have the strength to aim the thing accurately. But he didn't need to aim well to kill Vivi. Not at that range.

I was in motion already, my boot whipping up to crack into the big guy's jaw. He reeled backward with a shout. Then the old man scooped the dazed Vivi up, arms locked under her armpits, gun shoved in the hollow of her cheek.

"Deal with him!" he yelled. "Meet me at the rendezvous point!"

The big guy lunged at me with a knife. Part of my brain dealt with weaving and dancing to avoid the blade, while the rest of me watched in brief flashes through my peripheral vision as the old man herded the stumbling Vivi to the driver's side of the van, and climbed in behind her, jabbing the gun into her ear. I could hear the man's shrill, scolding voice, yapping unintelligibly.

The van's engine roared, the lights flicked on. It squealed backward and accelerated out of my line of vision.

Nothing to concentrate on now except not getting cut, and keeping that berserker son of a bitch too busy to get near the guns lying on the floor. I arched back to let a huge boot whoosh through the space where my face would have been, then spun to the side to avoid a knee to the gut. I took an uppercut to the nose that sent me spinning into a rib-crunching *whack* against the cement-block wall.

Pain and lost breath cost me a precious fraction of a second. The blade whipped down. I jerked to the side. The tip hit cement, bounced, skittered, and slashed the top of my shoulder. My knee jabbed up into my opponent's balls. He lurched back, bellowing.

We circled each other, breath rasping. The other man lunged, and I saw the movement broken down to infinite increments. Parry with my forearm, spin until I was side to side, seize the knife hand between scissored wrists, torque until the guy screamed, doubling over. The knife clattered to the ground. I applied more pressure, whipped a vicious side kick into the side of his knee, guided the top of his head toward the wall—and swung it hard, like a battering ram.

The asshole flopped to the ground. The crown of his head was wet with blood. There was a dark, bloody smear on the wall. I stared down, breath jerking in and out, every limb trembling. Hard to think, with combat hormones flooding my system.

Sirens wailed, far away. Myra had called the cops. Good, but I could not stay to talk to them. Every second that passed widened the space between me and Vivi.

I touched the guy's carotid artery. Still alive. I was tempted to kill him, just to have one more player off the board. But I would have to change into a different person to kill an unconscious man. I couldn't bring myself to do it.

The cops could take care of him. I scooped up the guns and leaped over the bulk of the fallen man to jerk open the bathroom door. Edna leaped into my arms, whining. I ran for the truck and tossed the frantic dog into the passenger's seat.

I burned rubber turning out of the lot, as sirens approached from the opposite direction, and finally fishtailed to a shuddering stop at Dwayne Pritchett's gas station.

Dwayne jogged forward, his big, ruddy face alarmed. "Jesus, what the fuck? Were you in a car accident?"

I realized abruptly that my nose was streaming blood, all the way down over my chin. My shoulder was bloody as well, from the knife wound I'd taken.

"I'm fine," I said tersely. "Did you see Vivi's van?"

"Yeah, I seen it come by here, going hell for leather. Didn't stop at the sign. Took the turn on two wheels. Big fuckin' hurry. Did Vivi do that damage to you? Jesus, she must have been pissed as hell. Wadja do to her, for Chrissakes? You want to come in and clean up that—"

"Which way did she go?" I roared.

Dwayne nodded toward the northbound road. "Thataway."

I gathered up the shivering dog, pushed his door open, and shoved the animal into Dwayne's arms. "This is Vivi's dog. Look after her for me."

"But ... but I ... but you—"

"Later!" The truck leaped forward, squealing toward the exit.

Chapter Twenty-Two

Vivi

"Faster!" Haupt shrieked. "Drive faster, you stupid bitch!"

I pushed down on the accelerator. Not much point telling the guy that my decrepit van was already making a valiant effort, and didn't have any more speed in her. The frame of the vehicle shuddered and groaned as it was.

Or maybe that shuddering came from inside my own self.

We were on the northbound Kaneset Highway, which looped alongside the steep-banked, meandering Kaneset River. Haupt rolled down his window, stuck his empurpled face out to drag in air.

I was in conflict as to what to do. The road had given me options, and a quick, fiery death after a few seconds of falling through midair was a far better death than the one Haupt had described for me.

But what about Jack? He'd come back for me.

In back of the panic and terror was that haunting thread of

emotion, like music in my head, sweet and poignant. I hung on to it, and with it, to my sanity.

He'd come for me. How had he found me? How had he known I was in trouble? It made the prospect of driving off a cliff oh, so much harder to swallow.

I concentrated on high-speed driving. No future, no past. Just this breath, into my lungs. Just this heartbeat, then the next, and I was grateful for every one of them, even with a gun to my head. I hoped he was okay. *Please.*

He'd come back for me. Put himself on the line for me.

"What are you smiling at, you insolent slut?" Haupt shrilled. "Are you laughing at me?" He jabbed the gun into my ear.

The van lurched and wove. "No! I wasn't, I wasn't! Not at all!"

I reached down with my left hand to grab the tire iron. The road ahead did a hairpin and started to gain altitude. Farther on, the road was very high over the canyon. Any further attempt to drive off the road once I drove higher would result in certain death.

This turn that was coming up was my last chance at a slightly more favorable compromise with certain death. Right ... *now.*

I widened my turn, wrenched the wheel, and braked, violently. Haupt lurched forward, holding out his arms to brace himself. I whipped the tire iron down over his forearms. *Crack.*

He screamed. The gun dropped. I spun the tires in the gravel, accelerating, gaining the crest ... and tipped over the top.

We were sliding and bouncing down the other side, tipping crazily. Haupt screamed, scrambling for the gun, but the van bounced wildly in every direction as it rattled down the steep slope of rock and shale—

It hit a large rock at the river's edge, knocking us forward.

The van teetered, tipped, hung on two wheels for what felt like eternity.

Then it flopped onto its side into the river, Haupt's side down. I slid down on top of him. Icy water flooded from the open window into the van.

We were a screaming, struggling knot, fighting, clawing. I couldn't let him find that gun. His desperate, strangling grip was like the gigantic kraken of the abyss. The water bubbled in, swirling, getting higher.

I struggled up, yanking the steering wheel, trying to trample him down beneath my feet. The van was tipping, moving. If water covered the top of my side, I'd never get the door open. I shoved the door over me, expecting a bullet to punch into me at any second from below.

Haupt still struggled, but his head was underwater now. The water was up to my chest, gurgling and swirling.

Haupt seized my ankle and bit me, savagely hard. I screamed, struggled, kicked at him with all my strength. He looked up from beneath the water, a blaze of mad hatred in his eyes. Bubbles rose from his mouth. The water gurgled higher.

I thought about my tattoos, the ones he had intended to keep for his precious album of mementos. My hair, which he had wanted as a trophy. I put my feet on his shoulders, pressing him down as I shoved myself up, and pushed the van door open.

The van was moving with the current. I saw Haupt's briefcase, bobbing on the surface next to the steering wheel, and grabbed for it. His hand still clung to it.

I yanked on it, and he let go, his eyes blank. Dead.

I clambered out and pitched myself into the river, shocked by the violence of the current. It tossed me like a twig. I couldn't swim in any direction. All I could do was try to stay somehow afloat as I whooshed along, fighting my way slowly closer to the rocky shore. I almost let the briefcase go, but I couldn't bear to. We had suffered so much for those necklaces.

I struggled with the current. The van had floated behind me for a little while, but it had soon gone down. A half mile or so later, I managed to grab onto a rock at the edge of the water.

I crawled up onto it, shaking so hard I could barely function. My teeth were going to fall out for the clacking.

I clung to the rock like a wet rag, just trying to breathe.

Chapter Twenty-Three

Jack

I jerked to a stop at the skid marks on the cliff, my heart thudding. I leaped out, staring at the jagged trough the vehicle had made as it slid down into the water. My guts were knotted with terror. My mind still rejected the most probable outcome, but the rest of me shook with raw fear.

I vaulted over the gravel slope of the road's shoulder and slid in the loose shale to the water's edge. I followed the current, hopping rocks, clambering on boulders, slogging through water. I had to swim through cliff-lined channels, prying myself out of the current's grip just before getting sucked into the rapids.

I finally spotted her, all the way across the river, spread out on a rock as if she'd washed up on it. Facedown, wet hair spread around her. I screamed her name over and over. She did not move.

I dove back in, fighting the water. Got across it, God alone knew how. I crawled up on to the rock and rolled her over with shaking hands.

Her eyes opened, locked into mine. I was so relieved, I burst into tears and dropped my face against her chest. Jesus Christ, her skin was ice cold.

But she was still alive. My soul shook with terrified joy.

It took us an interminable, staggering time to get back to my truck. I would have carried her if I could, but we couldn't go back the way we'd come, not with those channels, those sheer cliffs. I couldn't dump her into that icy current again, and the only alternative was to climb straight up to the road far above us. Which meant that we had to scramble and claw our way up slippery rock faces, over shale and thorns and brambles. Vivi could barely keep herself upright.

My relief at finding her alive was undercut by growing fear. Her face was so white, her eyes so shadowed. She couldn't stop shaking. She kept falling down. She could hardly speak. When we finally crawled onto the asphalt of the highway, I picked her up.

She murmured something at me, but her voice was weak and slurred.

I got back to my truck and sped to town. Squealed to a stop outside the emergency room at the hospital. We caused a big stir, and things moved with gratifying speed as the EMT techs got Vivi squared away.

I was annoyed to find some of the staff wanted to fuss over me, too. Big waste of time. I was fine. They should all concentrate on Vivi.

I begged a cell phone off one of the EMT techs and called a guy I knew in the local cop shop. "Hey, Tim? It's Jack Kendrick."

"Holy shit, man!" Tim exploded. "Where the hell are you?"

"Later for that. That son of a bitch who was lying unconscious in Unit 42 of Evergreen Acres. Do you guys have him in custody?"

Tim hesitated. "Uh ... are you okay, Jack?"

"I'm fine. What about the guy in Unit 42? That son of a bitch is a serial killer."

"There was no guy in Unit 42," Tim said. "Just a trashed room, blood on the floor, and a bunch of bullet holes. Whatever happened in there, we missed it. Would have been really helpful if you'd been around to clue us into the serial killer thing, because he didn't hang around, either. And the chief was unthrilled with you for fucking off before you could give a statement. What were you thinking?"

I blew out a long shuddering sigh as the cold sank even more deeply into my bones. "You have no idea," I muttered.

I closed the call as he was still talking, passed the phone back, and ripped the IV needle out of my arm, ignoring the scolding lectures. I grabbed a chair and situated it outside the curtained cubicle where Vivi lay, a vantage point that gave me a clear view of both ends of the corridor plus the lobby entrance. I was almost hoping the guy would make a move.

I wanted to fucking finish this, already.

Chapter Twenty-Four

Vivi

I drifted in and out of consciousness on the drive into Portland, but even when I was awake, I kept my eyes closed. I didn't have the nerve to talk to Jack. To ask him how he felt. What it all meant. If he had changed his mind about the two of us, or if he was just being righteous and heroic. A guy's gotta do what a guy's gotta do, yada yada and all that. His grim, taut face discouraged confidences. Didn't seem like the right time.

He had bullied the hospital into letting me leave after only twenty-four hours, and there had been a big kerfuffle about it. Lots of shouting about security and danger and attackers. The angry doctors made me sign a waiver accepting responsibility, which I'd been glad to do, though my fingers barely felt the pen, floating in a Demerol cloud. Even stoned out of my mind, I knew what side my bread was buttered on. When it came to Snake Eyes, the doctors and nurses were no protection.

Jack Kendrick was my man. Hands down. He was my best shot.

Margaret had come by that morning, bringing Jack some clothes, and one of her own warm-up suits for me. It was eggshell blue, spattered with yellow daisies. Wow. Very special. But still, I was grateful.

"I'm flying to New York," I announced, bracing myself.

"That's the last place you should go!" Jack said sharply. "John told you he'd hired an army. We've warned Rafael, your sisters and their men. Do you want to face an army now? Those guys weren't enough of a challenge for you?"

"It's not that," I said. "I just can't live like this anymore. I have to resolve this thing. No matter what. You do what you want. I'm more grateful than I can ever say, but I'm flying to New York. I want to meet with my sisters, now that we have the necklaces back."

Jack muttered something foul under his breath, but he gave in eventually.

The earliest flight we could find with seats available left the following morning. Way too long to wait, but we had no choice. We checked into an airport hotel. When we were locked in our room, Jack laid his pistol on the kitchenette counter.

"I'm taking a shower," he announced. "You all right out here?"

He waited for my nod, his eyes still doubtful. "Don't open the door," he added.

Hah. As if I would. I rolled my eyes, and he disappeared into the bathroom.

I felt like a puppet with strings cut when I didn't have his hot, vital energy to struggle against. I curled up on the bed and thought it through.

I had to be realistic. Hard-nosed. I had nothing to offer Jack except a crushing burden of danger, financial drain, and constant, grinding stress. He'd already risked his life, dodging bullets and knives, diving into wild water. A man couldn't marry a risk like that. Or plan a future. I'd be stupid and selfish to demand promises from him now.

This, however, did not mean that I was going to deny myself the comfort of his body. Life was short and uncertain. I was seizing every day and night from now on.

I listened at the bathroom door to the shower hiss. I caught a glimpse of myself, in the prim, daisy-spattered warm-up suit, and sputtered with laughter.

I stripped it off, folded it carefully, and waited for the shower to stop, shivering in the air-conditioned chill.

When I opened the door, his startled face made me smile, catlike. I laid the gun on the counter by the bathroom sink. The room was a fragrant fog of steam. The bruises on his face were taking form.

Maybe I was presuming too much. Maybe he was too stressed, too injured and exhausted—or, um ... maybe not. His cock pointed straight at me, in seconds flat. That seemed promising.

"What's this, Viv?" he asked.

I touched the dripping, gleaming contours of his body. "I'm just living in the moment, Jack."

He flinched. "Don't throw that in my face. We need to talk."

"No, we don't," I said. "No past. No future. Just now."

He looked worried. "How long do we have to play this game?"

"How long is irrelevant, when you're in the moment," I told him. "Only now exists. You should know that. Aren't you the expert?"

He stared at me with haunted eyes. "You're a real hard-ass, Viv D'Onofrio, you know that?"

"I've had tough teachers." I gazed into his face for a moment, and finally relented. "Look, if I ever have a normal life again, with no axe hanging over me, and you still want to have a conversation about our future, we can have it. Until then ... no." I reached out, seized his cock and stroked it boldly.

"And until then, you just want to fuck me?"

My mouth twitched at his sulky tone, and I sank gracefully to my knees. "I ask it ... respectfully," I purred, trying not to smile.

He let out a stifled burst of laughter as I swirled my tongue around his cockhead. "Oh, God. I've never gotten respect like this in my life."

"Your time has come," I murmured, then sucked him into my mouth.

He was so thick and broad and hard, but I was inventive, hungry, and aching for his every shudder and gasping sigh of pleasure. I used my hands, my tongue, and, bit by bit, pulled him deeper into my throat, long suckling strokes that made him quiver and groan.

I kept it slow, kept him trembling on the brink until the ache of my own yearning grew too sharp to bear. Then I rose up and turned to face the mirror. I parted my legs, arching my ass so he could see everything. How flushed and gleaming wet and eager I was for him. "Take me," I said.

He seized my hips, stroking them. "I don't have condoms."

"Of course you don't. You've been too busy saving my life to pay attention to stuff like that."

He looked worried. "Viv, this is exactly the kind of thing we need to talk about—"

"No talk. Give it to me before I start to scream."

He eased past my body's resistance, sliding and circling his cockhead around in my lube, deliciously seductive and teasing. Then drove himself slowly, deeply inside me, surging tenderly, sliding over my most sensitive spots. I clutched the kitchen counter, staring at my own flushed face, whimpering at each slick, slamming stroke. We held each other's gaze in the mirror as if the fate of the universe depended on it.

He reached around and caressed my clit, tipping me over into a huge, wrenching climax. When I finally had the strength to prop myself up, he was still waiting for his own release, his face tight with self-control.

"I want to come inside you," he said.

I thought about it for about half a second. "Go for it."

His eyes widened. "You're sure? You're okay with that?"

"I want it all," I blurted. "I want everything you have to give me."

His eyes flashed, and he gave it to me, pumping deep and hard. One last shove, a shout, and he came, explosively.

I hung over the counter, limp and soft. Light as air, soft as a cloud. One thought floating in my mind in a perfect shining bubble of hope.

Of how much I would love to make a child with him.

Jack set the shower running and washed me with sensual thoroughness. That interlude ended as one might have expected, with myself pinned against the wet tile wall, legs draped over his elbows, sobbing with delight as he nailed me deep and hard.

Not a thought about bad moments in my past. No dread for the future. Not a thread of panic, of nausea. No "danger keep out" signs. My old phantoms were gone.

They could not withstand the bright light that was Jack Kendrick.

Afterward, glowing and relaxed, I sat naked on the bed and examined the three necklaces that I had retrieved from Ulf Haupt's briefcase. I laid them out on the bed, fiddling with them. Studying the patterns of gold that decorated each pendant.

Something about them tickled my mind. The setting was different on each pendant. On my own, there were tiny open spaces in the coils of gold. On Nell's, the lacework was flat, with a slight protrusion on each side. Nancy's also had those protrusions.

It made me think of a sculpture I'd done back in art school, one of the pieces that had been mangled in Snake Eyes's second break-in. Three female figures, made of motley chunks of glass, pebbles, and bits of plastic, all wired together. But their stylized hair swirled out like halos, hooking and tangling together, linking the three figures.

I had entitled it *The Three Sisters*. Lucia had loved it. She had displayed it proudly, right next to her priceless bronze Cellini satyr.

I placed the pendants side by side. Nancy, Nell, Vivi. I felt a strange, dreamlike feeling of being gently guided as I slipped the little protrusion of my own pendant into the open space in Nell's. A push, and *click*, the openwork linked together, seamlessly.

My heart gave a heavy thud of excitement. "Jack," I whispered, my voice shaking. "Look at this."

He looked, and his eyes widened. "The other one? Does it fit, too?"

"Let's see." I slid the protruding part of Nancy's pendant into the openwork of Nell's. *Click*. The pieces were all united. Three pendants, side by side. Locked together.

Jack held out his hand, and I passed the pendants to him. He manipulated them delicately, putting pressure on every point. One of the protruding bits on Vivi's pendant moved. At first, I cried out in dismay, thinking he'd broken it, but then I saw that it was a lever, moving smoothly down—

Click, once again, and something snapped out of the bottom. Three fine, shining, miniature sheets of gold, flush to each other, as narrow and sharp as a blade.

We leaned closer. Something was written on them, in letters so small, I could not make them out.

Jack pulled out his phone. He held the thing up under his camera and zoomed in, magnifying the image. *"Salve Regina Mater Misericordiae,"* he read slowly. He turned it over and studied the back. *"Primus Modus Doricus."* He looked up at me. "Latin, right? Can you make anything out of that?"

"No, but Nell could. She's studied Latin." My voice was high and shaky. I pressed my hand to my mouth, fighting to control my face. It was too soon for tears of joy. I had no idea what this might mean. It was by no means a triumphant win.

But it was something. Finally, a window had opened, letting in some light to illuminate our helpless confusion. We had a place to begin.

"This was the part of the puzzle that I was supposed to figure out," I said.

Jack raised his eyebrows. "How do you figure?"

"In the draft of the letter we found, Lucia said it was our love of art, music, and literature that would solve the puzzle. I don't know the first thing about music or literature." I thought about *The Three Sisters,* and the pride that Lucia had taken in it, and tears sprang to my eyes. "But this part was just for me."

I felt as if I had just received a tender message from beyond the grave. A wave of love and faith and encouragement from Lucia to her youngest adopted daughter.

"Oh, God. I'm losing it," I whispered. "I miss her so much."

"Go ahead," Jack said. "Lose it all you want, for as long as you want. You're entitled."

He stroked my hair while I hid my face in my hands. I

raised my face after a moment. "I want to call my sisters," I blurted.

"It's three a.m., New York time," he reminded me gently. "We'll be there tomorrow. We've waited this long. Can't you wait a few hours more?"

"Okay," I said, sniffling. "I guess."

Jack laid the united necklaces on the bedside table next to the gun and slid between the sheets. He held the covers up for me. "Will a hard-ass broad like you allow for some cuddling in bed?" he asked.

"Oh, hell, yeah," I said, sliding between the sheets and into the hot, lovely rush of his tight embrace. "I may be a hard-ass, but I'm not an idiot."

I let his warmth relax me for a few moments and then turned up to look searchingly into his face. "Thank you for coming back to save me," I said.

He gazed back. "Anytime," he replied. "But the truth is, I was saving my own ass. Thank you for still being alive when I got there."

Tears prickled in my eyes, but if I gave in to them again, I was afraid they would drown me.

Chapter Twenty-Five

Jack

Duncan and Vivi's sister Nell met us at the airport. Nell was horrified when she saw the battered-looking, hollow-eyed Vivi, and insisted on sitting in the back with her little sister and holding her hand while Duncan and I debriefed.

At one point, I looked back and found Nell's eyes sparkling at me. "What does that Latin phrase mean, anyhow?" I asked her hastily.

"Hail queen, mother of mercy, first Doric mode," Nell told me.

"Does that mean anything to you?"

Nell shook her head regretfully. "Not in particular, no. It's just a common phrase from the Catholic liturgy."

We headed to Nancy and Liam's place, and I bucked up my extremely depleted social energy to meet two new people. Fortunately, they both seemed mellow and sensible, and disposed to be friendly and approving. Liam struck me as intelligent and canny, the older sister Nancy likewise. I felt at ease with them immediately.

Liam had prepared a juicy and appetizing pot roast with a mountain of gleaming potatoes and vegetables. I dug into it gratefully. Afterward, we gathered in Liam's workshop around an unfinished dining room table, upon which he had set Lucia's unopened safe.

"So?" Nancy asked briskly. "Do we try just keying in the letters of the phrase? In Latin, or in English?"

"Try them both," Vivi said.

"You're sure it won't explode in our faces if we get it wrong?" Duncan asked, his eyes wary.

"Only if we try to crack the safe," Nancy reassured him.

Duncan looked far from reassured, but Nancy just got to it, frowning down at the keypad as she keyed in the long sequence.

The little button flashed red. The door remained locked.

"In English, then," Nancy said, undaunted. She keyed in the new sequence. The light flashed red again. "Nope."

We all pondered the safe, discouraged. Nancy held up the linked pendants. "Hail queen, mother of mercy," she repeated slowly. "I've seen this translation. First Doric mode is a musical term. This was sung, not ... oh. Oh, my God. *Yes.*"

"What?" we all demanded, in a ragged chorus.

"Just a minute. Let me get something." Nancy leaped to her feet and scurried out. She came back moments later, a CD in her hand.

"Novum Gaudium!" she announced. "They're a Gregorian chant choir that I represent! I took Lucia up to see their concert last Christmas, at the Cloisters Museum concert series. She loved it! She even bought the disc." Nancy pried out the liner notes. "Let me see ... it's a Marian antiphon, and the phrase 'hail queen, mother of mercy' is the incipit. This is in Doric mode. I wonder if she meant for us to somehow get a code out of the music. But how?"

Jack spoke up, his voice hesitant. "I don't know anything about music," he said. "But could the tune have some sort of numeric correspondence?"

Nancy's eyes lit up. "Hell, yes, it could. In relation to the Doric mode, you bet it could. Liam, give me that CD player on the workbench."

Liam unfolded his tall, rangy self, grabbed the player, and plugged it into the wall socket near the table. She selected the track. A haunting tune began. Men's voices, deep and reverberant, singing in perfect unison. The sounds rose and fell in ancient patterns that sounded somehow familiar.

Nancy listened to a fragment of the piece, brow furrowed. She hit "stop" after a few moments, then let it play again. And again. And again, scribbling numbers after each time.

Around the eighth time, she held up a scrap of paper with a long sequence of numbers. "Twenty-five digits," she announced.

"Try it," Vivi urged.

Nancy keyed it in. They held their breath. The light flashed red. Nancy sagged. "Hell," she said, dispirited. "I'm all out of ideas."

"Try adding PDM for *Primus Modus Doricus*," Duncan suggested.

Nancy shrugged, and punched in the numbers again. "Okay, guys. Here goes nothing. P... M ... D," she said.

The light flashed green. The door of the safe popped open with a *click*.

None of us could quite believe it. We stared at the thing, almost afraid of the seam of darkness behind the crack of its opened door.

Liam touched the door gingerly with the tip of his forefinger and swung it open.

There was only one item inside. A piece of yellowed, ancient paper in a plastic sleeve. Thin and limp and tightly covered with cramped handwriting.

Nancy took it out. "It's in Latin," she said, passing it immediately to Nell.

Nell put on her glasses and peered at it. "This must be Marco's treasure map," she said, in a wondering tone. "This is a list of what look like Latin flower names, and instructions that say to move from this flower to this flower, et cetera, et cetera. At the end, it says to go down into the ground four hand spans and turn three times counterclockwise. No wonder Marco thought the treasure was in the palace gardens. The gardener at the Palazzo de Luca said that the garden had been dug up more times than he could remember."

She laid the piece of paper down with a sigh. "Well, phooey," she said. "We've exchanged one puzzle for another. And I, for one, am burnt out on puzzles."

Liam got up. "I'll go get dessert," he said, sounding resigned.

Vivi got up to stretch her legs and wandered around Liam's workshop, touching various items with her fingertip. She turned to me.

"This is all Lucia's stuff," she told me. "Things that Liam and Nancy were able to salvage from when John trashed her house." She fingered a mangled thing made of glass, pebbles, plastic, and bent wire. "This is one of mine. *The Three Sisters*. I think Lucia meant for me to think of it so it would occur to me to put the pendants together." She petted the twisted knot of materials and wire. "I'm going to restore this. In memory of her."

"Excellent idea. Liam's doing that with Lucia's *intaglio*

table, too," Nell said. She laid her hand against the plane of a beautiful carved oak table that lay on the workbench. It was cloven in two splintered pieces.

"This is the famous table Duncan told me about?" I asked Vivi. "The one from the Renaissance that had the hidden drawer?"

"Yeah." Vivi traced some brutal scratches on the surface with her fingertip. "These marks were carved on it by the SS men, during the Nazi Occupation. The men who served under Colonel Haupt, Sr."

I leaned down to take a closer look. "Amazing detail," I said. "I can tell in a glance what all these plants are. Common wildflowers, and whoever carved these spent hours looking at them. Look. *Centaurea scabiosa.* Here's *Achillea millefolium*, and *Linaria vulgaris*, and *Senecio jacobea*—"

"What did you say?" Nell demanded.

"Oh, yeah," I said, embarrassed. "Sorry about that. I meant, knapweed, yarrow, toadflax, and ragwort. And this one here is—"

"No, not that! Repeat what you said in Latin!"

"Oh." I was taken aback by the sharp, almost frightened look on her face. "Ah, let's see." I glanced down at the table for reference. "I just said *Centaurea scabiosa, Senecio jacobea*—"

"They're in it! They're in Marco's map!" She turned toward the door. "Duncan! Liam, Nancy! Get in here!" She collected the map in its plastic sleeve. Liam, Duncan, Nancy, and Vivi gathered around the splintered table, wide-eyed and breathlessly silent.

"The first one on the map is *Senecio jacobea*," she said. "Ragwort, did you say?"

She waited for my nod. "It says to go from there to the nearest *Knautia arvensis*. Do you see that?"

I studied the table for a moment, and pointed. "Right here,"

I said. "That's scabious, in English. There are others, but this is the closest one."

"Okay. *Achillea millefolium,* then," Nell said.

My finger moved down a few inches. "Yarrow."

A breathless tension was building. I was starting to feel intimidated by it. Like a huge electrical charge was building up.

"Do you see anything named *Anagallis arvensis?*" Nell asked.

"Scarlet pimpernel," I said, scanning the table and pointing. "Right here."

"And *Trifolium repens?*"

"Clover," I said. "Here it is. Down at the corner."

Nell frowned. "And this is where it says to turn to the earth and go down four hand spans."

I thought about it for a second. "Go down the table leg," I said.

Vivi looked at me, wide-eyed, and leaned over to give me a kiss. "How'd you get to be so smart?" she asked.

"Don't jinx us. See if I'm right, first," I murmured. "Then reward me."

"You can count on it," she said.

Vivi's sisters exchanged winks and nudges, but Liam was already examining the carved table legs that lay on another work surface. "I labeled them when I removed them," he said. "Relative to the direction that the flowers are growing, this one is the front left leg. Right under that clover." He laid it gently on the table.

Nell leaned over it. "Four hand spans," she said. "Let's assume they're a man's hands. Liam, measure four, please."

He did so, and his hand finished up right next to a carved knob adorned with a relief of climbing vines and morning glory flowers.

Liam looked up at me. "I'll hold it steady," he said. "Three full turns, counterclockwise. Want to do the honors?"

I seized the smooth knob, felt the texture of the morning glory vines beneath my hand, and applied pressure. It did not budge. I tried again. Still nothing.

"I'm afraid of damaging it," I said.

"It's been eighty years or more," Vivi said. "It's bound to be stiff."

I applied pressure once more, and this time felt a tiny *crack*, and then a squeak. The leg began to turn. One time, two, three. Fragments scattered, but it came free.

The bottom part in my hand was hollow. Threads had been carved into it, caked with blackened wax. I tilted it, and a cylinder of parchment dropped out of the hollow. It was ancient, yellow and brown at the corners.

I held it gingerly in my fingertips, and passed it swiftly to Vivi.

"Here," I muttered. "I'm afraid to touch it."

"All this time," Nancy whispered. "And it was right here, all along. In Lucia's table."

Vivi accepted it and laid it on the table, gently loosening the roll. The pieces of paper were not large, but they were very brittle, threatening to crack.

Vivi unrolled it ever so slightly, pressing it just far enough to peek inside. She stared for a long moment, and when she lifted her face, her eyes were huge.

"Oh, guys," she said. "This is ... I think that this might actually be ... oh, my God, this is scary. I'm getting dizzy."

"What?" I snapped. "Out with it, goddammit!"

"I think this might be the big L," Vivi said, staring first at Nell and then at Nancy. "Just look at it. At this bit of sketching, of the angel. Look at that face. And look at the writing below it. That script. It's backward."

Nell and Nancy gasped. "No way," Nancy whispered.

"I can't believe it." Nell's voice ended in a squeak.

"Who the fuck is the big L?" I said, frustrated.

Nell turned to him. "Leonardo," she explained. "As in, da Vinci."

"Oh." I closed my mouth abruptly. "Oh. Holy fucking shit."

There was a moment of dead silence. "I need a drink," Liam said, turning toward the door.

"Bring the bottle back with you," Duncan called after him.

A few restorative swallows of fine single-malt Scotch took the edge off our collective freak-out, and a half hour later we were all sprawled on the couches grouped around the coffee table in Liam's living room, staring at the roll of parchment that sat in the middle of the table as if it were an unexploded bomb.

Which, in a sense, it was. After all, it had almost gotten all six of us killed, at one time or another.

"We have to tell the press," Nancy said. "Get it on AP. All over the Internet. If the sketches are no longer secret, and that bastard knows that it's now in the hands of experts getting authenticated, there'll be no more reason for him to attack us. There will be no profit in it."

"Wrong," Vivi said, regretfully. "I'm so sorry, Nance, but that would only be true if you were dealing with a normal, reasonable criminal asshole. But John is special. He's over-the-edge bat-shit, blood-hungry insane. I don't think John even cares about the money. He's just pissed. He wants payback. He wants to chop us into chunks."

"Which means that we'll be looking over our shoulders for the rest of our lives?" Nancy said, dismayed. "God, I am so sick of it!"

"One thing's for sure," Liam said. "I will not have that thing in my house overnight. I've lost enough sleep lately."

"It's been in your house for weeks of nights," Nell reminded him.

Liam gave her an eloquent look and tossed off another swallow of whiskey.

"I'll take it," Vivi offered. "My friend Jill has a big rare-book and antiquarian gallery in the city. She'll be able to tell us how to take care of it, and store it, and get it authenticated. Somebody lend me a phone, and I'll call her right now."

Vivi wandered into the kitchen to make her call, and I listened to the animated rise and fall of her voice as she told her librarian friend the crazy tale. I felt beaten down, exhausted. Scared. Impressed about the famous art and the big *L*, for sure. Very cool, zowie, but only a tiny part of me really gave a shit. It was only parchment and charcoal and ink, after all. No matter how famous and charged with history and talent and genius it might be.

I was far more focused on the danger that bastard John posed to my living, breathing, beloved Vivi. And her sisters, of course.

Vivi came bouncing out and tossed Nell's phone back to her. "It's all set up. Jill just about had a stroke when I told her. She'll make the arrangements for authentication, and she can store the sketches in humidity controlled her rare-book vault."

"The sooner you get rid of them, the happier I'll be," Liam said.

Nancy gave him a soothing kiss, but the guy looked unsoothed.

Vivi was holding up the necklace to her sisters. "Should we detach these again? Do you want your necklaces back now?"

Nell and Nancy looked at each other. Nell took it from Vivi's hand, flipping the lever to retract the three planes with the miniscule writing.

"Not yet," she said. "Let's stay united. When this is sorted out, we'll get the chains fixed and wear them again. For now, you keep it, okay? Like a talisman."

There were tears, at that point, and group hugs. I averted my eyes until Vivi's voice caught my attention.

"Nancy, can I borrow your Jetta to drive into the city?" she asked.

My whole body seized up. "What? You're going to just stick that thing in your purse? You mean to carry it around on the street?"

"I'll put them carefully into the table leg where they've resided for at least eighty years, and I'll put the table leg into a big shopping bag. No one will know they're there," she soothed. "We'll all breathe easier when those sketches are safe in a vault somewhere."

"I'll breathe easier when that son of a bitch is dead," I said.

Vivi kissed the top of my head. "Well, yes. That goes without saying. Afterward, we'll drive out of the city. Find ourselves a hotel, okay? If Nancy can spare the car."

"Sure, but the Jetta is kind of unpredictable these days," Nancy warned. "The window in the back's come loose, so don't even try to roll it all the way up. It got smashed in by crackheads and methheads one too many times."

"It couldn't be more rickety than my van was," Vivi said, wistfully. "My poor, beloved, drowned van. I owe that van. It gave its life for me."

My urge to fight drained away. I was whipped. I was following that chick around like a panting hound, doing exactly as I was told. But the thought of a night in absolute privacy with her alone in a hotel room was too tempting to resist.

I wanted to have that talk that she had promised me. To thrash things out between us, so I could just go buy her a goddamn engagement ring already.

I wanted to close this deal and move forward, with her. Into our shared future.

But my patience came dangerously close to its end when I realized that she intended to stop at Lucia's house in Hempton on the way.

"There's something I need to pick up there," she insisted.

"At a time like this? What in holy hell could be so important?"

"It's a secret!" She frowned at me. "You'll understand later! Now just take this exit, turn to the right at the bridge, and stop arguing with me!"

I snarled obscenities as I flicked on the turn signal, and guided Nancy's battered, coughing little car off the highway, following Vivi's directions to the quiet street where Lucia's house was located.

I jerked to an angry stop in front of it. "So? Now what?"

"Thank you," she said primly. "You're very obliging. So polite, too. Do you want to wait here while I run up and get it?"

"You think I'd let you go into a dark, abandoned house all alone?" I pulled out my gun. "Bring those sketches in with you."

"As if I'd leave them in a car," she scoffed. "Let alone a car that has its back window held together with duct tape."

I kept hold of her arm. The street was quiet at this hour, just a few of the houses lit, the bluish flicker of televisions here and there. But my senses were buzzing, my hairs on end. There was no way anyone could know we were here—unless Lucia's house itself was watched. But who would watch an empty house? For weeks?

Get real, I told myself, as Vivi pushed the door open.

She didn't waste time in the sad, quiet house, just flipping on the light over the stairway, and then the light for a steeper stairway leading up to the attic. I followed her up, fuming. My discomfort grew as she pried open box after box. "What the fuck are you looking for, Viv? Christmas decorations?"

"Shut up and let me concentrate," she replied calmly.

She finally found what she sought, although she would not let me see it. She hid it with her body, wrapping it in a big plastic sack.

"Okay," she announced. "We can go now."

I led the way down the stairs, muttering imprecations as we went back to the car.

Vivi frowned as I opened the trunk for her. "I wish you'd relax a little," she complained. "You're making me tense."

"I'm making *you* tense? Jesus." I opened the car door for her, circled around, slid in, and started up the engine in one movement. "Let me tell you about *my* tension level, Viv."

That instant, I registered the smell. Sour halitosis, heinous body odor. But it was already too late. There was a rustling sound, like a flock of bats. Panic exploded inside me—and Vivi's gasp choked off into a squeak.

A heavy arm was clamped across her throat. A gleaming blade was pressed beneath her eye.

John grinned from behind Vivi's car seat, a panting, stinking death's head, his face swollen, bruised and shiny. The point of the blade traced its slow, cruel way down over her cheek, leaving a thin red line in its wake. It ended up jammed against her throat. Point digging in.

"One move, and she'll bleed out in forty seconds," John rasped.

Chapter Twenty-Six

Vivi

My system was so burnt out from adrenaline overload, I barely reacted. I felt blank. Empty. No matter what I did, no matter how hard I fought, the way out of this trap was always barred to me.

"I'm sure it would be fascinating to hear about your tension level," John said, with a wheezing laugh. "We can compare it to your tension level while you're watching me cut your little fuck buddy here into bite-sized bloody pieces."

Jack's hand moved. John pressed the knife tip harder against my throat and clucked his tongue. "Not one muscle. Hands where I can see them. On top of the wheel. *Now.*"

Jack complied. I wanted to look at him, but I was afraid the knife would jab right into my jugular. My larynx bobbed against it, stinging. "It's too late to get the sketches," I said, my voice tight. "I've told everyone. Curators at the art museums. Sotheby's, the press. I've scanned pictures to the *New York Times,* to—"

"Don't bother, you dumb bitch," John hissed. "I know you haven't done any of that yet. I watched you. I have video cameras all over Knightly's house. What a bunch of careless, stupid fucks you all are."

"Cameras?" I was startled. "At Liam's house?"

He laughed, and the hot cloud of his foul breath made me gag. "All that time they spent in San Francisco with Liam's dear old long-lost dad," he said. "I rigged his house. I saw every minute. You never called the press. Just that curator bitch— what was her name? Jill Rosseau. Is she cute? Should I put her on my list?"

I gathered my nerve. "You still won't be able to sell—"

"You think I give a fuck about that?" His laughter was shrill and explosive. "If I can't sell them, I'll wipe my ass with them the next time I take a shit. All I want is to hurt you. Make you squeal like a little pig." He jerked my head back, dragging the blade over my tendons. He stank, of sweat, and something worse. Something rotten.

"With Haupt dead, there's nobody left to pay you for the job, right?" Jack remarked, in a conversational tone. "Damn, that's unfortunate."

"Oh. Haupt. That's another bone I have to pick with you, slut. You killed the old bag of bones before I got a chance to do it myself."

"You mean you're doing this for revenge?" Jack sounded casually interested.

My hand clenched in the folds of the dress Nancy had lent me. It closed over the linked pendants that Nell had slipped into the pocket. I slid my trembling fingers inside, felt for the lever with my thumb.

"I'm doing it because you guys fucked me," John announced. "Nobody fucks me. You pay for that."

His voice was shaking. So was the hand that held the knife. I pushed the tiny lever of the linked pendants, feeling the thin gold blade snap out, pressing against my thumb. Sharp as a box cutter.

"Must have hurt you quite a bit, with that head smash," Jack commented. "You must have one motherfucker of a chronic headache."

"Fuck you," John said. "Shut your mouth."

"And that kick to the knee. Did I fuck up your knee? And don't you have a bullet wound? Your arm, or your shoulder, or something? Has it gone septic? Smells like gangrene, man. You should have somebody look at that. You probably need IV antibiotics. Maybe an amputation."

"Shut up!" John bellowed.

"Come to think of it, you look like you've got a fever, too," Jack offered. "You should pop some Tylenol. That smell is intense. Whew."

"Fucking bastard! Shut the fuck *up!*" John whacked his hand across Jack's face.

I used his instant of distraction to whip the pendant up, slashing it into John's cheek. He shrieked, jerked back. Jack twisted—

Bam. Bam. Bam. The pistol blasts were deafening in the small car.

The force of the bullets punched John back against the corner of the backseat. His big, heavy face went slack. Eyes blank.

His head tipped slowly and heavily to the side, mouth slack.

We waited several seconds, hearts pounding, before Jack reached back, gingerly, and pressed his finger to John's carotid artery for a long, careful moment.

"Gone," he said, his voice hoarse and exhausted. The gun slid from his hand, thudded to the floor. He sagged, breathing hard.

"Oh, Jack." I lunged for him.

We rocked together, in a tight, trembling embrace.

It was over.

Chapter Twenty-Seven

Jack

Several hours later, after a long, complicated, emotional stint at the police station, Vivi and I finally managed to get to our hotel. We had scrounged yet another car from Vivi's long-suffering family, since the blood-drenched Jetta had been sequestered, and it was past dawn by the time we checked into our room.

Vivi's sisters had begged for her to come back to stay with them in Hempton, but Vivi had quietly but stubbornly insisted on some time alone with me. I was pathetically grateful for that small grace. Her sisters were great, and I liked them fine, but the conversation I needed to have with Vivi required privacy.

Vivi flipped on the light, dropped her bags by the door and left the blackout curtains closed against the morning sunshine. She sat on the bed, her eyes big and solemn. She looked like a girl from another century, hair tangled and soft around her like a red cape. She wore a blue dress that one of her sisters had lent her, but it was too big for her. The neckline drooped low over her bosom, showing off her tattoo.

She followed my gaze and smiled. "Hey, buddy," she said. "Are you looking at my *Eranthis hyemalis?*"

"I can't keep my eyes off you," I admitted. "Does it make you nervous?"

She reached up to touch the little yellow flower on her bosom, giving me a smile that made my jeans suddenly feel too tight. "Not in the least."

I sank to my knees in front of her. "You promised me that if the axe was lifted, we could have this conversation," I reminded her. "About us. And our future."

"So I did," she said demurely. "The axe is gone. And here we are."

I stared searchingly into her face. "Why were you such a hard-ass, Viv? Were you punishing me for being a dickhead before?"

She shook her head, and laid her hand against my jaw, stroking it. "Hell no," she whispered. "I was just trying to be a grownup. How could you hook up with a woman who was nothing but a black hole of problems? What kind of a future could you possibly plan with a woman like that?"

I laughed. "I don't care. I'd marry you anyway. I'd marry you if those fuckers were banging on the door this very minute."

She pulled me closer, between her knees. I leaned forward against the swag of her full skirt, seeking more contact.

"I thought it would be better not to make plans, or get attached to the future," she said. "Since I thought I might not even have a future. Better to stay in the moment. Since you'd already taught me how."

"Ouch," I grumbled. "Would you stop it with that?"

"I don't mean it as a judgment." There was a smile in her voice.

"The hell you don't." My arms slid around her waist, and I nuzzled her breasts, dragging in a deep lungful of her sweet scent, rubbing his cheek against a glossy lock of dangling hair. "This is the thing, about staying in the moment," I said carefully. "There's a lot to be said for it, but certain things require a longer arc. Like planting trees. A flower garden. You plant, you wait, you weed, you water, and finally, eventually, you enjoy. It takes months. Years. Or waiting for those *Eranthis hyemalis* seedlings to take root and spread into a floral carpet. That takes time. That's not a momentary thing. They won't even bloom until February. Understand?"

"Oh, yeah," she whispered, her mouth touching my ear.

I was shaking, deep in my core. "Opening a gallery shop of wearable, usable art, for example," I went on, doggedly. "That's another long arc. Or, uh, making a baby. Although I don't know ... now that you're a potential mega-zillionaire, things might be different for you. You might want to live a glamorous, jet-setting sort of life. What the fuck do I know."

"Mega-zillionaire, my ass." She shook her head, smiling. "If I ever do see any money from that mess, the only difference it'll make is that I'll be able to hire a girl to help me at the shop. So that I can work on my art. And, ah, the baby. Of course."

I was grinning like a fool. I wanted to roll over backward for joy, wave my legs in the air like Edna. I controlled the impulse with some difficulty. A proposal of marriage should be digni-fied, goddammit.

She slid both hands into the hair on the back of my head and leaned her forehead against mine. Her hair fell down, fragrant against my cheek.

"You told me a few weeks ago that I'd pack up my van and

drive away as soon as I realized what it meant to look at the same place, day in and day out," she said. "Or the same person."

"I'm sorry." I nuzzled that fragrant hank of hair. "I was a dick. I know it."

"No, no. I wasn't roasting you. Let me finish. I just wanted to say that, um, I think I've realized what it means."

I pulled away, gazing at her with narrowed eyes. "Yeah?"

"Yours is the face I want to look at for the rest of my life," she said. "Day in and day out. I want to see it echoed in my children's faces, if we get lucky that way. While seasons turn, with rain and snow and wind and sun. While flowers bud and bloom and go to seed all around us. While seedling trees grow way up into the sky. A long arc. Decade after decade after decade. As long as life gives us."

I hid my shaking face against her chest again, letting secret tears soak into her dress. "Just one more question, Viv," I ventured.

"And what's that?" There was a soft smile in her voice.

"What the hell was that thing you had to stop at Lucia's house to pick up last night? The suspense is killing me."

She burst into startled laughter. "Oh! I forgot all about that, what with one thing and another. I'll show you right now. It's actually kind of a silly joke." She retrieved the plastic bag from where she'd left it by the door and gave me an embarrassed look. "This makes me a little shy."

"Out with it," I prompted. "You're killing me here. Don't make me wait."

"Behold, my famous thigh-high black lace-up boots," she said, whipping them out of the bag. "You said you wanted to see them. So here they are."

I stared at the boots, and started to laugh, helplessly. My tension started to unwind, into shaking convulsions. "Oh, God. I can't believe it."

"I no longer have the ripped fishnet stockings at the moment, unfortunately," she said. "I'll have to go shopping to complete the look for you."

I wiped my eyes. "They'll work just fine all by themselves," I assured her. "They're perfect. Put them on. I'll show you just how stimulating they are."

And that was exactly what I did.

I hope you enjoyed Vivi and Jack's story in the Edge Trilogy! If you missed the first two exciting installments, find them here https://books2read. com/u/4D75Gg. and here! https://books2read. com/u/bMMJEk
Join my mailing list right here, http:// shannonmckenna.com/connect.php.,
to hear all about my upcoming projects and book announcements! I also have several juicy free stories exclusive to my newsletter subscribers, so come on down!

And if you liked the Edge Trilogy, try The Unredeemables! Read on for a tantalizing taste of Master of Lies, Book 1, a nonstop adventure full of passion and peril ....

Excerpt: Master Of Lies
The Unredeemables, Book 1
Chapter 1

Jed

Well, would you look at that. So Sandee was a real, live girl, after all.

I shuffled forward in my shackles, eyeing my penpal through the glass barrier with wary fascination. She hadn't noticed me yet from her place in the line by the door, but I knew her from the photos she'd sent. At least the ones that got through the prison censors. They were grubby and dog-eared by the time they made it to my cell. Letters, too. Long, gushy letters, packed with too much information, including but not limited to her hard-luck past, her loneliness, her intense longings, her sexual fantasies.

The girl was a hot mess, and desperately in need of therapy, but I'd read all of the letters multiple times. I'd pored over them, in fact.

So I had no business judging anybody else's twisted coping mechanisms.

I had plenty of empty hours in prison to study Sandee's

letters and pictures. Up until right now, I'd been convinced they were a fantasy front. Just too damn pretty. Not realistic. Somebody photoshopped the living fuck out those photos. I was sure of it.

My guess had been that Sandee was some lonesome, tragically plain girl, or maybe someone housebound or disabled, looking for a virtual boyfriend. Or else maybe a guy who wanted to be a girl but was afraid to make the leap, so had chosen this way to live out his/her/their fantasy. Something along those lines.

But no. What the hell was a woman like that doing here? I couldn't see what the payoff could possibly be, the way she looked. That body, those tits, those eyes.

The pleated red plaid skirt fell a few inches above the knee, showing off bare, shapely legs. High-heeled red ankle boots. A tattoo on her ankle that I couldn't make out from here. She had hot pink streaks in her jagged blonde bob. She was rocking a rumpled, sexy anime schoolgirl look. The sweater was red, skin-tight. She'd followed the visitation modesty rules, but still managed to look like a walking wet dream. How she'd gotten through the visitor intake process like that was anybody's guess.

Worked for me, though. Oh, man. Worked great.

The glaring white light illuminated her white-blonde mop. Her full, sexy red lips gleamed hotly, all glossed up and sticky looking. If I were inclined to criticize, which I wasn't, I'd say she wore too much makeup. But she could be painted gold, for all I cared. I would lick her clean. Slowly.

Her look was so exaggerated, it had to be some kind of mask. Then again, I was probably overthinking this. I'd been undercover for too long, and prison shook a guy's grip on reality. Her letters and pictures seemed so real. So intensely vulnerable, they made me uncomfortable. And aroused. And seriously fucking confused.

According to the letters, Sandee lived in a rented trailer in a nowhere town with a shuttered factory, rampant unemployment, fentanyl, meth. She bartended at a skeevy roadhouse. Slimebag boss. No family support. And a thing for bad boys.

She'd heard about me from a friend whose husband was inside for mail fraud, and hunted down my mugshot, which was posted online on a booking photos website.

That had been unwelcome news. Like I needed any more attention.

She'd fixated on me, deciding to save some worthless fuck-up from himself by the power of her love alone. She might as well dive into a shark tank. But everybody had a right to his or her own brand of self-destruction, myself included.

Still. Something about her surprised me. I couldn't put my finger on it. That posture. Despite the sexpot outfit, she seemed elegant. Ladylike, almost. That dignified quality stuck out like a sore thumb in a maximum-security hellhole like this one. That gorgeous face, what I could see of it behind the shaggy, choppy blonde bangs. Sharp eyes, looking everywhere but at me. Like she didn't even know I was there.

The CO prodded me to enter the room. My shackles dragged and clanked as I shuffled toward the seat.

The fuck she didn't know I was there. She had positioned herself carefully, and then struck a hot, sexy pose for me. To give me a good, long gawk. That was calculated.

Sandee could be a honeypot, sent by Boer. If Boer had fingered me in here, then I was in imminent danger. Mickey, too. My team outside. They could all be in danger. I needed to contact the Unredeemables right now and put them on their guard.

I hesitated, gripped by panic, and the CO who held my arm stumbled into me with a curse. Goddamn. This was a mistake. I should have kept refusing to see her.

Chapter 1

I'd changed my mind because I wanted to do the girl a favor by ending this fantasy of hers—definitively. To scare her to death, make her run before she drew any more unhealthy attention to herself. I wanted her miles away, back in Nowheresville, mired in whatever boring routine she was trying to escape from. *Run, Sandee, run.*

The strategy had seemed smart at the time. But now I felt danger prickle on my skin. Whether from her, or for her, I did not know. One thing was certain. I should never have touched this live wire. Not even once.

She could fuck me up. And idiot me, I'd agreed to this partly because I was bored, and curious. I had to know if she really looked that good. If anyone could.

She did. Score: one for my dick, zero for my brain.

I was so close to my goal. I'd been in Kalaharee for months, getting close to Mickey Savalletri, ingratiating myself to him by protecting him from predators. At long last, he'd agreed to give me the info I needed to run down my ex-colleague, Wex Boer.

Once I got my hands on Boer, I could torture intel about Shane's location out of that murdering shithead. I looked forward to that with every fiber of my being.

But Mickey would only provide the intel after I busted him out of the joint. That was his price, and it was time to pay up. A man had to stay focused while planning a prison break. There was no time or space for a frivolous crush on my sexpot penpal.

"... dee McGillis? For the last time! Sandee McGillis!"

Here she came, right at me. Too late to change my mind.

Want to give Master Of Lies a try? Find it here!

Also by Shannon McKenna

The Edge Trilogy

Edge of Whispers

Edge of Secrets

Edge of Ruin

The Unredeemables

Master of Lies

Master Of Secrets

Master Of Chaos

The Hellbound Brotherhood Series

Hellion

Headlong

Hellbent

Heedless

Havoc

The Obsidian Files Series

Right Through Me

My Next Breath

In My Skin

Light Me Up

The McClouds & Friends Series

Behind Closed Doors

Standing In The Shadows

Out Of Control

Edge Of Midnight

Extreme Danger

Ultimate Weapon

Fade To Midnight

Blood And Fire

One Wrong Move

Fatal Strike

In For The Kill

Standalones

Return To Me

Hot Night

Meet Shannon McKenna

Shannon McKenna is the NYT and USA TODAY bestselling author of over thirty novels, ranging from sexy contemporary romance to action packed, turbocharged romantic thrillers. She loves tough and heroic alpha males, heroines with the brains and guts to match them, terrifying villains who challenge them to their utmost, adventure, blazing sensuality, and most of all, the redemptive power of true love.

Since she was small she has loved abandoning herself to the magic of a good book, and her fond childhood fantasy was that writing would be just like that but with the added benefit of being able to take credit for the story at the end. The alchemy of writing turned out to be messier than she'd ever dreamed, but whatever, she loves it anyway and hopes that readers enjoy the results of her experiments. She loves to hear from her readers. Contact her by email at her website, http://shannonmckenna.com, or find her on Facebook at https://www.facebook.com/AuthorShannonMckenna/ to keep up with all her news! Follow her on Bookbub to get new release and discount alerts! https://www.bookbub.com/authors/shannon-mckenna

If you'd like to know when new books will come out, and hear about discounts, giveaways and promos, join Shannon's newsletter at http://shannonmckenna.com/connect.php. She has special goodies waiting for you there, exclusive bonus stories that are just for her subscribers, and a free Obsidian Files novella!

She hopes to see you there!